The Power Within

The Chronicles of Hollyglade Wayrender

Steve Barker

First Printing, 2017
ISBN: 978-1-7750284-0-6

Published by Steve Barker
Canmore, AB Canada
T1W 1R1

Meet the Author at
www.facebook.com/Stevebarkerauthor
stevebarkerauthor.blogspot.ca

Cover Illustration by Brayden Sato
Cover design by Taylor Sato
www.satodesigners.com

E-Book Edition also available

I : FLIGHT

The ground was cold, and beginning to freeze with the approaching winter. As she ran, the rough terrain scraped the skin from the bare soles of her feet, mercilessly grinding her down. Yet Hollyglade would not let herself slow the pace of her flight. She had to keep moving as fast as possible. The goal was to put distance between herself and her pursuers. Desperately, she scanned the edge of the forest for somewhere to hide, and take some much-needed shelter. She felt incredibly exposed, having been running at this pace, and in her state of nakedness for far too long.

The sound of hoofbeats, most likely the armed men in pursuit of their prey, could be heard ever closer. She pushed herself to quicken the pace. The onset of an unusually dark night gave her hope she might lose her pursuers, even though it was getting more difficult to navigate as she approached the untracked forest. She feared the effects of the cold as night continued to close in, and her fingers, her feet, and most of her body began to go numb despite the exertion of running. Though her feet had been toughened by many years without shoes as a young child, she had known the comfort of boots in recent years. Now she was suffering greatly under her relentless retreat across frozen ground.

The solidity of the winter-hardened earth was also both helpful and harmful. She would not leave tracks that would easily be followed. Only the most skilled trackers would be able to find the minor disturbances of the dust she left behind, but her feet were being cut with every stride. Now she was bleeding. Blood was easy to see. Easy to follow. She knew that she could not outrun men on horseback indefinitely, but a certain trepidation made her hesitate to leave that hard plain for the forests.

Hollyglade slowed, and decided that one place was going to have to be as good as any other. She had been running for what felt like an hour. Though she was a fit teenager, whose seven-and-a-half-foot tall frame made for long strides and therefore a very quick pace, she was naked, cold, and her feet were bleeding. She knew she could not keep this pace any longer.

Taking an abrupt left off the road, she moved into the thick undergrowth along its edge. The bushes scratched the skin from her feet all the way up to her collarbone. This was the time of night when many of the more foul and dangerous creatures roused from their daily slumber. Though she had no fear of bears, wolves or feral dogs, Hollyglade did not wish to meet any crocottas, shug monkeys, wyverns, adanncs, or any other magical creatures. Dealing with magical creatures required magic, and such power was not something Hollyglade was keen to use. Still, she hoped to avoid both classes of predator, as there was a much more immediate threat she needed to focus on.

Though the giantish half of her heritage lent her extremely good vision in the dark, this was a cloudy moonless night which left her feeling for a way through the dense undergrowth. Finding her way through the first few strides into the underbrush, she heard the approach of the men on horseback. Two at least, from what she could tell. Her elvish half lent her a sense of hearing to be envied. The cold air, the thunderous beating of her own heart, and the fight to control her own breathing made it difficult for Hollyglade to decipher exactly how many pursuers were nearing. They drew closer by the second, and she feared they would be upon her at any moment. Hollyglade looked about her immediate surroundings and found that just to her right there were several small bushes bunched tightly together which might conceal her. She made for the clump of foliage as quickly as she dared move, fighting not to make a sound. As she crouched, she tried to slow her breathing and relax her heart rate, hoping she would not be heard. She began to shiver, fighting to stop her teeth from chattering as the riders approached.

Hollyglade began to feel a panic creep in as the riders slowed their pace. She feared they had spotted her trail. Slow your breathing Holly. Relax and don't let your teeth knock together. She struggled to calm herself. In all her days of living on the streets of Magnaville she had never been in such exposed peril. She had lost her weapons, and here there were no back alleys with back doors to escape through, no corners to disappear around.

She was naked and freezing, numb and slowed by the cold. She couldn't hope to fight two armed and armored men on horseback. Is this really it? I'm to be raped and slain naked in the night on some gods-awful road in the middle of nowhere? Dammit Holly why did you have to take that bath? She began to fight with herself, within her own mind. She possessed a terrible power. Power she had been born to, but feared. You can't, Holly, You can't. How far will it spread? Who else would you harm? It had been many years since she had used that power. It had been in self-defence. It had been an instinctive reaction, wild and uncontrolled, and it had cost her everything.

As Hollyglade crouched in the thicket, the two riders came to a stop on the road. Turning their horses to either side, they began searching the area. "Eh! This looks good! As good as anything we seen so far," the shorter one shouted to his companion as he dismounted. "Come 'ave a look closer and light that lantern of yours."

The tall rider turned his horse back toward the side of the road where Hollyglade was squatting in the bushes, and trotted over to see what his partner had discovered.

"Looks promising. Let's walk in a bit and see what we 'ave. I'm tired of all this chasin' ghosts," replied the tall rider, as he too dismounted.

"We'll 'ave to walk the 'orses in, but it looks like we might not 'ave to far to go," remarked the short one.

Hollyglade braced herself. She could feel power rising up within her, begging to be released. She fought it, battled within herself to control and contain it. Breathe Holly. There will be another way. You can find another way.

She felt the the intense pain of cold in the mangled soles of her bare feet, and now lamented pushing her pace to the point of causing the skin to break. As a result of running at a pace beyond what her bare feet could handle, she had left a trail of bloody foot prints which could easily be followed. She could not tell if her feet were still bleeding, because in the darkness she could not see them. Neither could she feel any blood through the numbness taking hold in her fingers. The two men were only a dozen yards from her now and she was sure that the light of their lantern would soon fall on the bushes where she hid. As she peered through the leaves still clinging to their branches in this first cold spell, it became clear that the men were following a narrow path. She could not yet tell how far off that path she might be.

Hollyglade tensed up, ready to spring out of the copse. Her hope was to use surprise to her advantage and somehow incapacitate these men. She had been forced to defend herself many times in Magnaville's filthy Red Lanes, when the occasional soldier, drunk tradesman, or traveller thought they might try being with a tall girl. She had always been just quick enough to get away, but usually not unscathed. This was different. This was going to be worse.

Magnaville was warm. Like most towns on the coast, the poor children could run through the streets mostly naked. They would never have to feel the roughness of the frozen ground, never worrying about the cold making them slow and weak.

Here and now though, it was cold, and unlike Hollyglade, these men were clothed and in footwear.

Half a dozen yards now.

Hollyglade gritted her teeth, and clenched her fists. She stepped back slightly with one foot and prepared to launch out of the bushes once the moment presented itself. She had learned how to pick pockets from others who had grown up in Magnaville without parents. Every orphan in the Red Lanes knew that when picking a man's pocket it is best to do so from behind. When picking the pocket of a man with a friend, it is best to take from the man who brings up the rear. Hollyglade was not looking to pick either man's pocket, but she assumed the same principle applied when attacking two armed men in the woods at night while naked and weaponless. She waited as the two men approached, praying she had concealed herself well enough.

Three yards now.

Suddenly, the short one turned slightly to his right, followed by the taller one, and both moved into a small clearing. They stopped, walked around the edge of the clearing and nodded to each other. "This looks fine, fine indeed Hern," the short one said.

"Aye. It'll do. Well spotted, my dear Tom. Let's tie the 'orses 'ere and get a fire goin'. I'm starvin'," replied the tall rider. "I'm tired of ridin' after someone or something that some farmer we posted at that crossroad thinks 'e saw. It's been near an hour, I reckon, and we ain't seen no sign of that girl that was at that cottage. She's disappeared, and we'll probably find her naked and frozen to death someplace tomorrow."

Hollyglade began to see stars whirl about her. She could feel the anxiety rushing through her body, sticking in her muscles. Could she have been so lucky? She nearly fell over, and had to put a hand on the ground to stop from plunging into the bushes. The tension in her muscles refused to release. These men were so close, yet to Hollyglade's amazement, seemed not to have found her. What could she do? She could not move, and was in no state for stealth. Any movement would surely be heard. There was no choice but to wait.

"Hern. Pass me them fire irons will ya? It looks like someone's camped 'ere before and left us a nice ring o' stones. I'll get this set up with a pot." said the short one as he examined the fire pit. "Grab us a bit of wood, will ya?"

The tall rider nodded and handed the short one a set of two iron rods. "'Ere,'" offered the tall rider "You get that set up, but I'm cookin'. I've 'ad enough of yer burnt porridge on this endless 'alf-breed 'unt already. If that Dancer fellow wants us to 'unt day in an' day out, the least 'e could do is feed us a decent meal at an inn before 'e puts a knife to the innkeeper, for once". He turned to set about securing the horses.

The Dancer, thought Hollyglade. In the gods names, how am I being hunted by him? She had heard him mentioned as a bounty hunter of sorts. The stories were not good. They invariably involved a trail of blood and death. Hollyglade knew that as a half giantish, half elvish girl, she was less welcome in Loria now than she had been only a few months ago. She had heard that King Harford was less tolerant of non-humans than his father had been. So far, he had only directed his soldiers to encourage those from the Elder races to move along when they encountered them on routine patrols or during other duties. She had not heard that they had started hunting the Elder Folk, and bounty hunters were not the kind of people a king hired. They have the army and garrisons for finding people. But why me? she wondered. Why hire him?

While on the streets of Magnaville, she had occasionally drawn the ire of an upper-class citizen. Stealing bread or eating a meal at an inn and not paying for it, were among her survival driven indiscretions. She had never been violent unless defending herself, and had never left anyone any worse for wear than with a black-eye or a bruise.

She didn't like violence. It was too intimate in the wrong way. She was capable of knocking most men down and taking their change purse if she caught them by surprise, but sleight of hand and a bit of misdirection seemed far more palatable. She also preferred to be far away when rich men discovered they had one less coin purse than when they had left home.

"Ahoy old Hern! I've made us fire, and soon we'll 'ave some warmth," cried the short man. "What 'ave you got in mind to feed us?".

"I," replied the tall man, "'ave some meat!"

"You wut, now? Where'd ya get that!?" exclaimed the short man.

"I pocketed it in that inn we was in this mornin', while The Dancer was inside with that new recruit of 'is, 'avin' at that lady innkeeper. I reckon it's pork. She 'ad a few pigs out the back of 'er place".

The short man grinned widely and pulled something out of a saddle bag. "A carrot and an onion!" He smirked as he replied.

"Right," offered the tall one, "you get that fire goin' nicely, and I'll get the stew in the pot." The tall man took the pot, emptied a water skin into it, and began to cut the meat and vegetables.

Hollyglade's legs were beginning to cramp from squatting in her clump of bushes for what seemed to her like hours. She knew it had not been more than ten minutes, yet without the willingness to sit or lay down and expose more bare skin to the frozen ground, she was left in an extremely taxing position. To make matters worse, the fire the two men had built was glowing invitingly, yet she was too far from it to feel any heat. The pot the men had placed on the fire was just starting to simmer, and the smell of food wafted toward her, making her stomach growl.

Why the feet? She groaned inwardly. Why not the nose, or the stomach? Why did it have to be my feet that went numb? She thought about sitting on her hands, just to lift her feet a for a moment. Anything had to be better than letting the numbness slowly creep up past her ankles. She thought better of it, knowing there would be a need to keep the feeling in her hands if she planned on engaging one or both of these men in a fight. She questioned whether or not she could even stand up, let alone fight.

Cold, cramped, shivering, and starting to feel light-headed, her lips were going numb along with her knees, buttocks, elbows, hands and feet. She had to wait, believing that her only hope was for these men to eat, drink, and fall asleep quickly. If she could make it until that happened, she may have a slim chance.

"What ya reckon this one done?" Hern asked his companion. "I mean, why is it we're chasin' a tall girl through the night? I 'eard she burned someone's 'ouse down. Must 'ave been someone important."

"Dunno for sure," Tom grunted. "But I did 'ear it was more than an 'ouse. I 'eard it was an entire village," he remarked while chewing a mouthful of stew. "It still don't fit the usual kind of job The Dancer takes. I 'eard 'e usually don't go for somethin' that's not a payback for some kind of killin'. Like, killin' of someone important. I 'eard that village she burned down was just some farmin' village.

"Last job The Dancer 'ad was findin' whoever it was that killed prince what's-his-name of Loria 'ere. The Dancer was 'ired by this king 'ere, and went down to Demaria and brought back some nobleman or other, and turned 'im over to King 'arford. I 'eard they tortured 'im quite a while looking for some information er other." He paused to drink the last of his stew. "That there Dancer never fails to get 'is man".

Hern looked down at his bowl, and drank the remains of his meal. "Well, 'e's an 'arder man than I ever met before. I worked for a few bounty 'unters in the past. Usually goin' after some bandits or other been botherin' some villages, or who bedded some nobleman's wife, but none of them's used quite the same tactic as the Dancer.

"Whatever," he sighed, "as long as 'e pays me, I don't rightly care too much who we nab. Maybe we'll 'ave a bit o' fun with 'er first before we take 'er to 'im, if we're the ones lucky enough to catch 'er," Hern mused.

Tom chuckled in response. "I'll drink to that." He smirked as he raised his mug. "I've never 'ad an elf, nor a tall woman. Ha ha! I can 'ave both at once! You reckon she'd put up a struggle? I like it when they put up a struggle. Makes it more interestin'."

Both men drained their mugs and chuckled to themselves. "Now then, my dear Hern," Tom continued, "let's get some rest. We're supposed to make it to that town by first thing tomorrow and report back by midmorning. We've got a fair bit o' ridin' to be done, and I'm 'opin' there'll be a trail to find in the light. And if we plan on 'avin' a little fun with this 'uge bitch you're gonna need some rest!" They both howled.

"Aye," Hern replied, "I'll be dreamin' of tall ugly women!" He snickered.

As Hollyglade watched the two men roll out their sleeping packs, she felt dizzy from the anxiety caused by all she had overheard. She squatted with her arms hugging her knees, trying to conserve what little warmth was left in her numbing torso, and hoped her pursuers would fall to sleep quickly. She felt her anger begin to swell as she observed these men who had come upon the cottage where she had managed to find a room earlier that day. They had murdered the woman who lived there, who had allowed her, a half-breed non-human, to rent a bed for the night. For Hollyglade, their timing had been impeccably bad.

Again, she cursed herself for having been so careless as to take that bath. She knew better. She had always found a stream, pond, lake, or river and bathed in the dark of night where she would not be so likely to be set upon by a stranger whose intentions were less than honourable. But she had been dreading this year's turning of fall to winter, and the idea of a warm bath enticed her when she had learned that the innkeeper was blind, and would not have been able to discern that she was renting a room to one of the giantish, elvish, dwarvish, or a half-breed.

Hollyglade felt an odd sense of loss for that bath. Usually, she did not care for the heat of baths found in inns. She had grown accustomed to bathing in various natural sources of clean water. But the allure of warmth, and real soap, had overcome her better judgement. Now, it was that heat she lamented having left.

She also felt a sense of guilt over the old woman's death. She felt the two senses of loss, for the bath and the old woman, competing within her, and chided herself for allowing such internal contention. Was this some callousness that had begun to grow in the years she had spent wandering alone from town to town since leaving Magnaville? Or was it just the intense cold numbing her mind, as well as her flesh? She closed her eyes, recalling the events of that morning.

Hollyglade entered the small village with a measure of caution. Having been on the road for over a week, she was tired of travel, but could not assume this town to be any safer than the last. She had been forced to leave in a hurry when the local garrison commander had made it clear to her that non-humans were unwelcome. There had been a mix of both good and bad luck with villages and towns this last month. Life in general had become more difficult for her ever since King Harford, the new young heir to the throne of Loria, had decided that all non-humans were of a lower class and did not deserve citizenship in his newly inherited kingdom.

Some towns still may have work for a girl with Hollyglade's skills. However, those would-be towns without the presence of a royal garrison, that may not have heard this latest decree, or didn't yet take it seriously. In most towns there were farmers who needed their horses or oxen trained for the plow. Sometimes there would be a horse breeder who needed young animals trained for riding and carrying soldiers into battle.

Hollyglade's giantish half came with the inherited ability to communicate with animals on a level no human could. She almost always had to explain to a prospective new employer that she could not speak the animal's language, but that it was more like sharing a knowing look between friends, one that only they would understand. She never let on that it was much deeper than that, and in truth is was like speaking their language. With some nobler species of animals, it was the sharing of thoughts.

Hollyglade was also careful to conceal that, if she wished, she could influence, maybe even command or compel an animal on a subconscious level, to do anything she required of them. She had always been careful of this. Impressing a farmer with how quickly she trained a plow team, and boggling their mind by making an animal do something completely out of character for any beast, were two vastly different things.

Over the last few years she had been able to scratch out a decent living, wandering from place to place, finding work for a time with some good-natured farmer or another. Occasionally, she would even be able to rely on an employer's recommendation to find the next job, rather than approaching someone cold. It was not the kind of work that would make anyone rich, but Hollyglade found it satisfying. She did not much like interacting with people, and preferred the company of the animals. Perhaps it was because she always knew where she stood with the animals, or that they never tried to take advantage of her, or that they were endlessly loyal and honest creatures. Whatever the reason, she was content with her life.

As Hollyglade approached the first few buildings in the town, she took note of the disposition of the townsfolk who were about the street. She got a general sense that the town was laid back and welcoming. The road was dry and dusty, as it had not rained in over a week. As a result, her throat was parched from having drunk the last of her water when she awoke earlier in the morning. The sky was blue and cloudless as well, and she felt a sense of disappointment, knowing the dry weather would continue.

She approached what looked like a tavern or an inn, with the intent of looking for a good meal and a room for the night, and hopefully a lead on someone who might be in need of some animals trained. Usually, a competent farmer could train his own animals, but she excelled at convincing them it was worth their while to let her do so for a modest fee while they continued with regular work. She was most often successful in gaining work from coach drivers wanting to replace an animal on their team who had gotten old, sick, or who just did not fit in. It was most common for her to find leads for such work in whatever place the locals regularly gathered.

Hollyglade climbed the steps at the front of the building and ducked as she entered through the open door. At her height, most doors were lower than her chin, and it had been a year or so since she had not had the need to duck through a door. As she stepped into the main room, the warmth of a fire coming from the hearth in the centre of the room met her invitingly. The smell of stew and baking bread wafted through the air. Hollyglade's stomach growled. She had not eaten any hot food in days, and it had begun to feel like forever since she had eaten anything she could call a full meal.

Looking around the room, she saw several sets of small tables and chairs, all of which were empty. A large shaggy dog lay sprawled out close to the central hearth, and a woman stood stirring the pot hanging over the fire. Hollyglade took a couple of steps further into the room and stopped, politely waiting for the woman to finish with her stew. After a moment the woman turned and looked up at Hollyglade. The innkeeper was not very old, but had a tanned complexion and flaxen hair. Her dress was simple, light brown, and floor length, with a well-worn apron over top. Her eyes widened, and her mouth fell open slightly as she took in Hollyglade's seven-and-a-half-foot tall frame. She paused for an instant and looked Hollyglade thoroughly up and down.

Hollyglade was not dressed as a lady, but her riding boots, trousers, doublet and surcoat were somewhat neatly put together. Her long red hair, woven in a loose braid, hung over her left shoulder and reached to her waist. For those who knew such things, it was a dead giveaway that, though she had the slim build, soft facial features, and slightly pointed ears of her Elvish half, she was also half Giantish. Hollyglade did not carry a sword, but kept a long knife, the type commonly used by cattlemen and farmers, on her hip.

The woman finally came to focus on Hollyglade's face. "I'm sorry deary, but we can't serve you here. King's new orders I'm afraid. You'll have to keep moving".

Hollyglade relaxed her eyes, now that they had adjusted to the lower light of the interior of the building. "Pardon my intrusion madam," Hollyglade replied. "I meant no disrespect. Things seem to be changing recently, and I find places I had previously been welcome, I am welcome no longer. It surprises me not, that in places such as the capital, Elder Folk are less welcome, but in truth it does give me surprise that farming towns such as these now dismiss the good business of honest travellers."

The woman seemed impressed with her demeanor. Hollyglade had spent much time in the vicinity of the noble class while in the markets of Magnaville. She had a keen ear and did her best to learn to speak as they did. She found that people often judged others by the class of their speech as much as their general appearance and attire. She found this to have its greatest effect in the country, where she could make herself sound different from, and of a higher class than, the people she hoped to convince to accept her. Hollyglade had sensed a sort of apologetic tone in the woman's initial response to her appearance at the door, and thought it worth trying to gain a little information before moving along.

"Madam, I will not intrude on your fine establishment," Hollyglade continued "I wonder though, if I may ask you if there is still a place here, or perhaps in another nearby village, that a woman like myself might find hospitality, and perhaps even work."

Even though she was only fifteen years old now, Hollyglade had recently begun to refer to herself as a woman, rather than a girl. It seemed that all anyone wanted from her when she labelled herself a girl, was to ask her where her parents were, rather than what kind of work she could do. She would not normally have been so bold as she was with this woman, but she had not eaten in more than a day, and badly needed rest. She was by no means opposed to sleeping out amongst the trees, but when there was a chance of sleeping in a warm bed, it felt like something worth pursuing. So far, the worst rejection she had suffered was from the local garrison in a town a few days walk back down the road, who had simply asked her to leave town.

The woman walked gently across the room toward Hollyglade, and offered an apologetic half-smile. "Well you're as forward as you are tall, aren't you! Listen, there's none of them Kingsmen in town today, but I can't have you being here should they arrive tomorrow." she said plainly.

Moving closer to Hollyglade, she lowered her voice and continued in the apologetic tone once more "I'll tell you that there is a small cottage just out the far side of town. The old woman, whose husband passed this past spring, has been known to let travellers, even such folk as yours, pay for a night and a meal. She may even have a bath you might use, though I'd guess you'd be heating your own water.

"Before her husband passed on he used to have a few of the dwarvish folk tending his field. Why years ago, I recall he had a giantish man cutting wood for him for a time. I tell you, until recently I had a young Gnomish lad, who could play lovely tunes and sing like a bird, entertaining the guests. But once that young pushover of a king took his father's pretty chair, that lad moved on from here. Not brave folk, the Gnomish.

"Anyway, my dear, you try her, out the end of town. But I'd not spend more than a night there, were I Elder folk."

Hollyglade nodded, and bowed slightly as she turned to duck back out the door. "I thank you, good lady," she offered, and stepped back into the street.

Hollyglade had heard that same apologetic dismissal from an increasing number of innkeepers and tavern owners recently. Many other people like this woman made their living by being as welcoming as possible. There were not many who would happily obey a new ordinance that so negatively impacted their ability to earn a living. It was true, that the Giantish, Elvish, Dwarvish, Gnomish, and other Elder races, were becoming rarer in this part of the world, but they were all paying customers.

Hollyglade continued down the road. As she strode through the town, she received various looks ranging from nervous, to apologetic, to fearful. She was never quite sure anymore if those looks came in response to her particularly unique appearance or that she was obviously a member of the recently outcast and outlawed races. She walked with an upright posture, her lips in a hard line, her gaze fixed on the road ahead, her long red braid swaying slightly. She studied the town as she progressed toward the cottage she had been sent to. It seemed only to consist of the one road and, besides the Inn there was only a handful of houses on the street, obviously home to families who worked the outlying fields.

It was now just before noon, and as Hollyglade approached the last home on the road, just slightly farther away from the other cottages, she hoped to find it as the innkeeper had represented it. Hollyglade still carried a few coins, and was confident they would cover a room and a meal. The small house looked much older than the others she had passed. It was covered with ivy, and surrounded by a low stone wall which kept a number of goats, chickens, ducks, and a lone cow within its boundary. A thin plume of smoke escaped from the chimney which poked through a straw thatched roof, signalling that someone must be home, and that it was warm within.

Hollyglade approached the gate and opened it, stepped through, careful to re-latch it behind her. At her height she could easily have stepped over the gate, or any part of the wall for that matter. She entered via the gate knowing politeness was most often the best currency with small town folk, especially those as elderly as she had been told this woman was.

The animals seemed to take little notice of her as she moved gently across the yard to the cottage. She stepped to the door, gave three firm raps, and stepped back while folding her hands in front of her beltline, presenting as unimposing an image as she knew how. After a few moments, there seemed to be no response, so Hollyglade knocked once more on the cottage door and softly called out to whomever might be within. "Is anybody home? I'd like to inquire about room and board, if such may be found here. I'm led to believe you may rent rooms to travellers from time to time."

Finally, a woman's voice came from within. "Hold your horses friend, I'm not the spry thing I used to be." The voice was soft, yet it crackled while letting out the words.

The door handle rattled as the old woman took great effort to make it turn in its housing, worn out from its many years of use. The door opened inward to a darkly lit room, into which Hollyglade could not see more than the first few feet, and a gnarled hand sticking out the end of a tattered sleeve beckoned her to enter. "Come, come my dear. My old bones aren't suited to these cooler days. Come in."

Hollyglade ducked through the small door, and took a couple of steps into the room to let the old woman close the door behind her. "I thank you madam," Hollyglade offered, as she glanced around the inside of the cottage. The ceiling was low, and Hollyglade was not quite able to stand fully upright, and so she had to slouch not to rub her head on it. She noticed a small stone hearth in the far corner of the room, and two doors along the near wall. There was an empty pot beside the fire, a small table with a couple of simple chairs, and one larger chair in the corner at the front side of the cottage with several furs draped over it.

"You say you're looking for a bed, my dear?".

Hollyglade turned her attention back to the woman, whose long white hair went in every direction imaginable as it tumbled down over her shoulders and onto a long brown dress. Hollyglade's eyes quickly adjusted to the lower light in the room, and she noticed that the woman was not looking directly at her, but rather in her general vicinity. Hollyglade could not help but notice the thick, white-grey haze which covered the woman's eyes, indicating that she was most surely and completely blind.

"Yes, madam." Hollyglade's mouth felt suddenly much drier. The woman struck her as being impossibly old. In her experience, the poor people she had lived with, in the Red Lanes of Magnaville, would never have been capable of surviving to such an age, and the more well-off who may have lived as long, would not venture into the gutter Hollyglade had called home in their later years.

"I would indeed Madam." Hollyglade thought, as she responded, that she had never seen such long and deeply trenched wrinkles before. "I've been travelling on the road for a fair number of days now." Her back felt empathetically sore as she noticed the exaggerated hunch of the old woman's back. "I've not had the pleasure of a warm bed this last week." She felt her stomach tighten as her attention returned to what she was saying. "And I'd gladly pay for a meal, if one might be available."

The woman's brow furrowed slightly as she turned and shuffled toward the fur covered chair by the window. "I've a room you're welcome to for a silver a night, but I must apologize for the lack of a hearty stew. It has been some time since my good husband passed on, and I don't see many travellers these days, and am not often hale enough to give my energy to making a meal for those who may call at my door.

"But, if you are the type of woman who's handy with meals and would do some work with the animals in the yard, I'd be glad of it, and you could keep the silver for the room. There are too many days the eggs go wasted, and the cow goes unmilked. It's been some time since I've heard a good travelling story. I'd enjoy a good story from such a young lady." She gave a lopsided grin, which displayed more gum than tooth, as she eased back down into her pelted sitting chair.

Hollyglade wondered if the old woman would ever get up again. "Madam, I thank you for your generous hospitality, and I would be glad to be of service to you in return for your room. If I may, I would set my things in the room and tend to your animals first. I'm by no means a trained cook, but I'll make us a stew that you'll find welcome enough." Hollyglade wasn't sure how to relate to this old blind woman. She could easily take advantage of her in a number of ways. She had done so to many unsuspecting patrons of the Magnaville central market who liked to carry their coin in excessively fancy, and therefore easily fingered, coin purses. She felt pity for the old woman. These days Hollyglade was determined to make an honest living, and had done so for almost two years now.

"The room on the right, my dear. Once you've finished

with getting the stew on the fire, I'll point you to the bath. I might not be able to see you, but I can smell you." She gave an unrestrained giggle and sank deeper into the chair. Hollyglade dropped her nose to her shoulder and sniffed as quietly as she could, while feeling her cheeks flush with embarrassment. She stepped to the door of the bedroom, opened it and ducked through. It was indeed small, with a bed she would have to curl up quite a lot to get into, but it was warm and dry. She set her small satchel on the floor, ducked back out of the room and headed outside.

After finding the feed for the animals, convincing the cow let her take some milk into a bucket, and gathering several dozen eggs she managed to find around the roost and the grounds, Hollyglade set about making a meal.

The woman had a few vegetables in a small garden behind the house, and the planters around the edge of the house provided several herbs Hollyglade thought tasted pleasant. Once the pot had been filled and set above the fire, to which Hollyglade added a small bundle of wood for cooking, she took the pot of water she had heated for the bath and headed to the room next to hers. Closing the door behind her she poured the pot into the tub, set it down, and began to undress.

The woman had instructed her to leave her clothes outside the door to be washed. Apparently scrubbing clean her skin was only half the job the old woman required of her. Hollyglade placed her smock and trousers outside the door, closed it again, and sank into the bath. She was nowhere near the right size for the bath, but she made it work. It was a rare treat to have warm water and soap to bathe with.

As she cleaned every inch of her bare skin, washing away the dust she had gathered as she had travelled this last week, she smiled as her naturally pale colour was revealed once again. She undid her braid and began to wash her long, red hair. The deep red colour had come from her giantish mother, though Hollyglade's hair was straight and fine like that of her elvish father. She was often glad not to have to deal with the tight, course curls many giants were born with.

Once she had finished getting the week's dirt, sweat, and dust from her locks, she reclined and closed her eyes. She hadn't had a warm bath in as long as she could remember, and she was surely not stepping out of it while there was any heat left to be enjoyed.

Hollyglade woke to the sound of several voices. Immediately, she felt herself shiver. She had stayed in the bath too long. She shook her head, sat up, and pulled herself out of the bath, reaching for the sheet to dry off with. Her hair, which had been hanging out the back of the bath, was still damp. She was accustomed to being cold after a scrub this time of year, as most of them came in some creek, lake, or river. Clean and cold is better than dirty and cold. The anticipation of a hot meal by the warm fire quickly made her smile as she stretched out. She could smell the delicious aroma of the simmering stew through the door. She had just begun to dry herself, when her ears caught some of the conversation coming from outside the door.

"... very tall girl, looks like she's Elvish, rather thin, dressed like a man..."

Hollyglade tensed and scanned the room for her clothing. It was nowhere to be seen. Dammit old woman! Why did I give you my clothes! She pressed her ear to the door to see if she could make out more of what was being said. She could hear the old woman saying "..someone has been around but I'm old and blind and I've been asleep in my chair all afternoon. You'll know all about it if you're cursed enough to reach my age..."

Hollyglade was not in the mood for another run-in with some local garrison. She gritted her teeth. As she looked at the window to see if she could pry it open, she wrapped the sheet around herself. I hope to gods that woman has left my clothes on the line. Hollyglade figured she would employ a tactic she had used many times before in the side streets and alleyways of Magnaville. She would slip out the window and hide in the trees, wait for this group to move on, and then return to the cottage to collect her things before hitting the road once more. Next time though, she thought to herself, I would not trust the advice of some tavern wench.

As the window slid open, Hollyglade could hear the man's voice grow impatient.

"... then we shall have a look inside, and see who might, or might not be about."

Hollyglade did not wait. She squeezed awkwardly through the small opening head first, since there was no hope of stepping through a window this size. As she pulled her hips through, and attempted to brace herself on the ground with one hand, she slipped and tumbled head over heels into the vegetable patch. The sheet she had been wrapped in caught on some part of the window frame, and did not come with her. Great, she thought as she hit the dirt. So much for the bath.

As she scanned the edge of the yard for the clothesline, she heard someone rounding the far corner of the cottage. She quickly stepped backward toward the near corner of the ivy clad house. She moved quickly, but not quickly enough.

"Oi! Stop there!" someone shouted, "Lads she's 'ere". The husky man, dressed in leather, and hard boots, drew a sword.

Drawn sword. Not Good! Hollyglade gave one brief glance at the sheet hanging from the window frame, winced, and bolted in the opposite direction. She was not interested in staying to attempt to talk her way out of whatever this was.

Recently, local garrisons had given her nothing more than a 'move along, move along', but so far, they had yet to threaten violence or arrest. In her experience, when men drew their swords, they soon drew blood. Even if no sword had been drawn, she was not interested in enduring the kind of treatment women and young girls received from garrisons while under arrest.

Hollyglade moved swiftly, and as she approached the short stone wall, she did not slow down. She leapt over it with ease, continuing at a full sprint. The edge of the outer yard and the surrounding forest were close by, and she made the tree line in seconds. As she passed by the first few trees and into a thicket of berry bushes, she glanced back to see the man sprawled on the ground below the short stone wall, trying to collect himself up from the dirt. She paused momentarily to look for his companions, to see how many men she might have to outrun and hide from.

The sun was low in the sky, and she was looking directly below it. She could not make out how many men were responding to the shouts of the first, but she did not want to take the time to find out. She turned and began a brisk jog through the trees. Several indiscernible shouts came from the cottage, accompanied by the sound of shod hooves. They're mounted? Who do they think they're chasing for gods' sakes?

Hollyglade decided it was too risky to try and hide anywhere near the cottage. It was likely this group of men had come with more in mind than move along, and she expected that they would thoroughly search the woods near the cottage. Nimbly, she moved through the trees in a direction roughly parallel to the road, heading further out of the town. When she had approached the cottage earlier that morning, she had noticed a fork in the road a short distance from the edge of the old woman's field. If I can cross that road, and move beyond the far side of the fork, I should be alright. They're not likely to look for me that far from where they last saw me.

The riders were taking their horses along the edge of the woods. The underbrush was too thick for a horse to move through any faster than a walk. Hollyglade was adept at moving rapidly, and silently, through dense foliage, part of her elvish half she was thankful for. She paused and crouched low behind a clump of bushes as the riders came to within about a score of yards. She was sure that she was too far into the forest to be seen, but remained crouched. She did not like the idea of her red hair dangling at the eye level of a man on horseback where the sunlight would easily catch it.

The riders passed by, and after a few moments, Hollyglade began to move again. She assumed, if her sense of direction and gauge of the distance were correct, that she was just under a few hundred yards from where the road forked. As she approached, she heard the riders returning along the road, and stopped behind a large oak. She hazarded a glance, since they sounded further away now, and caught sight of them just before the fork, riding along the tree line on the far side of the road, in the direction of the cottage.

She stood up, hunched over slightly, and resumed her approach to the road. She decided that the best place to cross was at the fork itself, so that she would only cross one width of road, and only risk the exposure of a single crossing before she would have to circle back. She stopped and took one more look along the road. She flinched at what she saw at the fork, cursing under her breath. A man stood in the road scanning the trees. He was not one of the men from the cottage, and appeared to be a farmer, most likely conscripted by those men to stand watch. Hollyglade turned west again and continued through the trees.

The sun was now only a sliver on the horizon, and she knew that she would not make as much progress through the trees in the dark, even though her giantish vision would make it easier for her than for a human. She shuddered as she felt the air getting colder. Several minutes later, about a hundred yards west of the fork in the road, she moved to the edge of the tree line and peered through the failing light back to where she had seen the man standing watch.

The sun was now completely set, and she could make out only a silhouette. Thankfully, he appeared not to be looking her way. Silently, she stepped out into the road and headed for the far side, hoping to cross this road, the thin strip of trees, and then the next road. When it seemed safe, she would find a way to circle back to the cottage and collect her things after the men had given up and moved on. She kept an eye on the silhouette while stepping gingerly over the rough ground. Something further down the road, back at the cottage, caught her attention.

Several lanterns emerged from the cottage, and as

Hollyglade's giantish vision adjusted to the light, she could make out two men dragging the old woman by the arms. They brought her to the centre of the yard as the riders who had been scanning the treeline rode up to the cottage's stone wall. The two men, both of average build, one slightly taller than the other, wore various shades of brown. Another shorter man was dressed in creamy white riding clothes. The last was head and shoulders above the others, and stood a couple of steps away from the man in white, who now took hold of the woman for himself.

The man dressed in white passed his lantern to the tallest one. Next, he gently took the old woman's hand with his, bent slightly, and kissed the back of hers. Then, all in one lightning quick motion he straightened up, drew and swung his sword.

As the woman's white hair flew up with the force of the cut, Hollyglade abruptly sucked in a gasping breath of air. As if trying to put the noise back in, she clamped a hand over her mouth. The silhouetted man turned toward her.

"Oi! Who's that then?"

Hollyglade spun on the balls of her feet, and sprinted as fast as her legs would take her.

II : FEAR

Hollyglade scanned around the clearing looking for anything that might serve as a crude weapon. There were still several branches, which had been collected for firewood, lying on the far side of the fire where one of the men had dropped them. Hollyglade looked for the men's swords, but both had been smart enough to sleep with their weapons against them. Hollyglade moved to her left, and stepped around the edge of the clearing, slowly passing the snoring rider. She could not help but smell the foulness of his breath as he exhaled heavily. She grimaced and put a hand to her mouth and nose, observing the scarred and deeply pockmarked face of her would be captor.

After few more awkward steps, Hollyglade reached the pile of branches. She paused a moment to measure the distance between her and each of the men. It appeared to her that she could make the distance from the wood pile to either man with one long stride. This would put her in striking distance, should one of the pieces of firewood suffice as a weapon. She bent down to pick up one of the longer, heavier branches, and suddenly felt dizzy. Maybe it was the cold, or the lack of food, lack of water, or having been squatting in the bushes for so long, but Hollyglade felt entirely diminished in that one moment, and stumbled into the pile of wood. Several branches snapped, and she could feel deep pressure in several points on each hand, though the numbness of her extremities delayed any feeling of pain. A knee landed directly on a piece of wood, and there she did feel pain as she lost several layers of skin and felt the end of a twig drive into her flesh. She let out a small groan through her teeth as feelings of panic set in instantly.

The snoring turned into a single startled snorting gasp, as the man she had passed, and who was now to her right, threw an arm out of his blanket and pressed it on the ground to start to sit up. There was no stopping now. Hollyglade quickly glanced to her left, saw a blanket fly up, grabbed the branch she was touching, and stood up.

She loaded up on her right foot, stepped toward the snorer, and with her right arm swung the branch with all the strength she had. The blow caught the man in the cheek as she used every inch of her length to close the distance. The branch broke as it made contact, and without any feeling in her hands, Hollyglade could not maintain her grip, causing the remainder of the branch to fly out of reach. The man let out a scream as he grabbed at his cheek to find blood pouring from where the tip of the branch had swept across his mottled face.

As the branch flew into the surrounding bush, Hollyglade looked beneath her in search of another. From behind her, she could hear the taller rider getting to his feet. As her hand clamped around another branch, she felt a sharp pain break through the numbness, as it travelled up her arm to her elbow. Fear came with it. She had been so patient in the bushes, suffering cold and numbness in order to await the moment when these two men would be at their most exposed, and now she was fumbling clumsily in the night, with a broken tree branch for a weapon, and still slowed by cold. She gritted her teeth, whirled toward the taller rider, and swung blindly as she heard his sword being ripped from its sheath.

She was very cold. Her feet were numb, and she was dizzy. The whirl and strike were full of fear and panic, and therefore wild. The strike missed, and she lost her balance, tumbling to the ground as the man's sword whizzed over her head. She landed flat on her back, as the hard ground met her unforgivingly and she felt the air being smashed from her lungs. She gasped desperately as the taller man stepped over her, raising his sword to deliver a downward strike.

She could feel power surging, magic building like anger within her. It threatened to burst forth in an uncontrolled release of rage, ready to tear and rend everything around her. She could not let it out, could not let it through the barriers she had built within her. Something so dangerous and devastating could not be allowed to be released without control. But she could not control it, did not know how, and so she held it in. She knew her only option was some other form of action.

Hollyglade reacted as swiftly as she could, pulling her left knee up, and thrusting her foot toward the man's groin. She connected squarely, and buckled him. He let go of his sword with one hand, pulling his knees together and covering his manhood. The tip of his weapon dropped down to the side, as he struggled to maintain his grip with the other hand.

Hollyglade reached for the branch she had been holding, found it, and used her length to deliver a massive blow to the head of the man standing over her. He tried to avoid the attack, but her kick had done its job, and as a result he was too slow. He crumpled, and fell forward, landing directly on top of Hollyglade. She tried to grab him by the jerkin, attempting to roll him off, as she looked to the smaller man she had bloodied, but her hands were numb, and she could not control her grip. Her hand slipped from the unconscious man's clothing, and his limp body continued to hold her down.

The short man, his face now bleeding heavily, was on his feet, and with one hand covering his cheek, and his sword in the other, he moved toward her. "You beastly witch! I'll do you for that!"

Hollyglade reached for the sword dropped by the now unconscious man, found it by her left side, and brought it up as quickly as her numb hands would move it. The unconscious man still lay on top of her, making the move difficult, and even clumsier than her numbness had already caused it to be. As the bleeding man's sword came down she managed to get the blade in front of it, and both weapons collided.

She was cold, and numb. The blow knocked the sword from her hand, but with the momentum of her blocking motion, she managed to roll the unconscious body off and onto the ground. The bloody, pocked marked rider wobbled as he tried to control his follow through. Hollyglade sprang to her feet and lunged for him. As she did so, she lowered her shoulder and knocked him straight at the centre of the fire, and onto the stew pot and fire irons. He howled as he landed squarely in the center of the fire ring, sending sparks flying, losing his sword on impact.

Hollyglade stumbled clumsily to her knees again and let out a sharp cry, feeling another intense shot of pain jump through her legs as the rough, frozen soil bit at her. She fumbled for another branch from the scattered pile of firewood, until her hand clasped around the middle of a large piece. She looked to her left and saw the man had moved to all fours and was feeling for his sword. He grunted and spat as he located the blade and tried to grip the handle. Hollyglade sprang to her feet once more, gripped the branch in both hands, took one step forward, and with all her strength delivered a blow to the back of the man's neck as she let out a scream. He went limp before hitting the ground.

Hollyglade staggered, stumbled and reached for the sword she had dropped. She paused to gain her breath, and listen for any sounds, or a sign that someone might have heard the commotion. She could sense nothing, and so she stood catching her breath. She was naked, cold, numb, thirsty, hungry, bleeding, bruised, scraped, and dizzy with the aftermath of fear and panic. She began to cry softly.

Pulling herself out of her momentary tearful malaise, she inspected both men, finding them thoroughly unconscious. She grabbed the nearest blanket and wrapped herself tightly. Finding a rope amongst the small pile of supplies, she took it and began to drag each man, one at a time, over to a nearby tree. She laid them both on their backs and stretched their arms around the tree, tying them by their wrists with the rope lashed about the base of the tree. Once she was confident in her knotwork, she took a knife from one of the men's' belts and cut the sleeves from the smaller man's shirt, gagging each of them.

Hollyglade yanked off the larger man's riding boots, and tried to pull one of them onto her own foot to no avail. Though she was half elvish, a race with famously dainty feet, she was also half giantish, and though she was yet but a fifteen-year-old girl, she had already grown to a size beyond which she had ever seen any human man reach. She cursed and threw the boots toward the bush. There were still a few branches of firewood left. She placed several on the fire, and then took stock of the supplies the men had carried. Unfortunately, these two had not carried much in the way of supplies. She had hoped to have the use of one of the horses, which would give her a way to put some distance between her and the others of this bounty hunter's group, but in the commotion, they had both pulled themselves from their tether lines and run off into the night. Hollyglade took a moment to close her eyes and feel for the horses with her mind. She could not sense the presence of either animal. Though she knew horses often returned to their riders once panic subsided, she did not have time to wait.

The taller man had a long knife in his scabbard, which Hollyglade had retrieved from the blankets where he had been sleeping. She took the largest of the blankets, cut a hole in the middle and slipped it over her head. She took the other blanket, and cut a strip from the length of it, about a foot wide, which she then cut in half to use to wrap each of her feet. As she did so, she inspected the damage to her hands and feet. The soles of her feet had suffered numerous scrapes and impact wounds during her run along the road and through the bush. The necessary haste with which she had fled left her feet so battered that even the prospect of standing made her cringe.

The skin on her right knee had been torn nearly to the bone. Another sleeve torn from one of the now subdued men's shirts would have to serve as a bandage until she could find some clean cloth. Her hands radiated with pain as the heat from the fire restored some warmth to her body. With each incremental rise in the temperature of her body came the return of feeling, and with that she discovered new sources of pain. Her right hand had the remnants of several twigs buried in the palm, and was missing a layer of skin over a larger area. Her left was only marginally better, having several scrapes on the palm. She took the long knife from its sheath and began the painful process of removing splinters.

After a short while, one of the riders she had tied to the tree began to rouse. Hollyglade gave a dispassionate glance across the fire at the man as he let out several muffled groans. He became quiet as his gaze caught her eye. She raised an eyebrow and went back to cleaning the splinters from her hands. Moments later, the second man regained consciousness with a jerk and a muffled cry of pain. Hollyglade pretended not to notice.

"Welcome, Trenon Var Toran. Congratulations on your successful capture of our Demarian friend Lord Casterin of Downwater. The King was very pleased with the information I was able to extract from him. The Lorain people loved their prince, and were glad to see justice served to Lord Casterin by the hangman. It seems you have served many, by the capture of one man." Ni'Morstrom, the old Sorcerer, did not look up from his work table spread with vials, flasks, jars and bowls of various mixtures, as he addressed his guest. He kept his face mostly hidden beneath the hood of his grey cloak, which he wore over black robes, cinched at the waist with a brown cord. His hands, which could be seen pouring liquid from one vial to another, were white, gnarled, and spotted with age.

"I appreciate the gratitude of his excellency the King, and of those in his service. I quite appreciate the opportunity to continue being of value, and the opportunity to earn the compensation that comes with it. Tell me, how does our young and excellent King believe his Demarian counterpart, King Dermond, will take the news of the execution of one of his Lords? Is it not customary for Kings to offer the return of hostages, at least hostages in positions of or greater than Lordship, for a price? Was it not the good King's own grandfather who returned the Demarian prince, now King of his land, for compensation in the form of the counties of Shoreford and Clearvale, which our good King now rules as part of our beloved Loria? I wonder who advised such a sudden and trial-free execution of Lord Casterin, to our good King. Well, in truth that's none of my business and not why I'm here, is it?"

Trenon Var Toran was known for such elaborate ponderings. Maybe it was the sound of his own song-like voice, or the game of making salacious claims or guesses as to people's motivations with the intent of provoking a telling reaction. He enjoyed looking the part as well, with his cream white trousers, shirt and Jerkin, covered by black short cloak, and his riding gloves hanging neatly from one pocket. He spoke with a wide smile, and eyes that appeared genuinely pleased with himself, regardless of the content of his monologues. He enjoyed the way this approach would unnerve those whom he interrogated.

"Yes, Mr. Var Toran, your work was appreciated, as was your discretion. So will be your continued discretion." Ni'Morstrom ignored the subject of what fallout may come from the morning's public execution. "I have asked you here for something more than to simply settle your fee." The bounty hunter continued to smile as he raised an eyebrow, allowing the Sorcerer to continue.

"I wish to offer you another contract. A personal one this time. You came very highly recommended, and have proven yourself worthy of the high praise which preceded you. I hope I can count on your reputation for never failing to fulfill a contract continuing to build with this contract."

"Yes, my Lord Sorcerer, reputation is everything, which is why I'm careful which contracts I accept, and from whom I accept them. In that regard, I must inform you that I have tentatively agreed to take another contract, hired men necessary for its completion, and am thus previously engaged."

The Sorcerer did not look up as he responded

"I respect your desire to keep your word, but if I read correctly your use of the word 'tentatively' I assume that you have not signed anything binding. And in that case, I would suggest you hear my offer before you commit elsewhere."

Var Toran smiled, acknowledging the Sorcerer's assessment

"Tell me, what is the nature of the contract? I must hear some detail before I agree to put myself, and the few men I employ into any binding agreement."

Ni'Morstrom finished pouring the mixture, set the vial down and stood up from his work table. "While I certainly understand your desire to measure the risk and determine if the odds favour your success, this is one task which must remain secret. I am, as you are aware, someone who values discretion. Should I present the offer of, and details for, a contract to someone who decides not to accept that contract, I may find that the knowledge of the nature of the task which I have commissioned spread to places I would not like to have it spread." The Sorcerer turned from his table of experiments, and faced Trenon Var Toran directly. "Unless you agree to take this contract, one which shall pay you triple what the King contracted you for, I can tell you only this: I desire that a certain girl be brought to me alive, intact and relatively unharmed, in less than a fortnight."

Var Toran's smile did not waver as he clasped his hands behind his back and stepped to look out the window over the city. The sun was low in the sky, and the sounds of the city market closing for the evening floated up toward the tower which housed the Sorcerer's chambers. Trenon Var Toran gazed across the cityscape as he pondered the Sorcerer's offer. Six thousand gold crowns was an enormously rich price, one that would make great risk seem worthwhile, but it was also a price that indicated the size of that risk.

Var Toran was intrigued. Who might this girl be, that a Sorcerer in service to a king as naive as this one would pay as much as the monthly earnings of a handful of Lords to capture her? He had to know. The test she might provide could be interesting.

"My Lord Ni'Morstrom, the price you offer entices me as much by its allusion to intrigue as its sum total. As such, I shall accept your offer of this contract. Now, as you have declared the need for haste, I suggest we discuss the details. Tell me about this girl with three times the value of a foreign

Lord."

dGerrie Theurbeault approached the two men standing at the side port to the main castle gate apprehensively. dGerrie had never been inside the gates of Whiterock. He found himself somewhat in awe of the implied importance of the man he was sent to meet here, one who now met with someone in the Royal court.

It was an oddly hot day for this time of year. As fall turned to winter, the days grew shorter, and the air grew cooler. It was rare to experience the desire to remove a layer of clothing as the sun began to lower in the sky. As he looked up and down the street at the vendors and shoppers in the central market, no one else appeared to feel the heat as he did.

dGerrie was also experiencing a measure of trepidation over the way he had found himself in this situation. He was not entirely comfortable with signing on with one employer, only to leave several weeks later for employment with another, but this was not wholly his own doing. He had been in the employ of the King's city garrison in Magnaville for less than one month. That job would have paid steadily and was not easily secured. This morning his commander had informed him that his contract had been purchased by someone named Var Toran. dGerrie had given mild protest, but when the wage that came attached to the new assignment was mentioned, he stopped questioning it.

One hundred gold crowns was more money than he could make in a year with the garrison, but he did wonder to himself why it had been him the commander offered up, rather than someone higher ranking or more senior. Either way, dGerrie was not complaining when he was sent to meet the other men he would be working with.

Still dressed in his city garrison's uniform, dGerrie stood out on the crowded street. He generally did so anywhere he went, for at age 20, he was nearly 7 feet tall, had shaggy blonde hair, a light brown beard, and was somewhat skinny. He strode with confidence, which when combined with his stature, usually led to the crowd parting in front of him as he walked. He carried a short sword and a long knife on his hip, a longsword along with a mid-sized archer's bow and quiver on his back, and various other blades hidden about his body. dGerrie was fond of having plenty of options when it came to weaponry.

As he reached the side port, he cleared his throat to get the attention of the two men, who seemed engrossed in some private conversation.

"Excuse me lads, might you be Var Toran's men? I've been sent by the city garrison's commander, who informed me I'm to meet you here."

"Aye" replied the taller of the two men. "We been told 'e 'ired some new blood. You ain't small, is ya? This here's Tom, and I'm called Hern."

Hern, was slim, taller than the average man, clean shaven, and wore a fairly plain, brown leather jerkin over a long shirt and trousers. He appeared to keep himself fairly neat and clean, carrying a sword and knife on his belt.

"And w'o might you be called?" asked the shorter, stocky man, whom the first one had called Tom, seeming slightly disinterested in dGerrie. dGerrie noted that Tom seemed much less concerned with his appearance and cleanliness, had numerous scars and pockmarks on his face, and more than a few missing teeth. He was glad his height prevented the chance of a close face to face.

"The name's dGerrie. When might I speak to Mr. Var Toran? I'd like to know when we're leaving and what we're contracted to do."

"Heh." Chuckled Tom. "Don't be impatient boy. The Dancer never really gives out much detail before we actually 'it the road. Tends to be due to the nature of most of 'is work. We'll be on the road soon enough. 'E never gives us much notice when we'll be 'eadin out on a job, so you can be sure we'll be leaving tonight."

dGerrie looked to the west to find the sun only slightly above the horizon. The Dancer, thought dGerrie. I've heard that name before, and I don't remember feeling warm about it. His sense of discomfort remained. "The Dancer? I've heard him mentioned as a bounty hunter, but that's about it. Have you two worked for him long?"

"I'm as new as you, but Hern 'ere 'as worked for him a couple of times."

"Aye, I've worked for 'im these last couple of months. 'E's an 'ard man in many ways, but 'e pays well. And, 'e don't put on you the same kind of rules as that garrison you been slaving for."

dGerrie was not fond of the idea of working for someone with a disquieting reputation. Though he was beyond proficient with any weapon he picked up, he had only ever seen fit to use violence in self defense, the defense of a friend, or more recently, apprehending someone the garrison was ordered to pick up. Now though, he could not afford to be picky about the work he chose, owing to debts he had with several of the city's less law-compliant citizens, but he was still curious. "What kind of work did you do with The Dancer, if you don't mind me asking?"

"Ah, my towering friend..." dGerrie did stand head and shoulders above everyone on the street "If I told you that, 'e'd 'ave me 'ead. The Dancer, 'e usually takes the kind of job that requires a certain amount of desc.... Descre... of keepin' yer mouth shut"

As dGerrie absorbed the tone of warning in Tom's reply, he told himself to think about the money. With it, he was sure that he could clear his debts, and quite possibly find someway to improve his station in life, even if only marginally.

"Ah, I see. Then tell me, why The Dancer? Seems like an odd nickname."

Hern also looked at Tom for a reply.

"Well, I can tell you that, as I've seen the why of it me'self. 'E 'as an 'abit of takin' people by the 'and, people he's askin' questions of, and twirlin' them around like one of them fancy dances they do in Lord's and Lady's parties and weddings and such. I found it a bit odd myself, but it seems to make people real nervous, which I guess is 'is point."

Hern cocked an eyebrow as he looked away pensively. "And I 'eard he don't tend to leave them living neither" he added.

"No. 'E don't" Tom agreed.

dGerrie drew in a long breath and sighed. One Job, dGerrie. Just one. He sat down against the wall beside the door and waited. The two men traded stories about various conquests, both as mercenaries, and of women they tried to make the other believe they had been with.

dGerrie's mind wandered back along the path that had led him here. It had not been that long ago that he had been living in the Red Lanes, dressed in rags, and plying his trade as a pickpocket. He found himself missing certain aspects of that life. Though it was difficult in many ways, and there were plenty of days on which he had gone without a meal to speak of, he had always loved the company of the other boys and girls who had shared his plight as an orphan. It was a tight knit group, that gave meaning to the term honour among thieves. They often shared food when one had enough, though dGerrie was never under the illusion that certain scores weren't kept secret by the one who earned it, or more aptly, stole it.

dGerrie was glad to finally be earning a living more or less honestly. One of the things most of the orphans learned how to do well was fight. dGerrie, most of all. With his near seven-foot frame, he often found that he could use his length to keep other men at distance, and thus avoid any real damage in a fight. Eventually, he found that he had a knack for weapons. So far, there was not yet a single weapon, neither blade nor bow, that he had any real difficulty wielding well.

Maybe the life of a hired sword suits me. His unease returned as he noted to himself that neither of the two other men The Dancer had hired had been in his employ very long. You just hang back and do as you're told. Don't be brave, don't be stupid, and you'll be in the clear soon enough. With that, he sat and waited.

Ni'Morstrom motioned for him to sit, and Trenon Var Toran accepted.

"She is special in a number of ways I highly value for my work." The Sorcerer picked up a decanter and poured Var Toran a goblet of wine. "Have you heard the tale of The Great Destruction?" The Sorcerer spat out the word Great as though he did not like the term. Var Toran nodded.

"Well, I am sure there are some details, finer points that matter in this instance, that you likely do not know." He watched Var Toran for a moment to gauge his reaction. There was none, and so the Sorcerer continued.

"What most people are aware of, is that there was a great fire, preceded by an explosion that bent trees to the ground for nearly twenty leagues in each direction. The explosion seemed to originate at a small farming village in the centre the area of the Destruction. There were no known survivors, and many men of learning, wise and long-lived members of the Elvish race –even the wizard Artache– who could not give reason for the calamity. Some theorized that this was a natural phenomenon, like a previously unknown volcano, though in the absence of any evidence, that theory quickly faded from discussion.

"Others theorized that it was the work of a dragon, that perhaps this signaled the awakening of a member of their race. Though this theory gained some traction, the absence of any sightings or further activity suggests that their kind still slumber, as should be expected. Though the Golden Race has slept for near two hundred years, and the next stage in their usual cycle does draw near, this would be the earliest, in the recorded histories of men, that they would have ended their time of slumber.

"Some blamed the alchemists, suggesting that they were testing some sort of weapon commissioned by King Jerold.

Another easily dismissible theory based on, if nothing else, the late King's personality, character, and predisposition to be disinclined to the arts of war.

"An explanation, I may have, but for now that is not of your concern." He kept to himself the knowledge that he was sure of the fact that is was an immense unleashing of magical power, and not a large version of the kind of explosion the alchemists make with their mixing of powders.

"What will be of special interest to you," continued the Sorcerer "is that there was a survivor. One single girl was found by a convoy travelling from the western plains while en route to the city with grain for sale at the central market. This girl was brought here to Magnaville, and then shortly after that, when the man who had taken her under his protection was killed in some tavern dispute, she slipped away, and no-one can say with any certainty what happened to her."

He did not elaborate on the tavern brawl. He did not admit that he had heard the story from a witness to it, one who said that it was in fact, the young girl herself that killed her once saviour, when he tried to sell her to a less than scrupulous army commander for the night.

Var Toran showed a look of recognition "I have heard talk of this survivor, over the years. There are many terms used to describe her."

Ni'Morstrom raised an eyebrow, but did not address the almost mythical stature the stories had given the alleged survivor.

"The rumour I believe, is that she is the half-breed of a giantish mother and an elvish father. As you may be aware, half-breeds of humans to Elder Folk are not entirely unheard of, but are uncommon. Many explain the rarity of these pairings by the desire of most Elder Folk to keep the bloodlines pure. But nearly all those who give that explanation do not connect the reasoning for wanting the purity of the bloodlines to anything other than a sort of racial family honour.

"What most people overlook, and what is right in front of

them, is that all Elder races have naturally occurring magical abilities. The Giantish with their night vision, great strength, and communion with the animals. The Elvish with their long life, speed, and occasionally deeper magical powers. The Dwarvish with their tolerance of the cold, their ability to shape stone. The Gnomish with their lack of the need for much food, and their ability to work metal, and to breathe the thin air high in the mountains."

The Sorcerer did not mention that he was sure of the girl's magical abilities. He was sure of them because he knew that the only way a person could survive a magical outpouring of the magnitude of the Great Destruction, was that that person must have been the source of it. No magical ward could have withstood the power it took to make such a blast.

Ni'Morstrom paused and stepped to the window in a moment of deep thought. Var Toran took a draft of his wine and tilted his head, listening patiently. The sorcerer continued "When these elder folk breed with humans, the resulting offspring possess none of the abilities of their Elder Folk parent. Any subsequent children, whether they come from the half-breed and a human, or a half-breed and a member of one of the Elder races, are also bereft of these abilities.

"Furthermore, in my lifetime, I have never been able to find an example of a half breed with a human, where the Elder Folk parent was not either Elvish or Dwarvish. I have never so much as heard of a half-breed mix of two races of Elder Folk who has survived beyond infancy." He decided not to further elaborate on his knowledge of this girl's ancestry. The fact that he knew her parents to be a Giantish woman and a magically active Elvish man, would not likely help in this instance.

"Some, usually the wizards who devote themselves to the study of the natural world and its scientific mysteries, say that this is because such pairings produce offspring that are unable to survive. Others say that it is simply because such pairings are so rare, and that the bearing of mixed race children is forbidden by their clans. I tend to believe the former."

Truthfully, he knew more than that. He knew that nearly all pregnancies resulting from the joining of the Giantish, to any other of the Elder races, caused terrible miscarriages that most often took the life of the mother. He believed that it was some work of the father's magic that saved the child and the mother, and in the case of this girl, that this magic focused into the mother's womb may have been what caused the child to become as powerful as he believed her to be.

The Sorcerer turned back from the window and stepped over to his work table. "I believe it is most likely that this girl is the exception to the rule, and that she is more powerful than she knows. This is why I wish to meet her. I wish to study her, and determine whether or not she indeed has the power I believe she may. This was my wish ten years ago when I received word that a half breed child, one of two separate Elder races, had survived beyond the age of infancy, when most others that are not stillborn perish.

"Unfortunately, the envoy I sent to request that she and her parents join me here and allow me to examine her, perished in the Great Destruction." The Sorcerer would never admit to anyone that he had not sent an envoy, but rather a bounty hunter whom he had instructed to kill the parents and bring the child to him.

"How she survived, or what magical ability warded her, is something I must know, and wish to understand. Such knowledge could be put to great use in the service of our kingdom." The Sorcerer paused again, turning back to the window. His thoughts went momentarily to his work on devising a new ritual to transfer the magical power, from another magically active being, into himself. He was pulled from his thoughts by his guest.

"Tell me. How dangerous is she?" inquired the bounty hunter "You say she is half Elvish. The Elvish have been known to have among their kind wielders of great power. Have your sources given you any reports of her using magical power? Such knowledge would be useful for both our interests." Trenon Var Toran's perpetual grin did not leave his face.

Ni'Morstrom studied him for a moment, trying to decide how much more information to provide. The Sorcerer believed that this girl had tremendous power. Power that he wanted for himself. He could not let this bounty hunter know his true plans to take the girl's power from her. It was a risk to divulge anything about what he truly had in store for her, and it was also too risky to let anyone know just how much power he believed she truly possessed.

"The extent of her power is not known for certain. I have gained little information in that regard. Some of my sources say that she has power and fears to use it, or is unaware of how to use it, while others say she has no power at all. No matter the true extent of her power, I desire to find out for myself. The chance to study a surviving half breed of two Elder Folk, who likely has great power, is something I must pursue. As to your first question, you must consider her as dangerous as you deem her to be." Because if I told you how powerful I think she is, you would likely pass on the job, and my time is running out.

"She will be about 15 years old and therefore still very much a child, she will have spent her entire life living in squalor, she will not have been trained in the magical arts and should not have control over what power she may possess. More than that, I cannot say, but I would think you are well within your skill set, Mr. Var Toran." Again, Ni'Morstrom turned, and faced his guest.

"Perhaps it is so," offered Var Toran as he rose from the chair. "Well, as you have said, time is of the essence, so I will be on my way. There remains only the matter of my payment. As you are aware, I require at least one quarter of any contract up front." He stood straight and clasped his hands together in front, awaiting a reply.

The Sorcerer stepped to large set of cupboards along the wall behind the work table, motioned with his hand, and a door opened. He reached in and retrieved a small chest. Returning to the centre of the room, he handed the chest to

Var Toran.

"Two Thousand crowns. One third your contract. Remember Var Toran, one fortnight, no later."

With a widening of his ever-present grin, Var Toran accepted the chest.

"One more thing," added the Sorcerer "take this with you also. It may be of use to you." He handed the bounty hunter a letter and turned back to his work table.

Var Toran opened the letter and raised an eyebrow as he read the contents. "Our good King is generous, yet I doubt I'll need such assistance"

The Sorcerer turned to look back over his shoulder "Nevertheless."

Var Toran stepped back, straightened up, bowed, and made his way out of the room.

As he heard his guest make his way down the stairs from his chambers, Ni'Morstrom motioned the door closed with his hand and made his way to the corner of the room. There, he removed a large canvas cloth from a barred cell, in the shape of a large cage one might use to bring chickens to market, to reveal a bound and gagged Elvish girl. He walked over to his work table and picked up the flask he had been working with during the conversation with his guest.

Returning to the cage, he stretched out his hand toward the young girl. She groaned as she was forced upright and pulled forward to the bars of the cage by some working of the Sorcerer's power. With the flick of his wrist, the gag dropped to her neck, and she attempted to cry out, only to produce a hissing, gurgling sound as the Sorcerer kept his hold on her.

He came close to her, and moved his free hand to her chin, lifting her head slightly and forcing her mouth open. He began to pour the contents of the flask into her mouth, and then with a motion of his hand, forced her mouth closed and waited for her to swallow.

Once she had unwillingly gulped the vile liquid down, he released his hold on her, and stepped back from the cage. There, he raised the flask to his lips, and drank the remainder of its contents. He grinned savagely, and began to chant. Immediately the elvish girl's eyes rolled back in her head. She fell to the floor of the cage and began to shake.

As they rode into another small village, dGerrie felt the same apprehension he had experienced four days ago at the side port to the palace gates. There were several reasons he could cite to explain the feeling, but in truth, he was not entirely sure where to place that blame. He was aware that signing on with the city garrison would mean that he would have been, from time to time, assigned to a squad tasked with moving Elder Folk out of the city. He had seen the garrison performing this new duty, one resulting from a new order signed by the young king, and so far, it had been performed in an orderly manner without any real harm coming to anyone. Occasionally someone would put up a struggle, but for the most part the garrison's refrain of "move along" accompanied by their usual strength in numbers, was enough to get the job done peacefully.

This work was different. This was bounty hunting. dGerrie had heard the odd rumour about bounty hunters. It was not a common trade, as it was usually the King's garrisons, or the Royal army that were sent to find outlaws and criminals. But when rewards were posted for finding someone and bringing them in alive, often bounty hunters were the ones to claim the reward. Usually though, they were not like The Dancer.

Most of them showed the signs of being on the road for long periods of time. Most of them displayed a general lack of hygiene and plenty of scars to remind them of the fact that criminals do not usually come quietly. They were not generally the kind of men whose company one enjoyed. But this bounty hunter was different. He had not a single mark on him, dressed like he was on his way to a wedding, had a grin that never left his face –which dGerrie found unnerving at times–

and never seemed to stop talking about life and the way the world worked.

So far, they had not managed to pick up the trail of the girl they were looking for. dGerrie, having travelled the road south from Magnaville before, was not surprised that there had been no evidence in the villages they had passed of the person they sought. Most people who wished to avoid the army or the garrison, gave Magnaville a wide berth and travelled via the green river in the south, or one of the hill-to-sea roads that ran east to west, parallel to the Green river. Most of the Elder Folk who left the city as a result of the King's new decree, stayed off the main roads until they were well away from Magnaville and the King's garrison. dGerrie assumed that this was also the case with the girl they were after.

Trenon Var Toran, as dGerrie had learned The Dancer was properly named, had given them a reasonable description. She was said to be fifteen years old, extremely tall, had dark brown or red hair, and was half Elvish.

dGerrie had known several half-breed orphans in his time in the Red Lanes; a couple of them were half Elvish, and a few half Dwarvish. He knew it was quite a rare thing to be a half-breed, yet there was a small concentration of them in Magnaville. This was due to the number of children who were orphaned in the Great Destruction. Sadly, that catastrophic event had taken place right at the peak of harvest time, when many workers left their children with neighbours and relatives to go to the Western Farms to find seasonal work helping with the harvest.

dGerrie was one of those orphans himself, though not a half breed. His parents were both killed ten years ago while working a harvest contract on a farm just outside the village at the centre of the blast. He was ten years old at the time, and had been left with his father's cousin to help with the sheep he kept. dGerrie remembered not liking his father's cousin, and running away to the city after learning of his parent's death. So, in a way, dGerrie empathized with this girl.

Var Toran motioned for the men to stop at a one of the

first buildings on the road within the village. "Gentlemen, if we do not find what we are looking for here, you two" he pointed to Tom and Hern, "will take the southwest fork out of town, and we shall take the southeast fork. Spend daylight searching for leads, and meet back here tomorrow evening, where we will decide which direction to head next." dGerrie had noted that it was the bounty hunter's customary routine to lay out a plan for the whole day, and usually the day following, each morning. dGerrie found it to be an effective practice. He appreciated knowing what was expected of him.

The building appeared to be an inn, though there was no signage on the exterior, and Var Toran wished to go inside to speak to the innkeeper. As they dismounted, he instructed the other two to canvas the villagers who were out and about, to see if they could produce a lead. It was near an hour before sundown, and dGerrie hoped that they would stop here for the night. He could smell something delicious wafting through the open door, and would be glad to spend some of the silver he had been advanced on a bowl of stew and a mug of ale. dGerrie and The Dancer entered the inn.

As he looked around the interior of the building, dGerrie saw a small number of patrons at tables along the wall of the main room. There was a stone fireplace in the middle of the room where a pot hung over a small fire, simmering some sort of wonderful smelling stew. As they stepped toward the fireplace to warm their hands, a woman approached. "Greetings travellers! Are you looking for a room, a meal, a bath? I can happily offer any or all, so long as you got the coin."

Var Toran donned his ever-present grin and turned to address the innkeeper. "I thank you for your generous offer of hospitality, but we must not linger here I'm afraid. You see, we are about an important task. We are searching for a lost girl, in fact. We are in great haste and can not manage to delay, for her caretaker greatly desires her swift and safe return. We have come to your establishment in the hopes that you might be able to provide us with some assistance, which we would greatly appreciate.

"You see, so far we have been unable to find anyone who has seen, or heard any sign of the poor girl whom we are endeavouring to locate. It appears many of the people we pose our inquiries to, are reluctant to give us any information at all, and they all want to swear that they have not seen a single sign of the unique young girl we search for. I hope with all my heart, for her sake, that our luck with you is different. I hope that the people of your lovely and quaint little farming village have sighted her, and might take pity on her by offering us some information as to her whereabouts."

His mouth bore a smile that showed his clean white teeth, his eyes smiled, he spoke with a pace and melody that made dGerrie think he would break into a song at any moment. Yet there was always a hint of the underlying threat of violence, that if you knew him, or his reputation, you would rightly fear. dGerrie stood unmoving, silently observing. He was now well aware of The Dancer's disdain for being interrupted.

It was only three days ago, while questioning an innkeeper just outside Magnaville, that he was interrupted by the innkeeper's helper. When the young whelp had piped up to try to say that no one had seen a girl like that, Var Toran, without breaking his grin had drawn his dagger, turned and stabbed the boy in through one cheek and out the other. Without the slightest hesitation, he had simply stated "Interruptions are sign of very bad manners.", and continued his questions to the innkeeper as though nothing had happened.

Here though, Var Toran paused for a moment to allow the innkeeper to respond.

"Well, good sir..."

"No, No. I'm not a knight" He interjected. She was caught off guard, as it seemed clear to dGerrie that she was only trying to be polite, and fumbled over her next few words.

"Umm... er... yes me Lord.."

"Not a Lord either my dear."

His abrupt interjections seemed to make her nervous. "Well, er.. Could you tell me who it is that you are looking for? Maybe she may have stopped in here, or someone may have seen her passing through town."

He moved toward her, took off his gloves, and reached for her hand. She nervously allowed him to take it, and he pulled her close. "Well, as I said, she is quite unique in appearance. Though I have not had the pleasure of seeing her myself, she has been described to me. She is said to have brown or red hair. She is said to be extremely tall, maybe even taller than my companion here. She is about fifteen years old, and half Elvish." He pulled the woman closer and placed his free hand behind her back, and began to sway slightly.

"Now, my dear, before you give me an answer to whether or not you have seen such a girl, please allow me to lead you in a little dancing. You see, I find dancing to be a terribly relaxing and comforting experience. I find it to be so, for a number of reasons." As Var Toran began to turn with her slowly, she shot dGerrie a glance. Her eyes were widening, and her face was beginning to lose some of its colour.

"You see, dancing takes coordination and cooperation. The two dancers must pay attention to each other. The leader, which would be me in this case, must give his partner subtle cues about his intent. He must give no more than a hint, lest he give away his intent to the onlookers and thus spoil the pleasure they may take from the entertainment. We wouldn't want anyone else know just what we were going to do as we dance, for it must be a surprise in order to captivate the audience. No, the communication must stay between the dancing partners." dGerrie turned his head slightly, and watched out of the corner of his eye, as the people who had been sitting at the table filed out of the inn.

"Now, my dear, the other aspect of dancing, which helps very much while having a conversation in which one desires to know the truth, is the need for the follower, that would be you in this case, to pay attention to the cues of the leader, so as not to fall out of step. Furthermore, the need for concentration is two-fold. On one hand, the follower must pay attention to her feet so as not to miss a step. If she does not miss a step, it is more likely that she is paying sufficient attention to the dance cues of her partner. In doing so, she is less likely to be able hide any attempt to misdirect her partner in the conversation they have as they dance. And my dear, in polite society, the conversation one has while dancing is just as important as the dancing itself, for that is the entertainment for the dancers themselves.

"On the other hand, if she puts more concentration on the conversation than the dance steps, and makes an attempt to mislead her partner in that conversation, then she is likely to miss a step, or at least not be quite as smooth as she thinks she is, with her movements."

dGerrie noticed a bead of sweat starting to form on the woman's forehead. Her lower lip began to quiver as they turned about the floor in front of the fireplace. Var Toran led the woman through a few turns without saying anything, letting the tension build as his veiled threats hung in the air.

"Now, my dear woman, have you seen anyone matching the description of this girl?"

She nodded.

"Good! Fantastic! What wonderful news!" His smile widened, and his eyes lit up like a child receiving a present on their birthday. "Now, my dear, tell me when you saw her."

"Today. Here. This morning before noon." She trembled as she let out the words. Her eyes flitted between Var Toran, dGerrie, and the door.

"That's wonderful news! Now, can you tell me where she went from here?"

The woman grimaced, and turned nearly white with fear. dGerrie was beginning to think The Dancer's reputation had preceded him here, and that this woman may have heard of how the other people who had been questioned in this way, on this trip, had fared.

"I believe she went to try her luck at finding a room at the cottage on the edge of town. I swear to the gods, I know no more than that" She was visibly shaking now. His smile was unwavering, and the excitement in his voice reached a level that made the hair on the back of dGerrie's neck stand up, as Var Toran continued to turn her around the floor.

"And what makes you think she would seek a room there?"

"She was told she may find a room there."

"Ah." He continued his swaying, turning steps as he formed his next question. "And whom, may I ask, did the telling?" He cocked an eyebrow as he posed the question he seemed to already know the answer to.

She began to open her mouth to reply, and tripped over one of his feet. He caught her and steadied her momentarily as he pressed the question "My dear, it is polite to answer promptly when your dancing partner has asked you a question."

She looked at dGerrie, who gave her no response. He had been reprimanded severely for interjecting the first time he had been present for one of these interviews.

She began to panic.

"I told her to move on. I told her that the King's new decree meant she wouldn't be welcome here. I only told her that the old woman in the cottage at the edge of town used to have some of them Elder Folk work for her in the past." She stumbled again slightly.

Var Toran stopped dancing, let go of the woman's waist, yet held onto her right hand with his left. "You see Mr. Theurbeault, I have never had the need for uncivilized methods of questioning." Var Toran did not take his eye off the woman as he spoke. "But, my dear, you did mention the King's decree. So, I must now assume that you are aware of the entire declaration. You must know, that our good and beloved King included with his righteous decree, that anyone who provides shelter, food, coin, or other such aides to the Elder Folk, that he has so fairly required to leave the Kingdom of Loria, should be subject to punishment under the law.

"Now, though you did not provide one of the aides specifically stated in the good King's decree, I must make note that giving direction to where one might find shelter, food, or coin, would fall under 'other such aides', and I'm afraid, my dear, that that makes you subject to the good King's punishment under the good King's law."

She tried to pull away as she began to protest. He held her hand with a vice-like grip, pulled it to his lips and kissed the back of it. He then stepped back slightly, still holding her hand in his, drew his dagger and plunged it into her chest. She cried out as he drove the blade to the hilt. She fell to the floor as she slipped off the end of Var Toran's dagger.

"Mr. Theurbeault." Var Toran bent to wipe clean his dagger with the dying woman's apron, then stood and faced the fireplace. "Please locate the rest of our party, and meet me here. We shall proceed to the edge of town forthwith."

dGerrie nodded, as he watched The Dancer pick up the ladle from the stew pot, and sample the stew, giving a long mmmmm in approval.

dGerrie ducked out the door and went to find the other two men.

Hollyglade picked up the stew pot and examined what remained of its contents. There was nothing left of the stew but a mouthful of broth, as most of it was now spread across the ground where she had sent the second man tumbling through the fire. She brought it to her lips and sipped what remained in a single draft. She had tasted worse, but her stomach growled, and she gritted her teeth as she thought about the stew she had left over the fire at the cottage only a few hours earlier. Her mind wandered to what might have happened to it now that the old woman lay dead in the yard of her own house.

Had the man in white, and his tall companion shared it while she froze in the bushes? For some reason, it bothered her a great deal. Never mind Holly, you've got more pressing matters. She put the pot on the ground, and picked up the saddle bags the men had left by their respective sleeping positions.

She turned each of the saddle bags upside down, and poured out the contents by the fire. As she did so, one of the men gave a muffled protest, and she turned her head to see his gaze come to meet hers. She cocked an eyebrow and looked back down at the items from the saddle bags now spread in front of her. There were a couple of coin purses, with only a few silvers between them, a small knife, a flint, a small pouch of oats, a spare set of reins and a short length of thin rope. It appeared to Hollyglade that these men had not packed for a long journey, and seemed to expect never to be far from a town.

She had hoped to find some dried beef, or some other food for the trail, but she had no such luck. She did know, from hearing the conversation the two men had had by the fire earlier, that they would not be expected by the rest of their party until later in the coming morning, but she still wanted to start putting distance between her and the men who hunted her. She needed information, needed to know why she was being hunted, and on whose behalf.

Hollyglade repacked the contents of both bags into the largest one, and set them aside. She took both riders' water skins and drank her fill before tying them onto the saddlebag she planned to carry. She stood, and strode over to where she had tied her former pursuers, and seeing that they had both now regained consciousness, she removed the gag from the shorter one.

"You'll get cut for this, mark my words." the man spat.

Hollyglade smirked as she stepped back closer to the fire to continue to warm herself. "Why do you hunt me? Who contracted your employer to find me?" Both men looked at each other, then back to Hollyglade.

"What do you plan on doin' with us? Not much point in us answerin' if you're just goin' to kill us anyway."

"I have no plans to kill you, but that could easily change, and there are many methods of persuasion I could come up with to encourage you to talk with me, short of killing you." Hollyglade had no intention of doing further harm to either man. Violence did not come easily to her, and for as long as she could remember, she was sickened by the thought of one person harming another. Now though, she needed these men to believe she was capable of using violence, as she would be very unlikely to persuade them to talk without that belief. She could not afford to have her bluff called.

"Do you know what it's like to sit out in the cold for a night during winter? Have you ever felt your legs go numb from foot to hip? The intensity of the pain that breaks through the numbness when toes start dying and fingers freeze solid? It's not pleasant." She walked back to the short man and grabbed one of his legs, which he attempted to resist, and pulled his boot off. She then grabbed him by the other foot and removed that boot as well. She threw them toward the bushes, where in her earlier frustration, she had thrown the tall man's boots.

"This fire will go out once I stop tending it, and you'll soon know what real cold feels like. Sure, you have your trousers and shirts, but they can easily be cut off. I'd like to leave you with some way to retain some warmth, but that depends on what you decide to share with me." She returned to her position by the fire, holding her hands out over the flames, taking in the heat. She looked sideways at the men, awaiting their response.

"Alright, alright. I'll tell you what we know. We was 'ired by The Dancer back in Magnaville, four days ago. 'E went into the castle on the day we left, in the mornin', to meet with someone er other in there about a job. When 'e came out, 'e only told us who we was lookin' for. 'E only gave us just a description. Very tall, dark brown or red hair, and about fifteen years old, and a girl. That's it, I swear. We ain't even got a lead until this mornin'."

She waited, hoping her silence would evoke more in the way of a response. Someone in Magnaville. Who? I haven't been there in years. This is the closest I've been to the city walls in a very long time. I can't have angered anyone there recently, and when I left, I did so without anyone holding any grudges, as far as I can remember.

He continued "The Dancer don't tell 'is men much before a job. It's 'is way. 'E is very clear about only tellin' us what 'e thinks is enough. I swear it. Please don't kill me. I weren't goin' to kill you if I had been the one to find you."

She whirled around and aimed a finger at him. "No. Just have your way with me. You fancied being with a larger woman, wondered what that would be like. No, you're not a killer. Just a rapist." With that, she moved over to his waist, and undid his belt. He began to thrash, so she leaned over, and though it caused her considerable pain, put one knee on his belly, and the other on his crotch. She then pulled the belt from his trousers.

"Hold still, or this will hurt a lot more than it has too." She then moved to his feet, took hold of one trouser leg in each hand, and pulled them off. "Pity you're such a tiny and insignificant man." She let the insult hang in the air for a moment, and watched as the man squeezed his legs together to protect his now completely exposed manhood.

"I could have used a good pair of trousers." She bunched up the britches and tossed them aside, turning back to face the now half naked man. "Whom, did this Dancer meet with?" She spat the name at him, drawing out the rest of her question through gritted teeth as she pulled the long knife from the its sheath, and played with the tip. She took a step back toward the man slowly, to let him reach the fullness of the fear she meant to evoke.

"I don't know for certain, I ... I ... can only tell you what I saw." The man squirmed himself away as much as he could, clamping his legs shut and trying to pivot around the tree, until he came up against his still gagged companion. Hollyglade took a step closer, and ran a finger along the knife blade, then looked him in the eye and waited.

"Look. There could only be an 'andful of people who could afford 'im, and fewer still that you'd need to meet at the castle in Magnaville. My guess, would be 'e met with either someone in the King's Vestry, or the King 'imself. I can't make any good guess beyond that. Please! Mercy."

Hollyglade paused in thought for a moment. The King? Why wouldn't he just send a garrison, or the army? But his Vestry? That doesn't make any sense either. She turned back to the fire and rubbed her forehead pensively for a while, before stepping toward the still gagged taller man. She took the knife and pressed it to his cheek, held it for a moment, and then undid the gag.

"Anything to add?"

He shook his head. "No ma'am. E' told you the truth, and all of it. We ain't got no further instructions from The Dancer. Please don't kill us."

"No. I won't kill you."

Hollyglade took the sleeves she had used as gags, and rebound both men into silence, making sure they would not be able to work free anytime soon. Then, with the rope she had found in the saddle bag, tied both men's legs together and stretched the free end of the rope to a nearby tree, and secured it.

She picked up the second scabbard, and slung it, along with the saddle bag over her shoulder. She took a branch from the ground and used it to scatter the coals of the fire, eliminating any active flame, and hastening its cooling. Then, with a swift turn, she silently strode out of the clearing.

As Var Toran approached the short stone wall of the cottage, he motioned his men close. "You two." He pointed to Tom and Hern, "One on either end of the house, so that you can see around the corner, and you." He looked at dGerrie. "With me inside.

"Now, I have a conversation to strike up."

They tied their horses to the railing beside the wall's gate, and walked to the front door. Var Toran stepped up to the door and gave it several hard knocks. There was no reply. He sighed, and knocked several more times, saying something under his breath about manners and guests at the door, that dGerrie could not quite pick up.

After a moment, a voice called back from inside "Hold steady and save your knuckles, I'm too old to run for knockers at my door." A moment later the door opened, and dGerrie could see a short, white haired old woman, who looked to him to be older than his grandmother's grandmother.

Var Toran's grin presented itself in all its spine tingling glory. "Hello my dear. May we come in? I have a few questions about a missing girl."

III : ESCAPE

Ni'Morstrom entered Prince Harford's side chamber and stepped forward to the table at the centre of the room. "It is an auspicious day, my Prince. The gods have favoured you. I have come to wish you well before your coronation."

Nervously, the young prince looked up from his waist, where he had been struggling to properly adjust his belt, and nodded to the Sorcerer. He looked back down at the tailor who was finishing the last adjustments to his ceremonial vestments.

"Will you be by my side? You've been so helpful these last few months since…. Since the loss of my Father, and then brother. I would like you to be there."

"My apologies my Prince. There are other matters I must attend to, that cannot wait. It is several days after the new moon, and there are some things I must attend to before the coming of the next lunar phase. And besides, I am not fond of ceremony. Yet you know that I shall always support you and advise you well."

With a motion of his hand, the Prince dismissed the tailor. "Yes, you have always guided me. I thank you for your friendship." He stepped down from the tailor's box, and faced the Sorcerer. "How do I look?" The prince had chosen to have embroidered on his jacket his family's ancient crest, two bears facing each other standing and fighting, which signified the northern and southern arms of the western mountains, above strip of blue which signified the sea.

He had chosen the crest, rather than the royal insignia, a white shield with a purple sash.

"You look regal," Ni'Morstrom gave a slight grin as he looked the prince up and down "and soon, you shall be King."

"Yes. So I'm told. But isn't this all a bit fast? I know that my brother is missing, and that some have presumed him dead, but I believe he may still be alive."

"Your Grace, we have discussed this several times," replied the Sorcerer, raising a hand as he spoke. "You know the law.

The throne must not remain empty indefinitely. No, no body was discovered, yet it has been weeks since the Prince went missing. If Demaria had taken him, we would have received ransom demands. The same would likely have occurred if it were some upstart faction within Loria. He is gone. We must accept that and move on. It falls to you to rule." The Sorcerer paused, and turned to look out over the city before continuing.

"Have you given thought to my advice regarding the Elder Folk? I believe that your kingdom shall be much safer, once they have been moved to other lands. The Commander of Your Royal Forces still believes that your brother's murder was indeed the work of the Elvish. I want to make sure that you, and your people are safe from such threats."

"Do you believe it was the Elvish? They have never bothered us before. Father always said we should try to get along with everyone, that peace makes prosperity. He was always fond of the Elvish."

Slowly, Ni'Morstrom approached the Prince "That, my Prince, is why it is a much viler thing, the disappearance of your dear brother. The betrayal of your good Father's trust and friendship is no small matter. However, we may find that it was not the Elvish alone, who had a hand in your brother's loss. There are others who would seek to attack you. If you recall, my Prince, Shoreford and Clearvale were not always part of your kingdom. Though your family knows them as ancestral lands, they had been ruled by Demaria for nearly ten generations before your grandfather fought to reclaim them."

"Do you think that King Dermond would do such a thing? How would taking my brother help them reclaim Shoreford and Clearvale? Oh, I was not ready for this. I was always second to my brother. It was he who was supposed to succeed to the throne after our father. He was raised for that, trained for it. I spent my whole youth learning the arts, and being groomed to support my brother. I'm too young for this." He dropped his head to his chest, looked at the crest embroidered there, and sighed.

Deliberately, the Sorcerer came to the Prince's side, took

his arm and walked him to the window overlooking the mezzanine. "My Prince, fear not. I work day and night on a new way to aid your rule. It is part of a Sorcerer's life to continually seek greater knowledge, and greater capability. And in my case, to use such knowledge and ability to aid the one I serve. I believe I am very close to perfecting a new way to bring stability and peace to your kingdom. But my efforts require much concentration and focus, and the dedication of my time and energies.

"Nevertheless, I shall always be readily at your side should you need my counsel, or other service. Rest assured, once I have unlocked the secrets I endeavour to discover and to master, you shall never need fear for your kingdom. Together, we shall bring peace to the world." Slowly, he turned and moved back to the table.

"My Prince, let us not dwell on politics or the past, just now. Today is a great day for you, your house, and your Kingdom. Take heart. Once you are King, we shall move to set right the wrongs done against your house and your kingdom. For now, enjoy the celebration. Tomorrow we shall begin to shape your Kingdom to be pure and strong, just as its new King is pure and strong."

The Prince picked up his cup of wine and raised it. "To a strong and prosperous Loria."

"Yes, my Prince. Strong and pure."

The floor of the cell was rough stone. It was not like the cells below the castle's keep which were constructed block by block. It appeared to be carved from the rock as a single hollowed out room. Not that it could really be called a room when its occupant could not stand without having to bend to keep from pressing his head against the ceiling.

Jeron had not seen the sun for a long time. He wasn't sure if it had been days, weeks, or longer. His back, knees, feet, and hands had developed sores from constant contact with his rough-hewn hollow. The steel bars that made up the one wall that was not rock were no easier on him than the rest of the cavity he was confined to. In all the time he had been kept here, he had not seen his captor. A guard, who was disguised in plain and indistinct clothing, kept his face covered with cloth when bringing scraps of food, or removing the shallow bucket Jeron had been provided as a sort of chamber pot.

There was no light, but when the guard came in carrying a torch, Jeron was able to catch a glimpse of some of what lay beyond the bars of the cell. It appeared that there was a short hallway on this side of the door which the guard came through and exited from, and at least one more cell opposite his, which was now empty.

Until a few days ago, or what he assumed were days, there had been a young Elvish girl occupying the cell across from him. She did not speak the common tongue, so he had not been able to glean much from his attempts to communicate with her. He was able to understand that her name was Aleera. He had deduced, by the fact she spoke only her native tongue, that she had been brought here, wherever here was, from the Western Mountains somewhere beyond the source of the River High. That was one of the last strongholds of the Elvish, and a place where men dared not venture without an invitation.

The Elvish had lived there for longer than men can remember, and from substantially earlier than men began recording their own history. The Elvish fiercely defended their lands, and did not recognize the borders of men. Both the Kingdom of Loria, and their southern neighbours in Sudara, had tried to bring the Elvish lands into their own control, and both kingdoms had failed time and again.

The Elvish prefer the high mountains, and the thick forests of the foothills. Such places are nearly impossible for an invading force to gain a foothold. The Elvish are long-lived and cunning warriors, and do not fight battles the way men do.

Whomever it was that managed to capture this girl, must have gone to great lengths to do so, and must have had incredible resources at their disposal. But why? Why a seemingly random Elvish girl? And what could we possibly have in common? The questions gnawed at him.

In the time he had spent on the unforgiving floor of this crude jail, he had speculated on the many reasons a person could have had for wanting to capture him. Ransom was the chiefest among them, but he had dismissed that once his stay had grown to more than a few days. Ransoms were rare, but were never something prolonged. No one had come to try to extract information from him, so he did not suspect having been captured by a rival. There had been peace in the realm for a generation, and neither of the Kings, nor petty lords had more than small trade disputes.

The girl had been taken from her cell only a short time ago, yet it had felt like an eternity to him. Having lost the company of this girl, Jeron felt more alone than ever before. Though they could not speak each other's language, the fact that Jeron had someone else to talk to had given him hope. Even though they had not been able to understand each other's words, Jeron had felt an immense closeness to her. She had been the only person he had had any real contact with since he had been imprisoned.

His sense of loss ate at him. He hadn't even been awake when she was taken. He had fallen asleep, and when he awoke, she had been gone. Was she even real? Had she even been there at all? Have I been dreaming, or hallucinating? Am I saying this aloud? He had lost all sense of time, all sense of reality.

Jeron was truly alone. In the first few days of his captivity, or what he thought were days, he had demanded of the guard an answer as to where he was and why he was here, but he was given no reply of any kind. In fact, Jeron had not heard the guard speak to anyone. He had begun to wonder if the guard was mute. Over the course of that same span, Jeron had tried to devise a method of escape. He found none. The rock was solid, the steel bars were thick and set deep into the stone, and there seemed to be no door in the bars at all. It was as if the cell had been built around him with the intent that he never leave, neither alive nor dead.

He slept occasionally. Though he ate every morsel of food he had been provided, he was losing a considerable amount of weight. He had always been strong and fit, but now he felt like a shadow of his former self, weak and lethargic.

The day he last remembered being somewhere other than in his present captivity, he had been on his way to Westport, to visit his family's crypt and mourn his father in the Western mountains just beyond the seaside trading hub which lay close to the Demarian border. The journey was a three to five day ride from Magnaville, depending on how a group travelled, and Jeron had wanted to make it a short trip, so had decided to make the trip alone. It was not the first trip he had made on his own. He had spent several summers at the Hot Lake, and along the coast where the River Low meets the sea, with cousins from the southern plains. He had felt that this trip would not be a risk, even though it travelled along the border road, since there had been peace in the region for so long, and he planned to travel light and plainly dressed.

How wrong he had been. It was on the third night when camping by the roadside, something Jeron often enjoyed, that he had been set upon in the night. While fast asleep he had been taken by more than a few men, odds that he likely could not have overcome awake and armed. The men had rendered him unconscious, the lump on the back of his head had only recently healed. Jeron had awoken in the cell he still occupied. Neither questions nor answers had come since. He wondered how much longer it would be before he went mad. Have I gone mad already? Is this just a dream? Either seemed better to him than wasting away in his personal dungeon.

Jeron awoke to the sound of the outer door opening. He sat up and slid the shallow bucket to the edge of the steel bars and backed away, as was the expectation he had come to learn. This time something was different. It was not the guard who approached his cell. As he cowered against the rear wall of the stone cavity, a darkly cloaked figure stepped into view. Jeron's wavy black hair, which had grown noticeably longer since his incarceration, covered his face as he hugged his knees to his chest and pressed his side to the wall.

With one eye, he peered through his disheveled locks, and began to shiver as the veiled, arcane figure stood at the bars. Jeron could not make out a face through the shadow cast by the hood of the cloak, nor could he see the hands that were hidden in the long sleeves of the robe. Jeron thought about speaking, about posing the questions he had asked himself over and over, but he could not force out the words. He felt cold, fearful like never before.

Gradually, the sound of breathing seeped from within the hood of the cloak. One of the figure's hands appeared from it's sleeve and beckoned to Jeron.

"Come," called a deep and commanding voice.

Jeron couldn't move, wouldn't move. He felt both paralyzed with fear, and stubbornly defiant. The need to resist and deny the command at all cost was strong, yet something compelled him to his feet. His body started to move, though he tried to restrain himself. He clenched his jaw so hard that he felt his muscles burn as he attempted to keep himself away from the bars.

"No" Jeron managed to rasp "Who... are.... you?". He felt pressure on his neck and a sudden dryness in his throat. He thought that if he tried to utter another word, that his mouth would tear and start to bleed. He was on his feet now, moving slowly to the front of the cell. He put his hands up to stop himself for fear of driving his own head into the bars, and when he made contact with the steel, he found himself gripping it with all his strength.

This was obviously a person of incredible power. Jeron's mind raced through all the beings who could possibly have the magical strength which currently compelled him. This could not be a wizard, their order did not shave or cut their hair, and Jeron saw no beard protruding over the neck of the robe. This was no Elvish mage, they would not hide their faces, nor their intent.

This had to be a Sorcerer. Who could this be, and what does he want with me? Jeron had heard that there had been a sorcerer in the capital just before his father died, but he hadn't heard anything other than that, and assumed it was just idle talk. Is this that sorcerer, or could I be somewhere other than in Magnaville? Jeron's mind raced through all the possible scenarios that could have brought him here, but could come to no conclusion as he fought, and failed to regain control of himself.

From within the folds of his cloak, the Sorcerer withdrew a small vial with one hand, and a small knife with the other. He stepped toward the bars Jeron gripped unwillingly and pressed the rim of the empty vial against the fingers of Jeron's left hand. Then with his other hand, pressed the tip of the knife into Jeron's hand to break the skin.

Jeron winced and let out a rasping groan as the knife entered the back of his weakened hand. The pain was tremendous and overwhelming. Jeron was normally not a weak man and readily dealt with small injuries with a dismissive ease. After so much time suffering through dehydration and near starvation, he found that his nerves had become extremely sensitive and that he did not have the mental fortitude to endure even the smallest of cuts.

The blood trickled down the back of Jeron's hand and into the Sorcerer's vial. The warmth of his own blood surprised Jeron, as he had felt so cold for so long confined within this stone box. After a moment the vial was nearly full, and the Sorcerer stepped back from the bars. Jeron felt his grip on the steel release as he sank to the floor. He took his left hand in his right, and tried to stem the flow of blood, as he watched the Sorcerer place the knife somewhere within the folds of his robe, and bring out another vial. This vial had a cork stopper and contained a black liquid. Jeron watched as the Sorcerer used his thumb to flick the stopper from the vial, and then raise them both to his eye level. As he did so the lower half of the Sorcerer's face caught the light.

Jeron stared into the Sorcerer's hood to see the scarred and wrinkled face of this mysterious practitioner of the arcane. "What do you want with me?" he wheezed. The Sorcerer gave no hint that he had heard Jeron as he began to pour a drop of the black liquid into the vial containing Jeron's blood. As Jeron watched the blood and the strange black liquid mix, his jaw dropped at what he saw. The blood began to smoke and turn white. Quickly, the whole vial became as white as ivory, and the Sorcerer's mouth spread into a sinister grin revealing his graying teeth.

Reaching into his robe once more, the Sorcerer retrieved another cork and sealed the vial, and without a word he turned and left the cells. As the door closed and blackness returned to the crude prison, Jeron crept to the back wall of his hold, curled up in the corner, and began to shiver.

The morning came with rain from a thoroughly dark sky. Yesterday had been one of the warmest and sunniest days of the summer. The city had been full of people who had come from every region of the country to witness the coronation of Loria's new King. The festival of coronation was in full swing despite the rain. The tournament to celebrate the new king and give glory to the beginning of his reign was set to last twelve days. Knights and archers, minstrels and players, had all travelled from various parts of the realm to mark the occasion with tests of skill and displays of theatrics.

The young King sat at a table in his chambers overlooking the city. The desk was covered in various books and scrolls that the King had requested from his Royal Historian. He had been reading the histories of his family and of the kingdom, hoping to learn from the stories of his forefathers how he should rule, and what kind of man he needed become.

Prince Harford had ascended to the throne only a month after his father, King Jerold The Just had died, ending the longest reign of any Lorian king. Jerold's reign had brought about the longest era of peace the region had known. For generations the kingdoms of Demaria, Loria, and Sudara had fought over where borders were drawn, who had the rights to the trade routes along various rivers, and who controlled the Narrowlands, which sat between the Eastern and Western seas. Jerold The Just had been known as a wise and patient man.

In the first days of King Jerold's reign, the now aged King Dermond of Demaria had massed a large force along the border which spanned the Narrowlands, making many of the Lords of Loria fear an invasion. King Jerold, instead of matching troop for troop, and rather than sending an envoy of negotiators, travelled to the border himself under a flag of truce. The newly crowned King Jerold rode alone, accompanied by no soldiers or knights, and requested safe passage to treat with King Dermond.

With great suspicion and doubt, he was escorted to the Demarian side of the border, and sat for three days in the war tents of the Demarian army commander while King Dermond made his way from the capital of Rivershore, to see for himself if the Lorian King had indeed dared cross the border alone. They met for an entire day as the seventeen-year-old King Jerold the Just made his impression upon his northern neighbour.

Jerold's father had been a warrior, and it had been assumed that Jerold would follow in his footsteps, looking to make his mark on history by expanding his kingdom at the expense of his neighbours. This assumption by the advisors of the then relatively new Demarian King, was the driving force behind the build up of Demarian military assets at the border with Loria.

King Jerold was more interested in building a legacy of prosperity through trade, and managed to convince King Dermond that peace was the best climate for all the region's kingdoms to be able to prosper. History now tells that Jerold was so humbly charismatic, that he and his Demarian counterpart turned a war camp into a two day feast celebrating newly signed pacts of peace and trade.

Harford was no such king. He was young, a boy of only twelve years old, and had been second in line to the throne of

Loria. His brother, a man nineteen years of age, had been groomed for the throne, schooled in leadership and diplomacy, and trained in the arts of combat and war. There had been a plan for Harford to begin joining his older brother in such lessons, once he was closer to becoming a man, that he might support his brother's reign as many a king's sibling had done before. But their father had passed before his time, and their mother had long since been taken by the winter fever, when both brothers had still been boys.

Thus, after the disappearance of his elder brother, Harford was left to rule with the advice of those his father had chosen to serve in the King's Vestry, and the guidance of the recently arrived and newly devoted Sorcerer.

Ni'Morstrom had come to Magnaville shortly before King Jerold had passed away, but had not attended court in the castle until the late King's body was on route to be laid to rest in his ancestral Crypt. It was during this first appearance at court, that the Sorcerer had introduced himself to Prince Harford and pledged his service.

The young prince was advised by members of his Vestry not to accept the service of the Sorcerer, telling him that a King having masters of the arcane arts in their court was an old tradition, and one that had not been necessary since his grandfather had broken with the practice. But Harford was young and impressionable, and was afraid of insulting anyone who offered their service to him, and so the Sorcerer was granted a seat on the Vestry and space to work within the castle walls.

As the newly crowned King sat looking out over the city from the windows of his chambers, he recalled all the events that had taken place over the last few weeks. He missed his brother, and his father, and wished there were some way he could bring them back. He was so lost in thought that he did not hear the Sorcerer enter.

"Pardon the interruption my King. I have come with news about the disappearance of your brother."

With a look of impossible hope, the young King sprang

from his chair and took a couple of steps toward the Sorcerer "Did they find him? Is he alive? Where was he? What happened to him?" The questions flooded from him in a desperate desire for some knowledge of his lost sibling.

"Your Majesty, I must bear to you unfortunate news. Your brother is dead. I am truly sorry."

Despondent, King Harford slumped to the steps at the edge of his bed. Dropping his head into his hand, he began to weep. The King was instantly crushed. Though he was King, and ruled a powerful kingdom which was the region's centre for trade and its strongest military power, he was still a boy who loved his brother. With the loss of his father, and now his brother, he felt that everything he held dear had been ripped from his life. Burdens, the weight of which he could not have imagined, had been thrust upon him long before he could have hoped to have the strength to shoulder them. "No" he sobbed "What happened?"

Ni'Morstrom stepped closer to the mournful King. "Your Majesty, my sources have returned to me with word that your brother was taken by agents of the kingdom of Demaria. They tell me that word of your brother's plan to escort your father to his final resting place reached the court there, and that a small force was dispatched to take your brother. They tell me that the order given was to kidnap the Prince for ransom, but that your brother gave resistance valiantly and was slain defending himself in the melee that ensued. It was not clear whether the orders came directly from their king, or from someone within his court. Nevertheless, the men were identified by their sigil, a river delta on a sandy shore, for house Casterin of Downwater. A King is responsible for the actions of his Lords. You must give response to this crime against your kingdom."

The King was overwhelmed with the depth and weight of the implications that came with what the Sorcerer had relayed to him. He sat head in hands, drifting between the numbness of grief over the loss of his beloved brother, the righteous anger at the audacity of the kidnapping, and the fear of having to decide how to respond to it all. His mind started to go blank as his hands trembled and the tears rolled down his cheeks. The King wiped his eyes and looked up at the Sorcerer "Where is my brother's body?"

"It seems, Your Majesty, that his body was sent out to sea from the mouth of the river in Downwater. A final insult to your kingdom and family. For that, the Lord Casterin must answer, lest you appear weak."

With a sudden turn to anger, the King stood and raised a fist. "I'll send the army. I'll teach those blasted Demarians what it means to throw away my Father's peace and love. Call my commanders at once!"

Ni'Morstrom remained motionless as the King turned from grief to rage, lifting only a hand as he offered his counsel. "My King, may I suggest a different approach? It may be wise to delay a larger action that would be seen as an act to war, by choosing a subtler response. I may have the means to bring Lord Casterin to you, so that he may answer for his crimes against you, and you may dispense a King's justice. I propose that you allow me to send an agent with a small and stealthy force to capture the Lord of Downwater. If they are successful, you may be able to render a just verdict and avoid war. An eye for an eye, as it were, my King."

The young King paused in a moment of indecision. He knew that he must issue a response for the murder of his brother, but he was afraid of the magnitude of war. Having read some of the history of his Father's reign, he knew that a measured response was often the choice the late King preferred when reproach or insult were directed at the kingdom. "What did you have in mind, Lord Ni'Morstrom?"

"Has Your Majesty heard of the bounty hunter Trenon Var Toran, called by some, The Dancer?"

Hollyglade was exhausted. She had not slept in a day, and it would soon be dawn. Through the night, she had moved at a steady jog, despite the pain in her injured feet and knees, to put as great a distance as she could between herself and the men she had left tied between two trees several leagues behind her. Fatigue was beginning to take its toll once more, and though she now wore a crude assembly of blankets she had fashioned into some small protection from the elements, she was still cold.

Had she taken more time to warm herself by the fire built by her would-be captors, she may have felt revived enough to continue for another day. She had gone without sleep for days at a time on many occasions while living in the Red Lanes, before she was able to lay claim her own corner of one of the disused and crumbling buildings in the old quarter. She had also been chased before, by men she had pickpocketed and by vendors from whom she had taken a morsel of food. But she had never had to deal with both the lack of sleep and a determined pursuit simultaneously. Never had she been hunted.

Nerves were beginning to fray, as anxiety and fear compounded by a growing fatigue-induced delirium started to take its toll. Her feet, though they were now bound with the cloth she had torn from the blankets, were still aching. She could feel them again, but what she felt was throbbing pain from several punctures, and an overall bruising sustained from running along the rough ground just as the sun had set at the beginning of this trialsome night. She needed shelter, a place to hide and to rest. She had hoped that a by-product of the running would be warmth, yet she was still shivering.

Stopping to catch her breath for a moment, Hollyglade attempted to calm her body and slow her breathing and heart rate. While doing so, she heard the distinct sound of a horse blowing. Looking around and crouching, Hollyglade began to feel panic rise. Had the riders somehow freed themselves of their restraints, found their mounts and caught up to her? Were these their companions? She heard another blow, and began to relax. In her deteriorated state, Hollyglade did not at first recognize the sound for what it was, a relaxed release of air horses often emit while greeting one another.

After a moment, she finally saw the animal which had made the sound. Just a score of yards from where she had stopped and stood with her hands on her knees, was a fence line. At the fence stood a tall grey workhorse, the kind often used on the plow or to pull wagons or other farm equipment. Hollyglade smiled and approached it gently. As she did, she reached out to it with her mind, sending a calming greeting. It turned its ears toward her and stretched its muzzle forward as she lifted her hand to its nose. As they made contact, the great horse dropped its head slightly and allowed Hollyglade to rub her hands along its head and neck. The animal seemed to accept her as she stood caressing its coat with a gentle recipience.

Hollyglade realized that she must have come to the edge of a farm, and this horse had been out to pasture for the night. Often at this time of year, farmers would bring their horses into the barns in the evening, but this animal was much larger, and would be quite comfortable in the night air until temperatures got considerably lower. Hollyglade closed her eyes, and as she made a mental connection with the horse, she projected the thought home.

Almost instantly, the great beast turned its head and took a couple of steps away from the fence. Hollyglade sensed that it remained calm and relaxed as it did so. After it had taken a few more steps, the horse stopped and turned to look at her expectantly. Hollyglade understood that the horse was waiting for her to follow, so she placed one hand on the fence post and hopped to the far side, wincing in pain as she landed gingerly on her sore feet. She moved up to stand by the horse's shoulder, and placed a hand on its back. They began to walk together as the horse led her out of the trees.

Once they had emerged from the wooded area, and into a fenced field, Hollyglade could just make out the shape of a building no more than a hundred yards from the trees. Though it was still night Hollyglade expected the sun would be up shortly, and so she wanted to reach what she hoped would be a barn as soon as possible. As if in response to the thought, the horse quickened its pace slightly, and Hollyglade limped along as best she could to match it. A few moments later, they came to the side of the building.

Hollyglade left the animal there, and circled the building slowly and silently, to get a look at the entire area. This was indeed a barn, and there stood a small farmhouse a stone's throw across another fenced off yard on the far side of the barn from where she had approached. There was no light coming from the house, so Hollyglade assumed that whoever occupied it was still asleep.

Hollyglade returned to the spot she had left the horse, and approached it once more. Standing in front of it and gently taking its head with both of her hands, she reached out with her mind again and projected a general curiosity about the farmhouse. The horse made another blow from its nose, and responded with feelings of peaceful affection. Hollyglade was certain that whoever owned this farm and this horse was a good person, and treated his animals kindly.

Animals always associated strong emotions with their masters, and Hollyglade was familiar with the expression of those emotions. Animals may have respect for a fair master, even one that drives his beasts with a whip. They would express fear, and even hatred, for an owner or master that mistreated them or worked them too hard. The impression that this horse gave her, about whoever lived in the house, was one of affection. This horse genuinely loved its owner and likely served him for the pleasure of his company.

With that knowledge, Hollyglade made a choice to risk entering the barn. She believed that if the man in the house was gentle with the horse, he would also not be overly harsh to someone seeking warmth and refuge in his barn. Should she be discovered there, Hollyglade was optimistic that she could beg pardon and be on her way without any trouble. She made the decision to sneak into the barn with the hope of finding a hay pile to crawl into and steal a short sleep. With luck, she would be able to sneak back out undetected and move along after some rest.

It was no surprise to Hollyglade that the man door was unlocked. With great care not to make a sound, she slowly opened the door and slipped inside. There was no real light in the barn, but her eyes were well adjusted and her giantish low-light vision allowed her to see well enough to move carefully and confidently. Within the barn, she could hear a number of animals breathing and chewing the cud from the previous day's grazing.

The smell of cattle and horses filled the air, and Hollyglade smiled to herself as she inhaled the familiar scents she had recently grown to take comfort in. Farm animals were docile and generally trusting of people. With her experience and special abilities, Hollyglade was always able to move among a herd without disturbing or alarming them. Though most animals were slightly more sensitive to strangers, especially within the enclosed space of a barn, Hollyglade gave out a calming and soothing projection which seemed to result in the beasts within this barn taking no notice of her.

She eventually found a ladder to the hay loft, and ascended gingerly as the rungs created an uncomfortable pressure on the battered soles of her feet, even through the wrappings. Though she winced with each ladder rung she climbed, she made it to the floor of the loft without slipping, and peered about her surroundings. There were sheaves of wheat and barley next to rough bales of hay, and along one wall a pile of hay which was obviously a bale or two that had been pulled apart to be pitched to the animals below.

Hollyglade stepped slowly over to the hay pile and knelt in front of it. Carefully, she removed the scabbard holding the sword and dagger from her waist, and set them along with the saddlebags on the floor of the loft. She placed the second sword and scabbard with the first, and began to carefully spread apart a small section of the hay pile to make a flat spot to lay down and hopefully find some sleep.

Deliberately, Hollyglade lowered herself into the pile, lay on her side and curled herself up to retain as much body heat as she could. She placed the saddlebags under her head, and the swords in front of her before pulling enough hay about herself to become completely covered. After only a couple of minutes, she began to feel the insulating properties of the hay take effect, and fell asleep.

The sudden stabbing pain in her leg shocked Hollyglade into consciousness with a jolt. With a loud, startled yelp she sprang back from whatever it was that was attacking her. Scrambling desperately, she reached for one of the weapons that lay buried in the hay with her while flailing her good leg in the direction of the attacker hoping to drive them back.

Her foot connected with someone. With a mad flurry of motion which flung hay in every direction, Hollyglade stood up out of the feed pile with a sword in her hand. As she became upright, she saw the shape of a man staggering backwards. The man let out a confused and frightened shout as he tripped over his own feet trying to retreat from the explosion of cattle feed. Hollyglade winced at the pain in her leg, and then in the next instant gasped in surprise and shock as the man, holding a pitchfork in his hands, missed his next step and fell down the opening in the floor where the ladder to the hay loft stood.

Feeling a rush of guilt, Hollyglade limped as quickly as she could, to the edge of the opening as she heard the hard thud of the man hitting the muddy ground, followed by a deep groan. Arriving at the top of the ladder, Hollyglade looked down to see the man splayed out below her with his mouth hanging slack and eyes glazed. She paused for a moment and watched him.

Relief rose within her as she saw his chest rise and fall. Panic began to creep up, and she limped back over to the hay pile, collecting her things. She chided herself for sleeping so long. Now her plan to leave without a trace was impossible to carry out. She hoped that now she could slip away and at least remain a mystery. Quickly and quietly, she made her way down the ladder, carefully stepping over the unconscious farmer and making her way to the man door.

As she placed her hand on the door and pressed it open, she stopped abruptly. Her senses were suddenly overwhelmed by the outpouring of fear and concern emanating from the livestock within the barn. She flinched and gritted her teeth, turning around to look at the man who lay in the mud. She had once been a pickpocket, and thief, and even a swindler from time to time, but Hollyglade had never been comfortable with harm coming to an innocent person.

As she stared at him, she realized that the man had had no idea that she was hiding in his pile of hay, and had simply thrust his pitchfork into the hay pile to throw down the morning's feed to his animals. Limping across the barn, Hollyglade bent over and moved the pitchfork aside to check the man for injuries. She could not find any sign of broken bones, and so she took hold of both his arms and attempted to pull him into a sitting position. He remained limp as his body refused to return to wakefulness.

"Hey mister, wake up" She shook him gently and patted his cheek. Nothing. "I'm sorry. I didn't mean for you to fall. You surprised me." He gave no response. "Aah, for the love of gods. Why couldn't you have just been a little late to your herd today?"

The man was not large. He looked to Hollyglade to be middle-aged. His brown hair and beard showed no signs of greying. Hollyglade was young, but she had built considerable strength in the last few years working on farms such as this. Her leg hurt and was bleeding moderately, but she could not bring herself to leave this man as he was. She strapped the scabbard with the sword and long knife back to her waist, and put the saddle bags and the other scabbard over her shoulder. She took hold of one of the man's arms, bent down to place one knee between his legs, and pulled him across her shoulders.

With effort, she stood up holding the man across her back, and walked to the door. She shuffled, wincing in pain each time she put weight on her right leg, yet forced herself to go forward. Once she cleared the main door to the barn, which the farmer had left open upon entering earlier, she looked around to get her bearings. With an exhalation she began to head for the farmhouse.

At about half the distance to the farmhouse, Hollyglade saw movement in one of the windows. She continued forward, hoping there would be someone in the house, the man's wife perhaps, who would be able to help him. Suddenly the door to the farmhouse flew open, and a woman came rushing out followed by a boy holding a wood cutting axe. Hollyglade stopped in her tracks and raised one hand from the unconscious farmer's leg as she signalled her yield to the pair as they came into the yard.

"What have you done to him?" the woman exclaimed upon seeing her limp husband draped across the shoulders of a very tall stranger. The plain looking woman, her black hair reaching her shoulders, over her brown dress and grey apron, caught sight of the weapons about Hollyglade's waist and motioned for the boy to stop.

"Ma'am, I assure you that I mean neither this man, nor either of you any harm. I was lost in the cold of the night this past evening, and took refuge in your barn. This goodly man here, unbeknownst to him, surprised me from my slumber beneath the hay pile, and in my shocked awakening I in turn frightened him. In his alarm he fell from the loft to the floor of the barn. I could not leave an honest and innocent man lying hurt such as he was, so I chose to carry him to his house. Ma'am, I beg you to let me bring him in to you that you may tend to him."

The woman paused for a moment as she appeared to be taking in what Hollyglade had told her.

"You're bleeding also." She gave a look of skepticism as she motioned to the wound on Hollyglade's right leg.

"Yes Ma'am. He awoke me with his pitchfork not knowing I lay buried in the feed. Please, I wish to help him, it was my fault he fell though I had no desire for it, and I wish to see him aided."

"Come." she nodded as she waved them toward the house "Peter, get the door for us." She approached Hollyglade and gave what support she could as they made their way into the house.

Once through the door, Hollyglade immediately felt the warmth of the fire burning in the hearth. She took a half second to peer about the inside of the stone building, finding a small table and chairs, cooking area, and a couple of doors leading to other parts of the house. The woman motioned to one of the doors "In here. On the bed. Peter get a bowl of water and a cloth and bring it to me."

As they came through to the back room where a bed stood against one wall, Hollyglade knelt down and lowered the man to the bed as gently as she was able. He let out a groan as his wife placed a pillow under his head and began to examine him. Hollyglade stepped aside to allow the boy to bring the water and cloth to his mother. She dipped the cloth in the water, folded it and placed it on his forehead.

"He doesn't seem to have broken anything, but he does have a lump here" she noted as she moved the cloth to the back of his head. He winced and then opened his eyes.

"Lera" he whispered "what am I doing here? I was feeding the cattle." He tried to sit up and groggily moved his head about in an effort to gain his bearings. His eyes found Hollyglade leaning against the wall and a look of puzzled suspicion came over his visage.

"Don't sit up. You've had a fall. This one here carried you in from the barn. Says you and she gave each other a scare, and you fell from the loft."

"My apologies" Hollyglade stepped forward slightly and lowered her head "I meant to give no mischief to you. I regret the disturbance my intrusion has caused, and the injury that resulted. I sought only to escape the cold of the night, and had hoped to be on my way without your knowledge and having taken no more than the refuge I sought. It appears my fatigue was so great that I did not wake with the rooster's call nor the light of morning." She looked up at the man and his wife "Good people, I beg your forgiveness and ask your leave to depart in peace."

The farmer and his wife looked at each other as he finally sat up and felt the back of his head. He swung his legs to the floor and stood up, wobbly at first, holding the bed post until he gained his balance. The farmer looked Hollyglade up and down, taking in the dishevelled appearance of her hair which contained a considerable amount of hay, her lack of footwear and the wrappings she had fashioned in their place. He grinned slightly as he observed the odd conjunction of her makeshift clothing and the weapons and saddlebags she had loosely hanging about her. He gave a wry half smile and chuckled to himself as he took in her pitiful demeanor and vestment. His gaze finally came to settle on Hollyglade's bleeding leg.

"You're bleeding. What happened? And why are you dressed in sleeping blankets? Did you leave a pile of clothes in my barn?"

Hollyglade opened her mouth to begin to offer a reply, and paused before she could let any words out. She did not want to start trying to explain the details, or even the generalities of what had happened to her over the last days. Doing so could place this family at the same risk as the old woman whose cottage she had fled from the previous evening. Hollyglade could not imagine leading her pursuers to this humble family's home and causing them to suffer the same gruesome fate. She avoided the question.

"It is nothing sir, I'll wrap it and make do." She offered as she rubbed the area around the wound.

"Nonsense. That's a fresh wound and I won't have you leaving here dripping blood, much less leaving a mess for my wife to scrub from the floor. Caught in the cold last night you say? Then you'll stay for breakfast."

Hollyglade felt her stomach growl at the mention of food, and she realized that this was the third day since she had last eaten.

"We may be humble farmers, but we care for strangers in need, when such need presents itself. What's your name?"

"Hollyglade, sir."

"An interesting name. Well this is my wife Lera, our son Peter, and I'm called Eric. Come, let's patch you up, and you can answer some things for me over a meal."

Hollyglade wasn't sure how to respond, as she expected anger from someone she had caused injury to, yet they seemed genuine and charitable people. She had thought the same of the old woman whose cottage she had stopped at the previous afternoon. The thought that there were people in the kingdom who still valued hospitality toward strangers, even after the King's latest decree, encouraged her.

There was still the matter of the men who she knew were hunting her. That old woman's fate weighed heavily on Hollyglade's conscience, and made her hesitant to take the offer of hospitality. Yet she was still tired, very hungry, and the warmth that now touched her skin still had a fair way to go to bring the restoration of some vitality to her bones. She convinced herself that there must be at least a small amount of time she could risk staying here before moving on. She nodded and followed the family, ducking out through the door of the bedroom, and stepping back out into the main room.

Hollyglade sat down on one of the chairs and took a look at her leg. The wound was not very deep, and the blood flow had reduced to a slow trickle. The man tore a strip from a fresh cloth his wife had given him, and handed it to Hollyglade, along with a bowl of water containing a washcloth. She nodded in thanks, washed the wound, and wrapped the clean cloth around her leg snugly, tying the ends securely. She accepted a mug of warm milk from the woman, and drank it all in a single series of long draughts. As she set the mug down on the table and wiped the milk from her lip, the man looked at her with a raised eyebrow which then transitioned into a smile and a chuckle as he took the mug from in front of her and refilled it.

"Slowly this time friend" he said with a hearty laugh

"there's a meal to come still."

She blushed slightly as she picked up the refilled mug and made an effort to sip politely. Sitting down, taking his own mug in his hand and sipping, the man looked Hollyglade in the eye and leant back in his chair.

"Now, you must tell me how you ended up concealed in a pile of hay in my barn dressed such as you are, without proper clothes or boots. I'd welcome a good story over breakfast."

Dawn had not yet broken when dGerrie awoke. The night had been a difficult one, and he had managed very little sleep. dGerrie felt restless still, as he ate a rudimentary meal he had prepared over what remained of the coals still glowing in the hearth of the inn. They had ridden to another town after leaving the cottage, which had been occupied by the now deceased woman. There they had come close to apprehending the girl whom Var Toran had been contracted to capture. The events of the previous evening had not sat well with dGerrie. He had been made to stand by as two innocent women had been executed within an hour of each other by the man dGerrie had been contracted to.

Violence had its place in dGerrie's personal moral code. That place was reserved for times of necessity such as war and self defence. The violence which came so easily to Var Toran was not sitting well with dGerrie. There was a scale upon which dGerrie ranked one type of violence, and another. Murder of the innocent was on a level he would never willing reach.

He felt conflicted over the fulfillment of his contract. On one hand dGerrie took the fact that it was a contract very seriously, and this meant that he felt obligated to see this job to its end. This would mean capturing a young girl who obviously did not want to be caught, and was somewhat capable of escape and evasion, which hinted at other skills and abilities that may pose a danger. Skills and abilities, the use of which may provoke a strong response from someone like The Dancer. Though dGerrie could assure himself that he would not resort to the kind of violence that The Dancer seemed to prefer, he was utterly convinced that this girl would not be spared completely, that there would be some sort of cruelty or torture The Dancer had reserved for her.

On the other hand, dGerrie was not without compassion. Having been one of many people he knew to have survived growing up an orphan on the streets of a large city, dGerrie understood that people sometimes acted desperately, doing things that were outside the law in order to survive. As far as he knew, this girl's only crime was being half Elvish, something that as far as dGerrie could recall should only require being ushered out of Magnaville, and maybe being told to go as far as the southern end of the Western Mountains, the traditional territory of the Elvish Septs. The default attitude that he had been instructed by the city garrison to treat Elder folk with, was one of firmness balanced with respect and dignity. dGerrie was having an increasingly difficult time rectifying the intensity of The Dancer's tactics with what he knew of the King's actual decree.

As he sat by the hearth eating his crude breakfast and waiting for his contractor to awaken and outlay the intended strategy for the day's search, dGerrie's feeling of anxiety and discomfort deepened. Part of him hoped that he would somehow find this girl on his own and be able to guide her flight to safety, leaving no trail to be followed, with the hope that The Dancer would eventually give up. His misgivings only deepened as he concluded that Trenon Var Toran was not the kind of man, not the kind of bounty hunter, to give up on a contract.

dGerrie had the distinct impression that there were only two possible outcomes to this hunt. Either Var Toran captured his prey, or met some kind of untimely death in the attempt. Having seen some small indication of the skill with weapons possessed by the bounty hunter, dGerrie did not expect there to be many people in this world capable of delivering him that untimely end, least of all a fifteen-year-old girl.

His thoughts were interrupted by the subject of his disquieted reflection, as Var Toran entered the main room of the Inn, fully dressed for the road.

"Mr. Theurbeault, I trust you slept comfortably in this lovely little auberge. Isn't it just wonderful to be able to take advantage of the marvelous variety of accommodations available across this pristine land? I do enjoy the road, with its beautiful scenery, colourful people, and delicious cuisine. I find the people in these small villages so quaint and interesting. How much effort their lives must take. How creative they must have to be just to combat the boredom that comes with a life spent toiling to put food on the table.

"Did you hear the music that came from the barn at the edge of this village last night? Such wonderful melodies! And the whole of this community seemed to have been gathered there."

The smile that spread across his face seemed to go from ear to ear as the bounty hunter sat down at the far side of the hearth. dGerrie would have been moved by the observance, were he able to take the smile and the musings out from the context of the rest of this man. Instead dGerrie felt a sinking revolt within his stomach.

"I see you have eaten. Are you ready to return to our search?"

dGerrie silently nodded his reply.

"Good, good. We should expect the return of Mr. Webb and Mr. Brooker by mid-morning."

dGerrie found it odd that this bounty hunter never referred to those in his employ by their given names. Perhaps it was his way of separating himself from those around him, or distinguishing himself from other bounty hunters as being in a class above.

Looking over his shoulder, Var Toran called for the innkeeper to bring him a meal, then returned his attention to dGerrie. "Mr. Theurbeault, please make ready our horses. I shall be only a few minutes with breakfast. I never eat a heavy meal in the morning if I mean to ride shortly after. I find it makes the journey more comfortable not to have the extra weight in one's stomach. We shall return to the fork in the road where we last parted with our companions, and if they have not returned there we shall set out along the path they took. Hopefully they shall have an answer to what it was our farmer friend thinks he saw in the road at sundown."

dGerrie nodded again and collected his effects, turning and heading out the front door to the inn. He thought about the girl they were hunting, and hoped that the person the farmer had spotted was not her, and was instead one of the many townsfolk who fled to the woods as the word of Var Toran's slaying of the innkeeper had spread. He could not help but feel for this girl. The conflict within him continued to grow.

The horses had been boarded in stalls behind the building, and dGerrie set about saddling them. Once he had them both ready, he returned to the main entrance to the inn and hitched them to the rail, waiting there for Var Toran to join him.

Mid-day had arrived and there was no sign of the two men whom The Dancer had sent along the eastern fork in the road, which led out of the village where they had first found the trail of the girl they sought. dGerrie had been sent back to that village to be sure the two men had not returned there to rejoin with The Dancer and himself, rather than waiting at the fork as they had been instructed. Having not found any sign of either man in the village, dGerrie arrived back at the fork where he had left Var Toran.

"There was no sign they'd gone back to the village. I was not received gladly there. It turns out the old woman you dispatched was well liked, and her …. passing…. was not taken kindly." dGerrie chose his words as carefully as he could. He hoped that his own personal discomfort with the bounty hunter's methods would be masked by the impression that it was the cold reception he had received which truly bothered him.

"Well then, Mr. Theurbeault, it appears we must broaden our search to include our comrades. Let us hope they are simply delayed. Shall we?" He motioned along the eastern fork, and turned his horse up the road. With a nod, dGerrie followed.

Less than a league along the road, dGerrie spotted something odd. "There," he pointed to something in the bush about twenty yards in front of them along the side of the road, "a horse without a rider. Could belong to one of them." dGerrie nudged his mount to a trot and came alongside the stray horse. It wore a bridle, yet was without a saddle.

As dGerrie dismounted, and Var Toran arrived beside him, he noticed a strand of rope tied to the bridle, the end of which appeared to have been snapped. He placed his hand on the horse's neck and reached for the rope. The animal did not seem to mind and continued to feed on the grass at the edge of the road as dGerrie looked closely at the broken tether. "Something frightened him" he said as he looked off into the bush.

"Indeed Mr. Theurbeault, and that is one of my mounts. Let us have a look here and there and see it we might discover what befell the man to whom I lent it. I believe we may be in for the telling of an interesting story. Oh, I do like stories!"

dGerrie shuddered at the sickeningly gleeful tone with which the bounty hunter spoke. He could not help but recall meeting Tom and Hern back in Magnaville, and hearing that neither of them had been long in The Dancer's employ, and that short terms of employment seemed the norm for those he hired. dGerrie began to suspect that failure was treated by The Dancer in the same way as a lack of cooperation by those he questioned had been. The line he walked in service of this contract felt thinner and thinner by the day.

As dGerrie took the horse and tied the tether to his saddle, the bounty hunter began scanning the bush along the far side of the road. dGerrie walked both horses along his side looking for evidence of the two missing men. Less than a hundred paces further along the edge of the treeline, dGerrie spotted a narrow path, what he thought was likely a game trail, that led between some short bushes.

Stopping to scan the area, he spotted several sets of tracks. A single set of footprints with some spots of blood, left by long and narrow bare feet, that led into the bush at a seemingly random spot. A few paces away were two sets of boot tracks leading down the narrow path. dGerrie tied both horses to a low tree branch, and set about tracing the tracks. They were not hard to follow.

In recent years spent on both sides of the law, dGerrie had learned some tracking skill, both in hunting for food, and for fugitives. He had also learned, through taking a keen interest for various reasons, in how to mask his own tracks, a skill he had applied on several occasions in years past.

These tracks were quite obvious, and seemed to have been left without a care. dGerrie looked up to locate the bounty hunter, and gave a short whistle, waving The Dancer to come to where the tracks began. dGerrie did not wait for him to arrive as he made his way down the path.

A dozen yards or so down the trail, and around a slight right bend, dGerrie stepped into a clearing and stopped suddenly. His heart sank, knowing what would come as a result of that which he now laid his eyes upon.

With hands tied above their heads to one tree, and legs stretched out and tied to another, Tom and Hern looked him in the eye and began to emit muffled pleas through the strips of cloth they had been gagged with. dGerrie shook his head, and rather than move to untie the two men, he rested his wrist on his sword and leant against a nearby tree to wait for the bounty hunter to arrive.

Looking around the clearing, dGerrie took stock of the scene spread out before him. Small bits of firewood lay scattered about, a cooking pot and fire irons lay next to the small fire pit, and a pair of boots sat at the edge of the clearing as though they had been tossed there from afar. Looking back at the two pathetic captives, it struck dGerrie that neither man had their boots, their sleeves had been torn from their shirts.

Tom was naked from the waist down and his feet had turned a slight shade of blue. As dGerrie started to imagine all the possible ways these two might have ended up in this position, the bounty hunter arrived beside him.

"Oh my" The Dancer exclaimed with excitement "we will have a story Mr. Theurbeault. One I think we shall find most interesting. Please untie them so we may have the telling." He walked across the small clearing and took a seat on the stump of a dead tree, crossed one leg over the other and laced his fingers together over his knee. He leant back slightly and widened his now baleful grin.

dGerrie untied both men, starting with Tom who began frantically making excuses as he ran immediately to his trousers, put them on, and scooped up the boots.

"She done bewitched us sir!"

"I'm not a knight, but please…. Continue. I do love a story"

"She must 'ave used some kind of bewitchment on us! Made us fall asleep under her spell and set upon us in the night."

"Yes. Oh, a witch Mr. Theurbeault! Do you hear that? How exciting!" his eyes never left Tom as he giggled his excitement.

Tom bit his lip as he began to grasp the gravity of his situation.

"Tom, she threw into the fire with some unnatural beastly strength." interjected Hern as dGerrie finish removing his restraints. "She surprised me out of nowhere with a giant club of some kind. I never 'ad time to get my sword to 'er. She must be some kind of giant Elvish fire-haired naked devil! The Red Witch!"

"Naked you say? This girl you scared out the window of the cottage remained unclothed, shivering in the cold of the night, and still desired to attack you! I must meet her." The excitement in his voice took on a slight hint of sarcasm, yet somehow dGerrie believe he truly was fascinated with this girl.

"Yes, Mr. Dancer." Hern responded "She was a 'uge one,

too. Taller than 'im by an 'ead," he said as he nodded at dGerrie "and she moved like the wind. She must 'ave been under some sort of spell that made 'er immune to cold and gave 'er beastly speed and strength."

Both men now stood close to the glowing embers of what remained of the fire trying to rub some warmth back into their chilled bones. dGerrie returned to his tree and leant back against the trunk, crossing his arms over his chest.

"She took our blankets too" Tom continued "and asked us a bunch of questions about what reason we was lookin' for 'er. She wanted to know who you was and why you was chasin' 'er. She threatened to cut off me gentlemen's bits! She probably would 'ave used it in some dark ritual of 'ers!"

As dGerrie listened to the obviously exaggerated recounting of the night, he started to picture this girl in his mind. Red hair. Half Elvish. Taller than me, which is taller than the average Elvish woman. Quick, resourceful, doesn't let the cold stop her. It reminded him a little of someone he had known in Magnaville. Could that be her? She wasn't nearly that tall when I last saw her. But that was several years ago, and she should still have had some growing to do from then to now. But what in the gods' names could she possibly have done to deserve a bounty? She was always kind and gentle. It can't be her. Must just be a coincidence. His attention moved back to the clearing as the bounty hunter now stood and approached the other two.

"And what reply gave you, when she inquired as to your contracts?"

"Nothing more than that we was given a description of 'er, me Lord"

"I'm not a Lord." His smile did not waver.

"I'm sorry sir..."

"I did not become a knight between standing up from the stump and standing here with you."

Both men were now visibly disturbed by the bounty hunter's demeanor. Each took a step back as he rested his wrist on his sword and rubbed his chin.

"Gentlemen, I'm sure you are aware that everything in life has a cause and effect. For every action there is a consequence, good or bad, which we must accept and learn from, ideally."

The two men looked at each other sheepishly and then back at Var Toran.

"As you are aware, this contract, as with all my contracts, is one to be taken seriously. One's professional reputation must remain intact throughout one's career if one desires to remain employable. In order for me to continue to acquire contracts such as this, I must ensure that those who consider making offers, make them to me. Were the name Trenon Var Toran to be associated with failure, with delay, or with humiliation…" He paused and dropped his smile as he uttered that last word, before restoring his grin and continuing. "I would not be able continue to find such gainful employment, and in turn not be able to pass on the benefit of such gainful employment to those such as yourselves." He lowered his head and stepped around the fire pit, over the pot and fire irons, and in dGerrie's direction.

"Now, you see my friends, I must acknowledge that you have suffered some small consequences for your carelessness in the night, and that for the average bounty hunter, these consequences would be a sufficient lesson unto themselves. There would be a good laugh, some jovial ribbing, and then everyone would move on and continue with the job at hand.

"However, I am not the average bounty hunter, and such consequences as you have suffered will not be sufficient to serve as the lesson I wish to teach." He paused for a moment, and began to pace left and right as he once again continued to draw out his parlance.

"Now, the subject of our search seems to have shown us some of her skill, cunning, and most assuredly her lack of willingness to come along quietly. But in doing so, she has also supplied me with a valuable test of the capabilities, or lack thereof, in my men. So, you see gentlemen, I am left with a conundrum, one I must address somehow. I am a fair man, so

I have decided to give you each a chance to redeem yourselves." He turned and faced the two now extremely nervous men.

dGerrie held his place at the edge of the small clearing, having learned previously that any interruption of one of the bounty hunter's monologues resulted in a swift backlash.

"Mr. Theurbeault, may I please borrow one of your swords?"

dGerrie drew both of his swords, held them by the blades and offered them to Var Toran. He wondered how well either man would fare in what was sure to come next. dGerrie had seen many men fight, had crossed swords with a few skilled fencers himself. He had seen The Dancer make a few quick cuts with his various blades, which indicated a deeper skill level. Though dGerrie had a code of sorts that he stuck to regarding who he would and would not draw a sword upon, these two men fell into a category he felt should fend for themselves. If dGerrie was honest with himself, which he always was, he had no real issue with Var Toran's obvious next move in this situation. These men were fighters, would be armed, and had every chance to defend themselves.

The bounty hunter took the shorter of the two swords, which made sense to dGerrie as the longer one would really only be fit for a man of his height, and handed it to Tom.

"Mr. Brooker." His smile lessened, and an eyebrow rose up slightly, "I offer you the chance to strike first, for if you manage to cut me, you will have earned some respect and admiration. I encourage you to take seriously the opportunity I present you here. A chance to hunt a bounty as a member of my company comes neither easily nor without great reward.

"Mr. Webb, if you would be so kind as to stand aside to allow Mr. Brooker and me a little space with which to engage in our activities?" Hern looked at Tom, then to dGerrie, and stepped to the edge of the clearing. Both Tom and Hern seemed extremely wary of what was taking place, and as Hern made the edge of the clearing he began to look in every direction.

dGerrie took note of Hern's shifting eyes. He had seen the look of a man preparing to run, and was seeing it again now. dGerrie casually removed the bow from his back, placed one end of it on the ground and his elbow on the other, pretending to rest on it. He then turned his attention back to the bounty hunter and to Tom.

"Mr. Dancer, sir...."

"I'm not a knight" interjected Var Toran "Why do people keep assuming I'm a knight?" he said, looking at dGerrie. He drew his sword, and the grin returned to its shudder-inducing apex as he took a step forward, throwing a feint to provoke Tom into raising his sword.

"That's better Mr. Brooker. One should assume a proper stance if one is about to engage in swordplay. Now, are you the sort of man who likes to strike first? Or do you prefer to counter?" He waited a moment. Tom pulled his sword back, cocking it for a stabbing maneuver. dGerrie cringed at the sloppiness with which he signalled his intent. Tom lunged toward the bounty hunter in an attempt to impale his abdomen.

The Dancer's response was as delicate as it was instantaneous. With a half pirouette, he stepped away from the strike and slapped Tom's sword aside. With another half pirouette, he came around with his blade and slapped the side of it against the stumbling mercenary's buttocks.

"Tisk, tisk, Mr. Brooker." The bounty hunter turned and faced Tom and allowed the mercenary to turn and face back toward him, waiting for his sword to rise again. "One ought not to allow an opponent to see what one plans to do before one does it." The Dancer lunged forward with his sword aimed to his left, appearing to stab for Tom's right shoulder, feinted, pulled his sword back in an upward arc over his own head and brought it back down, slashing along the length of Tom's left arm.

The move was quick and effective. When Tom moved to parry the feinted stab, he exposed his entire left side. dGerrie was sure that if The Dancer had wished, that he could have ended the fight with that single move had he chosen to target Tom's head or neck. The Dancer was quick, and his footwork was perfect. dGerrie was certain that he was watching an experienced fencer, likely trained by a highly skilled instructor. The bounty hunter was obviously toying with the mercenary.

Tom looked at his arm, which was now bleeding heavily from the cut that ran from his shoulder to wrist, and became visibly unstable on his feet. He looked back at the bounty hunter, raised his blade over his shoulder, stepped forward and swung the sword with all his remaining strength at Var Toran. The bounty hunter stepped back with his right foot while raising his sword straight over his head, turned in a quick pirouette as the clumsy slash flew past his back, and brought his sword down in a backhand cut as he completed the spin. The tip of his sword landed cleanly across the back of the mercenary's neck, a blow perfectly aimed to slice rather than hack. The sword did not stick, and Var Toran's follow through was frighteningly precise, as he made another half turn and brought his blade up in front of his own face.

Tom hit the ground in a crumpled heap as blood poured out of the two cuts. He made no sound, and did not move. Var Toran stepped over to the dead man, and retrieved dGerrie's sword. "Pity" he declared "I would have enjoyed some exercise. Perhaps your friend will offer a chance for some exertion."

Hern looked at Tom, then to dGerrie, and then Var Toran. dGerrie read the look. Hern was going to run. In a split second, several thoughts flew through dGerrie's mind. I'm in this now. I can't just walk away. Either I show loyalty, or I test myself in crossing swords with him. He made a quick decision. Without time to consider other alternatives beyond the two that came so quickly to mind, dGerrie flipped his bow up to his left hand and simultaneously pulled and arrow from his quiver with his right. Notching the arrow at the end of the single motion he took to draw it, he pulled back the bowstring and fired without bothering to take the time or to set his feet and sight his target.

The missile found its mark, and Hern tumbled into the underbrush. dGerrie knew where it had pierced him, and let the bow drop back to the ground, catching the top end with his hand. He leant back against the tree and turned his gaze to the bounty hunter.

Var Toran glanced to where the man had fallen, gave a look of impressed approval, and turned back to dGerrie. "Well Mr. Theurbeault, it appears you and I shall have to be sufficient company for each other for a while." The bounty hunter's grin remained as he adeptly tossed the sword back to dGerrie, who caught the weapon and resheathed it.

"Let's not waste any more time with fun and games." He looked dGerrie in the eye and winked as he added with a laugh "We have a witch to catch!"

The meal was simple but more than enough, and having not eaten for several days, Hollyglade found herself surprised by how good a hard-boiled egg could taste. As they ate, she gave only a partial account of what had led her to the barn the previous night. She told the good-natured farmer that she had been chased out of the last village by the King's garrison, and out of a fear of the overzealous soldiers, she had fled with only the blankets since her clothes were being washed. She did not mention The Dancer, nor the men she had left tied up in the woods, nor watching the old woman lose her life as a result of her hospitality. She ate her fill and thanked the woman for the meal, apologizing several more times for the scare that led to the farmer's fall.

"So, what led you to that town in the first place? And what is a girl of your age doing with a pair of swords about her?" the man inquired.

"Well sir, I've been travelling much in the last few years, and generally look for work training various beasts of labour. I have considerable experience with horses, oxen, mules, and the like. I prefer not to stay very long in any one place, so I was embarking on my next journey, wherever that may have been. With the King's new decree regarding Elder Folk, I have had trouble finding such work this close to the capital, and have also begun to experience decreasing levels of welcome within towns and villages. Though I must say, these last couple of days have revealed a considerable escalation in the vehemence of the garrison's eviction tactics." She avoided his question about the swords, as she had not thought of any explanation that he might accept, nor one she could tell confidently.

The farmer chuckled as she mentioned the garrison, and Hollyglade paused, giving him a puzzled look.

"Young lady," he grinned as he spoke "I've not heard such high language from someone so young as yourself, especially someone so obviously not high born."

She blushed, thankful that he had not pressed about the weaponry. "I beg your pardon sir. I sometimes let my vocabulary get away from me. I meant only to show respect."

He laughed aloud "Just don't send me flying from my hay loft again and you'll be alright."

Her face reddened further as she bashfully dropped her gaze.

"Don't tease the poor girl, Eric!" his wife interjected "She's been through enough. Listen dear, I must find you something to replace that pitiful excuse for clothing. You're likely to freeze to death if you're out in that over the next week. Come with me. Over the past few years we have had some larger folk work the field with my husband. Last fall one of them left a bundle of clothes here when the season was done. They might not fit your waist in a way that flatters a young lady, but that's nothing a few minutes with a needle and thread can't fix."

She took Hollyglade by the hand and lead her from the main room into a storage pantry. "Up there my dear. Can you reach that bundle for me?" she pointed to a sack on the top shelf. Hollyglade retrieved it and handed it to the woman. She took the bag and untied the string which closed the top end, reaching in to pull out a long-sleeved shirt which she handed to

Hollyglade. "Now dear, don't be shy. Take off that sad blanket and try this on for me so I can see what we have to do with it."

Hollyglade undid the scabbard holding the sword and dagger, wrapped it and set it down. She slid the blanket up over her head, and set it down on an empty section of shelving. She pulled the cream coloured shirt over her head and shoved her arms into the sleeves, letting the shirt fall to her waist. It was definitely very wide on her slender frame, but the sleeves were a good length, and the shirt fell far enough that she thought it might tuck into a skirt or trousers.

"Well, I've seen a worse fit." the woman offered with a smile. "Here, try the trousers." She held out a pair of slacks for Hollyglade to take. Hollyglade took them, and looked at the woman bashfully.

"Oh deary," responded the woman with a grin as she turned to allow Hollyglade to change behind her. Hollyglade untied the cord holding the second blanket in place, and dropped it to the floor. She slipped on the trousers and pulled them to her waist.

"They're long enough Ma'am, but I'll need the rope to hold them in place."

The woman turned around and examined the size of the pants. She took the waistband and pinched it together in each hand as she leant back to have a look at the fit. "My dear, that just won't do. Hold there a moment." She pulled a couple of needles from her apron and pinned the trousers where she had pinched them. "Alright dear, off with those so I can get them right for you."

"It's really not necessary ma'am, I don't want to waste your time."

"Nonsense girl! I'll not have you wandering around with a waistband as sloppy as that!"

Hollyglade smiled as she could hear the motherhood emanate from the woman's reply. The woman reached further into the sack and pulled out a pair of shorts, handing them to Hollyglade.

"Here, put these on while I take in the waist on those

trouser. Oh look!" she reached into the bag once more. "Try these on. You might just be lucky after all!" She produced a very worn, yet rather large pair of boots.

Hollyglade was speechless for a moment as she took the footwear. The boots were obviously made for a giant, but that was good news to Hollyglade, as her feet were not small. She tried them on and smiled, as they were only slightly loose on her feet.

"I'll be honest dear. Those have seen a few people's feet. But I'm glad if they can keep yours off the bare ground. Now come have a seat while I fix these slacks." Lera took the trousers and went out to the table, picking up a pair of shears along the way, and sat down to begin her alterations.

As Hollyglade came back into the front room, she noticed that Eric had left the house to return to the barn to finish spreading the feed. It was midmorning now, and she sat by the hearth to further regain some warmth. Sitting by the fire, brushing the hay out from her hair and braiding it once more, Hollyglade's thoughts turned back to her pursuers.

She could not linger here. As soon as possible, once the trousers were sewn, she thought to herself, she would leave. She guessed that a bounty hunter would not give up when there was money to be earned through her capture. She knew the name of the bounty hunter, The Dancer. She had heard something of his reputation, one gained through fulfilling contracts, and doing so in a ruthless manner. She had seen the demonstration of his ruthless tactics played out upon that poor old woman the evening past. Hollyglade assumed that the same fate would befall this decent family if she stayed much longer. She knew that she had to leave, but it was difficult to pull herself away from the offer of warmth, food, and shelter.

After a short time, Hollyglade decided to make ready to leave. She collected the saddlebags, weapons, and the blankets she had worn. Sitting back down at the table, she watched as Lera threaded the last stitches into the trousers.

"Now dear, try these on again."

She offered the slacks to Hollyglade once more. Hollyglade

took the adjusted trousers, and slipped them on. They were a near perfect fit, and Hollyglade tucked the shirt into the waist and placed the blanket with the hole she had cut, back over her head, securing it all in place with the scabbard which held the sword and dagger. As she finished adjusting the clothing, and slid her feet into the boots, Eric returned with their son, having finished feeding the animals in the barn.

"You look much better prepared for the road, I must say. Do you mean to resume your trek?"

"Yes. I mustn't linger here. I intend to get further south before winter hits in earnest." Though it was not getting south that drove her, but getting as far as necessary from the clutches of her deadly pursuer. "But before I leave you, I must offer some compensation for your trouble, and your kindness." She took the second sword, and scabbard, and offered it to the farmer.

"I can not accept such a thing" he replied, "I would have no use for a sword, nor the knowledge to wield it."

"Please, sir, you must take it. It is well made and could fetch a handsome sum at a market, or if offered for sale through a smith. Please, I insist. You may have no use for it yourself, but someone who would find it useful would pay well for it. Besides, I definitely have no use for two swords." She held the weapon out to him with both hands, her face pleading with him to accept the offer. After a moment of consideration, he nodded and took the sword from her, setting it by the hearth.

"Maybe we'll mount it above the fireplace." he chortled with a wink to his wife "We can pretend we've got a whole armoury, and this is our spare sword." He continued to chuckle waiting for Hollyglade to return his smile. She finally relaxed slightly, blushed, and nodded as she moved to the door. Turning to Lera, she stopped and smiled "Thank you for the clothing, and for the food. You have restored me."

"It was nothing. But you are very welcome my dear. Now, get south before those useless King's men get to bothering you again. Before you leave, take this." The woman handed

Hollyglade a small loaf of bread, and wedge of cheese.

"Ma'am, you are too kind." She started to try to hand the food back, but the woman waved off the attempt. Hollyglade blushed, dropped her head, bowed slightly and then turned for the door as she offered one last goodbye. "Farewell, good people."

Hollyglade ducked out the door, and turned for the road. It was now just before noon, and she knew that whatever lead she may have on the bounty hunter was surely less today than it had been in the night. Thankfully, it was warmer today than it had been in the last few days, but she knew that would not be the trend. The weather was going to get colder, and she needed to cover some ground. Her leg was stiff and sore from the morning's accidental stabbing, and her feet were still raw from the punishment the rough ground had dealt them in the night. She knew her pace was not going to be quick, but she felt she had to push herself. She set off along the road as fast as she could move at a limp.

After a short time on the road, Hollyglade's ears caught the sound of hoofbeats. She quickly shot into the bushes and found a thick copse to hide in. As she settled herself in the dense foliage, she looked back down the road to watch for who might be coming this way. Fear welled up in her again as she wondered if this could be more men hunting her. She hoped that this might just be some travellers, as she knew this road to be travelled often enough. She was just under a mile from the farm, and could still see the farmhouse, and some of the road beyond.

As the riders came into view, her heart dropped. One rider was very tall in the saddle, and carried a bow on his back. The other, the one whom she could not mistake for anyone else, wore clothes all of cream colour. The riders slowed as they approached the farmhouse and rode to the gate of the fenced yard.

Hollyglade put both hands over her face and did all she could to hold back the tears that welled up in her eyes. She was a mix of rage, panic, and anxiety. Her mind raced over whether to flee, or to run back and help. She had a couple of weapons, but felt useless with them. She fearfully suspected the most likely fate of these good people would be the same as the old woman in the last village. How could she just sit there and let such a wrong, an injustice she would be responsible for, come to those innocent farmers?

Hollyglade felt a rush within her. She felt the swell of power begin to build. I could wipe them all out with a thought! She told herself. But she also knew that using her power would mean using another weapon she had no skill with, that she had no control over, one that she did not know how to wield with any level of discipline. They are going to kill that family anyway, so what's the added risk? But then her thoughts went beyond this farm, and to the other villages she knew to be close by. She could not assure herself that an expression of the power she possessed would be limited to the area of this one farm.

As she looked up again, both men entered the farmhouse. Hollyglade made a decision. As the second, taller man ducked inside, she stood, turned, and ran as fast as she could away from the farm. As she fled, tears began to stream down her face, and her sobbing made her limping gait even more ungainly. She did not look back, and she did not stop.

As dGerrie followed The Dancer into the farmhouse, the bounty hunter threw back the hood of his cloak and offered a jovial greeting. "Good day to you fine people. I wonder......" He stopped mid sentence and drew his sword, placing the tip at the neck of the man standing next to his wife and son. "Where is she?" the bounty hunter asked with a tone now underlaid with threats.

"Where is who, sir?" came the reply through fear and restrained panic.

"I'm not a knight. Where did she go?"

"I'm sorry me Lord, I know not whom you seek."

"I'm not a Lord either."

With a flick of the bounty hunter's wrist the man's neck was opened, and he fell to the floor. The woman screamed and tried to hold back the blood which came pouring out of her husband. Another swipe of his sword dispatched the woman as her son backed away in fear. With a turn, Var Toran looked at the boy who was now almost right next to dGerrie.

Turning to look at the boy, and then back to his parents, dGerrie raised his hand and swatted the boy across the face, knocking him to the floor unconscious. He then looked back to the bounty hunter who narrowed his eyes, lifted his hand to point a finger in dGerrie's direction, and pressed his mouth into a hard line, then turned and walked over to the hearth.

As he did so, dGerrie looked down to see the boy still breathing, then back at the bounty hunter, who was picking up a sword which had been leaning against the hearth. Var Toran looked at the sword and then to dGerrie.

"Search the barn. I'll search the house. Though this belonged to one of them, this was not left here by Mr. Webb, nor by Mr. Brooker".

IV : ANGER

Vernon Howe had ridden through the night and was now extremely weary as he approached the City of Rivershore. The capital city of the Kingdom of Demaria sat on the shores of the Western Sea at the Stone River's delta. The City was built on either side of the river, with Castle Waterstone built into the high cliffs where the southern tip of the Septen Mountains met the sea. Having been away from his home city for over a year, Vernon Howe was glad to be returning, though he wished it was under different circumstances.

His journey began on the morning of the previous day, in the city of Magnaville, capital of the Kingdom of Loria. Vernon was a Listener, and had been assigned a mission to make himself a member of the court at Magnaville, in order to covertly pass along information to King Dermond's Counsellor of Listeners, Lord Bellard Grange of River's Fork. Vernon had established himself in King Jerold's court, in the year leading up to the King's death. He had managed to do so by making himself one of the wealthiest merchants in Magnaville. This had not been hard to do, having had the support of the Demarian crown secretly ensuring that his shipments of various wares, spices, cloth, precious metals and gems, were always plentiful. Today, Vernon Howe returned to Rivershore to deliver a report to the King, one he knew he must deliver in person.

Vernon entered the city and headed for the palace gate. The city gates were open, as they had been for as long as he could remember. They had been built to withstand a great siege, yet in the era of peace that had lasted for a generation in the land, the gates had never been closed. As he rode through the great entrance, Vernon Howe could not help but think that he may soon see those gates closed for the first time in his life. He spurred his horse through the streets of Rivershore, avoiding the first few people in the street who had come to open their shops and stalls for the day's commerce. Dawn was just beginning to break as he arrived at the entrance to

Waterstone, the ancient seat of house Riaghlad, rulers of Demaria since before the kingdom's written history.

At the gate, Vernon Howe was met by the Royal Guard.

"Hail friend. What business have you at Waterstone?" This was the standard greeting. Hail Friend. In generations past, it had been a much less cordial Halt! Who approaches Waterstone? Again, Vernon Howe wondered how many things might change in the city after the delivery of his news.

"Friends, I am Vernon Howe, messenger and servant to Lord Bellard Grange. I bear a dispatch for the King and desire entry to make delivery." He had never uttered that first phrase, messenger and servant to Lord Bellard Grange, aloud before. As his true vocation had been covert and secret, in the last couple of years he had always introduced himself as Vernon Howe, Merchant. At your service.

"Friend, we know not of your service to Lord Grange. May we ask you for the seal of your house?" This was often the request for those the Royal Guard did not recognize. Vernon was frustrated by the delay, yet he knew that he must enter Waterstone via the proper procedures lest he be the cause of his own postponement.

"Good sirs, I carry not my seal, for I have had reason to keep it safe and hidden. Please, I beg of you to summon Lord Grange. He will vouch for me. The message I carry for the king is of the utmost importance, and though I desire to respect your duty to confirm my entry into the castle, I ask that you expedite the process as best you are able."

"Does the Lord Grange expect you?"

"I'm afraid there was not time to send word of my intent to return here."

"Very well, friend. Please wait a moment."

The guard motioned for one of the castle pages, and quietly instructed him to find Lord Grange and inform him of who it was that called at the castle gate. The page hurried off to execute the guard's command.

After a short time, the page returned with Lord Grange.

"Vernon Howe. I am surprised by this unexpected return.

Guards, let him pass. I am sure we have much to discuss."

"Thank you, my Lord" replied Vernon, as the guards opened the inner gate, allowing him to pass through. "I have urgent news which must be delivered to the King. Urgent enough, that I could not risk a courier. This news must be delivered in person."

"Now I am curious. Do you bear terms for the return of Lord Casterin of Downwater? Has the new Lorian King demanded as high a price as some have wagered?"

Vernon paused, and looked around to see that no one else was within earshot in the corridor they travelled on their way to the king's council chambers.

"No, my Lord." he whispered. "It is not terms for the exchange a hostage. It is the details of his execution."

Lord Grange's mouth dropped, as he was momentarily at a loss for words.

"When, in the history of our great nations, has a hostage been executed without a parlance between kingdoms? By the gods, this is the declaration of war! It is good that you returned, Mr. Howe. The King must hear of this. I shall send for the members of His Royal Council at once.

"Page! Page!" Lord Grange called for the page at the top of his lungs, and several came running, having properly interpreted the urgency in his call. "Boys, run with all the haste you can. Inform the members of the Royal Council that the King requires them to assemble at once. Tell them great exigencies demand their presence in the council chambers immediately."

Each of them nodded, and they quickly discussed between them who would deliver the messages to whom, and they left to complete their tasks.

"Come Vernon. You must be exhausted. We will have food and drink brought for you to the council's ante-chamber, and we shall await the arrival of the council there."

"Thank you, my Lord. I have much to tell."

"Your Grace. My Lords. I have travelled with great haste to deliver to you accounts of the happenings in Magnaville. Some of what I must report you will have heard versions of, while more of what I must report will be news indeed." Vernon Howe paused a moment to collect his thoughts. He had never addressed the Royal Council before. He had never been present within a meeting of the Royal Council prior to this. He was nervous.

"First, I must deliver the news that brought me with such haste. Yesterday morning. Lord Casterin of Downwater was executed publicly in the colonnade at Whiterock."

"Surely not!" exclaimed Lord Birk, commander of the Royal Army. The room erupted in protest and disbelief as the assembled Lords expressed their outrage and surprise.

Though there were few in attendance, the occupants of the room represented the full power and rule of Demaria. King Dermond kept appointed to council those whom he valued, for various reasons. Lord Birk was a proven military commander, Lord Orban was a shrewd negotiator and businessman, Lord Grange was connected across the four Kingdoms of the realm and beyond, and both the King's sons, Princes Dertron and Dornian were men raised for leadership.

Even in a room filled with such stolid men, the news of this blatant breach of tradition and convention, the breaking of the covenant made between King Dermond and King Jerold, produced deep shock and bewilderment. The only person to remain silent was the King.

Raising his hand to silence the room, Dermond Riaghlad turned to Vernon Howe

"Please continue, faithful servant. We must hear the details before we determine our response to this affront to our friendship." The King often referred to the diplomatic relationship with Loria in that way. King Jerold had done the same, during his lifetime. It had been their way of reminding all those in both kingdoms that peace was of foremost importance in the realm.

Vernon nodded and continued.

"As you are aware, the Lorian Crown Prince disappeared near our borders just over two weeks ago. Within the court at Whiterock, there was much speculation about the identity of the abductors. Of course, as you know, some immediately pointed their fingers toward Waterstone, though none here had motive nor desire to prevent the Prince from ascending to his throne. Others blamed the Elvish, claiming that they feared the Prince would alter the relationship built between Loria and the Elder folk by his late father. Some claimed that their motivation was to take advantage of Lorian and Demarian good will, to make a pre-emptive strike in a war for greater hold over their traditional lands.

"Some even pointed the finger to Sudara for various irrational reasons. As you know, the new Lorian King Harford, eventually sent covert operatives to abduct Lord Casterin. Though it is historically common for kingdoms and counties to take hostages when such conflicts arise, holding them to ensure that proper investigations are not interrupted, or to ensure all sides attend negotiations, there was no such intent in the abduction of Lord Casterin.

"Your Grace had asked, through our secret channels, that I make an investigation into the possible reasoning for the lack of customary demand for ransom in the case of Lord Casterin. I made much effort to gain insight into King Harford's deliberations on the matter, yet I was unable to glean his thoughts. During King Jerold's reign, his Vestry was made up of Lords whose general dispositions leant toward openness and sharing. Very little was kept secret from the other members of the court, and thus I was able to gain much knowledge. As you will remember, King Jerold felt nothing but love and friendship toward his neighbours, and thus my covert purposes in his court turned up nothing close to subversion, malevolence, or even a general negativity.

"However, once the young Prince Harford became King, the tone of court changed, as did the makeup of his Vestry, in one important way. As you may have heard, the Sorcerer

Ni'Morstrom has been granted residence within Whiterock, and a place within the King's Vestry. As is the case here in Demaria, in Loria such an appointment is unusual, and many at court felt unease at the swiftness with which the Sorcerer moved from being an unknown to the King's closest advisor.

"Several of the Lords of the realm counselled the young King against having any association with the sorcerer, reminding him that the practise of having such practitioners of the arcane ceased several generations ago when it was uncovered that many of them had used magic to influence the kings they pretended to serve.

"Many of the young King's decrees and decisions have gone against the advice of the majority of his Vestry, and instead followed other paths. These decisions have usually been presented to the court after the King has taken time for private reflection. Sources I have within Whiterock have reported the Sorcerer being granted admittance to the King's chambers during these times of reflection, which precede strange decrees such as the recent one regarding the treatment and expulsion of the Elder races from Magnaville and its surrounding areas.

"Some have theorized that the king has been placed under some sort of spell by the Sorcerer, and others have suggested that it is a case of a young and impressionable monarch being manipulated by a crafty politician. Either way, the consensus is that the young King would not make such rash moves as the expelling the Elder Folk, and executing a lord without demand for ransom or conditions for exchange, of his own accord.

"In the court at Whiterock, it is quietly seen as a shame and a tragedy that his older brother did not take his rightful place upon the throne." Vernon's gaze became unfocused as his thoughts drifted to what might have been.

The members of the Demarian Royal Council murmured and whispered to each other for several moments as the information presented by the Listener was absorbed.

Lord Orban spoke first.

"My Lords. Your Grace. It is clear we must respond, that

much I am sure we can all agree upon. But I must urge caution and restraint. While it is true, and undeniable, that the execution of Lord Casterin, and the false blame cast upon this Kingdom for the disappearance of the Lorian Prince are inexcusable, I urge this council to consider the long-term future of both Kingdoms and the prosperity through open trade that has come as a result of the generation of peace established by our great King and his former Lorian counterpart. Let us not rush to war."

Lord Birk's response was as quick as it was fierce.

"With respect my Lord, it is not we that shall rush to war. War is upon us. War is presently declared. The only question that remains for us has to do with strategy for that war, and the scale of our offensive." Turning to the King, Lord Birk continued "Your Grace, I propose that we make our goal nothing less than Whiterock. That we make our goal nothing less than to conquer Loria and bring it under your rule. I believe that anything less would simply result in endlessly escalating conflict. King Harford is not fit to wear his father's boots, let alone sit upon his throne."

The King did not immediately respond to his Lords. In his many years on the throne of Demaria, King Dermond Riaghlad had fought his share of battles. At the young age of sixteen, he had led his father's army against the rebellion of several houses within the Kingdom, and successfully put an end to the Northern Uprising. He had commanded his own forces, in the early days of his reign, in the three-year war with Ellendor, and being outnumbered by an overwhelming force, he fought to a stalemate and successfully sued for peace. He rooted out the bandits calling themselves The True Elders, and put an end to the raids upon the villages along the foothills.

King Dermond also did his part to bloodlessly negotiate peace with Loria nearly thirty years earlier when the council had then pushed for a Demarian invasion of Loria. He was a man who knew when to attack, when to wait, and when to talk.

"Friend, pardon me, but I do not know your name" the King said as he turned to Vernon.

"Howe, Your Grace. Vernon Howe."

"Mr. Howe. Tell me. You spoke of King Harford's decree regarding the Elder Folk. Many Elder Folk have sought sanctuary in Demaria in recent months, and so we have heard various reports of the methods used by both the garrisons and the army in removing them from their homes. But I would like to hear what is said at court, and more so, what you can tell us, if anything, about the King's own thoughts and motivations on the matter."

"Your Grace. I can tell you that, at first, it was the King's expressed wish that the Elder Folk be relocated away from Magnaville. It was very shortly after the issuing of his first decree regarding this, that he expanded the radius of the decree to the neighbouring counties. However, I will say that his written decree gave no mention of tactics, and when he gave instruction to his commanders, both of the garrison and the army, the King was clear that patience must be exercised, and that force was not to be used unless no other option of enforcement remained. To my knowledge, this instruction was adhered to.

"As to the motivation, none was made clear. It was a question many in the court strove to find an answer to, yet so far no one has been able to deduce the motive for the King's actions, nor any clear agenda."

"Tell me Mr. Howe, how many garrisons, divisions, troops or battalions does he commit to the endeavour?"

"Your Grace, I believe it is all of them."

"All of them?"

"Yes, Your Grace. In the last few weeks, the King gave orders to his commanders to engage the entirety of their resources to the task of purging the Elder Folk from his lands. In addition, I heard rumour that in the latest set of directives to those commanders, there were descriptions of particular persons of interest given. It was said that the King wished the capture of several of the Elder Folk. No reason for the need, or desire, for the capture was known."

"To be clear, friend, you say that the entire Lorian army,

and the King's garrisons are spread throughout the country about the task of purging the land of Elder Folk? That there is currently no gathered standing force?"

"Yes, Your Grace. That is accurate."

The King stood, nodded to Vernon, and then looked to the commander of his forces.

"Lord Birk, ready the army we have here in Rivershore, and meet with me here once you have issued your orders for preparation. Together we will define our war plan. Lord Grange, send word to Downwater and Westshore to ready fleets in both the Eastern and Western Seas. We ride at dawn."

"Father," Prince Dertron interjected "I will ride with you and bring you glory in battle."

"No Son. You will not. You are my eldest and heir, and thus you have some right to earn glory in war, but I have need of you elsewhere. You shall serve our house in this war. You both shall," he said as he looked to Prince Dornian "for I have others plans. Plans I will place in the hands of those I trust to see them through. You shall join us, and Lord Birk, here to discuss what I have in store for this impudent whelp who calls himself a king."

"Mr. Howe" the King turned to Vernon once more "you shall attend also. I may have further questions which you may be able to answer."

Vernon bowed his acknowledgement.

"Lords" announced the King. "you have work to do."

Each of the Lords bowed, and left to begin preparations for war.

Looking to the sky to find the position of the sun, dGerrie determined that it was about halfway between noon and sundown. It had been another day full of anxiety and tension. This morning, dGerrie had been forced to watch another innocent family lose their lives as a result of goodwill toward a suffering stranger. He felt some sort of solace in believing he had at least saved the boy. dGerrie felt sympathy for the young child, knowing what kind of life was now in store for the recently orphaned youth. He hoped that the boy might be lucky enough to have a relative take him in, someone better than dGerrie's own extended family, whom he had run from so many years ago.

As they entered the first town since leaving the farm earlier that day, Var Toran stopped to give dGerrie his instructions.

"Mr. Theurbeault, I must find and meet with the garrison commander in this town, as we now have the need for additional men. I would like you to canvas public houses, inns, and taverns in search of any sign of our missing girl. I recognise this little town, and suggest we meet at the Inn at the end of this road at sundown. You shall be able to find it by the carriage wheel hung on the railing outside the main entrance. If the girl is smart, she will have moved on by now, but we may at least hope for another lead."

"And if I find her?"

"I trust you are as capable knotting a rope as you are firing a bow, Mr. Theurbeault. Our contract requires she be intact and unharmed."

dGerrie nodded and nudged his horse into a walk, heading for the first establishment along the main road.

As he hitched his horse to the rail, dGerrie looked at his surroundings. The air was cooler now, as the evening was drawing near, and night would fall soon after. The roads were still dry and dusty, as it was now near ten days since the last rain. Looking up and down the road and side streets, dGerrie observed the hustle and bustle of merchants and traders, buyers, sellers, and townsfolk milling about and trying to make the last sales and purchases before closing their shops and booths for the day.

The people in town seemed a mostly bright and cheery sort. There was no sign of the rich, upper class that graced the markets in Magnaville, but these people seemed well enough off. Greenfield was one of the minor trading centres of the region, sitting at the crossroads to nearly all the southern roads. Usually, dGerrie would have enjoyed spending time is such a town, but his current reason for being here hung over him adversely.

Once again, thoughts of abandoning his contract and running across the nearest border flooded his mind. His anxiety returned as he recalled that The Dancer's most recent contract had been across the Demarian border, and that his reputation was built on the ruthlessly efficient completion of every contract, every hunt. dGerrie did not want to be the focus of the next hunt, especially if Var Toran were to take such a desertion personally.

Looking around him, dGerrie observed the street for a few moments to get a sense of the mood about town. Nothing seemed out of the ordinary, and it appeared that their presence here had not caused any alarm among the locals. Obviously, word of the exploits from the last few days, and the last few villages had not reached this particular town. dGerrie turned for the door of the building, which appeared to be an inn, and entered.

The smell of food coming from the kitchen, ales being drunk from large mugs, and the general odour of people who had been hard at work for the day, all commingled in dGerrie's nostrils, momentarily overpowering his senses. Taking off his riding gloves and walking to the bar, dGerrie caught the attention of the woman pouring drinks, and with an upward nod indicated that he wished to speak with her. She held up one finger, signalling she would be with him shortly. After delivering several drinks, she met dGerrie where he stood at the end of the bar.

"What can I get for you, beer?" the woman asked.

"No thank you ma'am. But I wonder if you might be able to tell me if you've seen someone." dGerrie hesitated before describing whom he was searching for. Several thoughts flew through his mind. Should I say why I am looking for her? Should I lie and say she's a friend who's missing? I don't want to scare this woman, nor tip off the girl I'm looking for by revealing too much here.

"I might. I might not. A lot of people come and go through the town, being on the cross roads and all." replied the woman. She pointed out a fact that made the need for haste that much more important to him. This town sat at the conjunction of several roads leading to and from the Hot Lake, the River South, the River Low, the River High, and the Southern Plains. If the girl did not turn up here, it was likely the search for her would take far more than the fortnight which The Dancer had been given to fulfill this contract. dGerrie did not like the idea of prolonging his time with Var Toran.

"Well" he began "I'm looking for my cousin. She's about fifteen years old, but very tall for her age, at least a head taller than I. She has long red hair, she's half Elvish, and she is likely dressed like a man or in riding clothes. If she passed this way, it would have been earlier today." He paused as he watched the woman rub her chin pensively. He felt the need to give further plausibility to his search for her, hoping to coax forth some information, or at least the desire to help.

"I've been looking for her for nearly a week since she ran off from my uncle's farm. You see she thinks she's old enough to be off on her own, but she's still a bit naive and likely to get herself in trouble. My aunt is worried sick about her and asked if I'd try to bring her home before she gets herself hurt."

The woman nodded along as dGerrie made his inquiry, but as he watched her expression he could see that nothing he was saying evoked any recognition from her.

"I can't say I've seen anyone that young, nor that tall in here today. But this is one of the bigger towns in the area. You might still find someone who's seen her. I'm sorry I can't be of more help." With that the woman returned to her customers.

dGerrie nodded his thanks to the woman and made his way back out to the road. He decided to check some of the other streets in the town, thinking that someone who knew they were being tracked might choose to steer clear of main areas.

The garrison commander's quarters were spartan, but seemed to serve well enough for the man who occupied them. He was a solid looking man with close cropped greying hair and at least a few days worth of stubble. The scars that lined his face accentuated the look of austerity with which he read the letter he held.

"This is the seal of the Crown. Though I must say I have not previously seen the signature of this new King of ours, I accept the authenticity of this document." He placed the letter in the hand of one of his officers, and looked at his guest. "So" he continued as he stood "I'm to loan you as many men as you require for a maximum of four days."

"Five days" Var Toran interjected "If I am correct about the date of the new moon, which a person who undertakes contracts with such deadlines as I have must be. You shall find that the new moon is on the fourth night from tonight, and should I find this missing girl, I shall require some of these men to transport her to Magnaville on the morning preceding the night of the new moon, which is when, at the latest, my very specific contract requires she be delivered."

"Five days." the commander's brow furrowed acutely. "Fine. Five days it is. I have twenty men stationed from this outpost. How many do you require?"

"All of them" replied the bounty hunter, widening his ever-present grin slightly.

"All of them?" the commander questioned. "Twenty men to bring in one girl?" He leaned his head back and let out goading laugh "Surely you jest. A man with your reputation needs twenty men to net one girl?" The commander shook his head as he allowed himself a chuckle.

"And yourself, Commander Tollison. Greenfield is not a small town, and time is of the essence. You and your men shall be compensated over and above your regular pay, as per the instructions in the letter. But we must begin without delay.

As you will recall, my reputation includes a perfect record of success. I shall not let today be the day that record receives its first blemish. I trust that your reputation as a capable commander is accurate and well deserved. Please have your men assemble here so that I may instruct them."

The commander's jaw dropped slightly as he came to grips with the seriousness of the bounty hunter's insistence on the use of the entire garrison. Var Toran turned to exit the commander's quarters and stopped at the door, looking back at the commander for a moment

"And as to the test this girl shall provide your men, I'll tell you that she managed to get the better two professionals who were hired to find her. She did so in the dead of night without the aid of any weapons, and completely in the nude." He paused to let commander and his aide absorb the information. "Have your men here in one half hour, Commander." With that, Var Toran left the barracks.

The back alleys of the town were typical of many villages and towns of the area. Businesses used the rear of their buildings for loading and unloading of wares, as well as disposing of various types of scrap, offal, and rubbish. Often the poorer members of society could be found sifting through the debris for anything edible, or otherwise usable in some way.

This particular alleyway was a bustling side market of sorts, where the poorer population sold various wares, fruit and vegetables, meats, clothing and trinkets from carts, or from a mat placed on the ground. Were he not here with a specific and time sensitive purpose, dGerrie would normally have enjoyed the stroll through the various peddlers' makeshift stalls, and likely would have purchased some sort of little souvenir for himself or a friend.

Stopping here and there, to interrupt the rummaging, or trading, of various people, dGerrie asked frequently if any of them had seen the girl he was looking for. Over the course of half an hour, he had no success. He was quite sure that some of the people he made his inquiries to would have told him they had seen nothing no matter what he had asked. He believed that no one had seen her, as he got the impression that no one was actually lying to him regardless of how little they wanted to indulge his questioning.

dGerrie felt his stomach begin to growl, as he'd not eaten since his crude breakfast at the inn that morning. A little way down the lane he noticed a small cart with a bit of smoke rising from it. dGerrie recognised it as a street vittler, though he had not yet seen one outside of Magnaville. He made his way to the vendor.

There was an assortment of meats sizzling on the make-shift grill.

"How much for chicken?" dGerrie asked, digging his hand in his coin purse for a copper.

"A half-copper for chicken, a copper for beef or lamb." replied the man from and toothless mouth on a weathered and dirty face.

"Chicken please" dGerrie replied handing the man a copper coin "No change please. It smells lovely"

The man nodded as he took the coin, and with his gnarled hand, lifted one of the skewers and offered it to dGerrie.

"You're most kind, sir," the man offered with smile.

dGerrie smiled back at the old man.

"Oh, I'm no knight" he chuckled "but your politeness honours me. I wonder if you might help me a little. I'm looking for my cousin who has run away from home, and whose parents have asked me to find her. You see, the poor girl is prone to bouts of depression and has run away before. She is only fifteen years old and my aunt and uncle are worried for her."

"Oh" muttered the old man as he listened "run from home you say. And what might she look like, friend?"

"Ah, well she is quite tall now. Almost a head taller than I, with long red hair. She often dresses in men's clothes, as she likes to ride and help my uncle with the farm. She may carry a sword, as my uncle's has gone missing."

The man's face gave a brief sign of recognition when dGerrie described the girl. As dGerrie finished, the man looked him up and down, pausing on the various weapons dGerrie carried. The keen observer could have seen the man's thought process as he weighed the pros and cons of whether to share his knowledge, or whether to attempt to lead dGerrie astray. Such a quandary was not uncommon for people such as this old man, when in fear of reprisal for failure to share information with people appearing to be of either the noble cast or the military.

dGerrie read the man's expression of recognition, and his hesitation, and offered reassurance.

"I assure you, good friend, that I am indeed this poor girl's cousin, and mean only to speak with her to urge her to return home to her loving and worried parents. Please, if you have seen her, point me to her."

The man looked at dGerrie, and then turned his head and nodded toward the corral a couple of buildings down the alley. dGerrie placed a hand on the man's shoulder, another copper in his hand, and nodded his thanks.

He took a bite of the skewer and marvelled and the pleasant flavours as he walked toward the stables the man had indicated. As he made his way to the corral, dGerrie looked to the west to see the sun nearing the horizon.

As the garrison troops assembled, Var Toran ascended the steps of the barracks and turned to face them.

"Good troops. I thank you for the loan of your service, for your time, and your expertise. I thank your Commander Tollison for his cooperation in this urgent search we must undertake. I am aware of the odd nature of the arrangement we have at present, but I am sure you will find the compensation for your efforts well worth your time. Now, let me explain to you the task we have at hand.

"We are in search of a young girl who is very dear to someone at Whiterock. Though my contractor's desire is to remain anonymous, their desire for the safe return of this girl is equally great. Though I can not tell you her name, I can describe her sufficiently, especially given that she has a rather unique appearance. The girl we strive to find is very tall, head and shoulders above your tallest man," he said as he pointed to one of the troops at the rear of the assembly.

"She has long red hair, is quite thin, and wears men's clothes. She is likely carrying a sword and dagger, and may know how to wield them reasonably well. Though she is young, about fifteen years old, she is quite capable, besting two men with skills similar to your own not more than a day and half ago. This knowledge adds to the difficulty of our task, as we are required to apprehend her without causing harm. The contract requires that she be returned to Whiterock intact, and unharmed. As such, I request that you conduct your search for her in pairs, as it is the best strategy to attempt to overpower her with strength in numbers, rather than steel.

"Your excellent commander and I shall wait at the coach house to monitor the junction at the main roads at the southern edge of the town. Report to us there with any solid leads, or ideally, the girl in hand." Turning to the commander, Var Toran signalled his consent to commence the search.

With a nod, Commander Tollison ordered his men to depart

"Be quick about it boys. There is every chance this girl is still in Greenfield, and I'd like us to get back to our regular duties as soon as possible. Dismissed."

Turning to the bounty hunter, Tollison extended his hand along the road, inviting Var Toran to head to the coach house.

Seeing that the corral was empty of people, at least in the holding area at the front, dGerrie ducked between the last couple of houses before reaching the stables. He wasn't sure where this girl might be, if she was even still within the corral, but he was sure that he could not simply approach and introduce himself without provoking a fight. Stealth was the better option. dGerrie was confident in his well-established ability to get close to an unsuspecting target without being seen or heard. Now was the time to employ patience and careful tactics.

Taking his time and moving furtively, dGerrie silently made his way to the edge of the last building beside the corral, making sure not to draw any unwanted attention along the way. Once at corner of the building, he paused and observed the stables for a few minutes. There was no sign of activity, aside from the animals in the yard, so dGerrie decided to approach the stable building itself. There was a man door facing the gap between the building where he stood and the stables, which appeared to be slightly ajar. Stepping lightly and drawing the shorter of his swords, one he would choose when expecting to have to do combat in tight quarters, dGerrie reached the door. Pressing his ear gently against the side of the stables, dGerrie listened for a moment, but could hear no sign of a person within.

dGerrie paused where he was and closed his eyes, counting to thirty. It was a trick he had learned from another bounty hunter. When entering a dark area from a light area, one could adjust one's eyes to the dark before entering, and thus not be disadvantaged visually upon transitioning to the dark. Thinking that if the girl were inside she must be resting, or reclining, dGerrie stepped back from the wall and aimed himself for the open door.

With lightning quickness, he stepped through the door while barely making a sound, raising his sword as he quickly scanned the inside of the stables for any sign of a person. He had been quick, and nearly silent, but not quick enough, nor silent enough. As he finally completed his visual sweep of the inside of the barn, and turned to the small area behind the door, he was met with a blade at his throat.

Taking up his chosen position at the edge of the porch on the outside of the coach house, Var Toran lifted one foot to the edge of the water trough and leaned his elbow on his knee. Turning to Commander Tollison, he grinned and struck up a conversation.

"Commander. I understand that, until recently, you served as Commander of The Cavalry in the King's Royal Army. The Southern Plains detachment, I believe. Tell me, did you see combat in the Sudaran conflict?"

"You are correct on all accounts, Mr. Var Toran. Quite well informed, I must say."

"Oh, thank you. I must admit that my livelihood can often depend on being well informed. Tell me, did your assignments ever take you as far as to where the border with Sudara crosses the Western Mountains?"

"I did venture that far on one occasion. It was in support of Commander Forjian's campaign. He found his infantry set upon from all sides by Sudaran and Elvish forces, but managed to get a courier out in time to make it to our location at the River South. We rode for five days to come to his aide. Though, when we arrived there was not much left of the company. We managed to take some of the Sudaran's by surprise, and open up an avenue of retreat. Forjian began his assault on the border outpost with four thousand men. We managed to aide the escape of only three hundred."

Var Toran's expression moved to one of fascination as he replied

"Ah, so it is true that the Sudarans and the Elvish fought side by side there. I have always wondered if the Elvish received Sudaran support in resisting Lorian rule where the traditional Elvish lands stretch north of the Sudaran border. Your experience would seem to indicate that such support was indeed supplied. I have also heard, and you must tell me if you know the truth of this, that the Sudarans had the help of one or more of the Golden Race. Many have dismissed this idea saying that they still slumber, while others have said the truth of it is evidenced by the total annihilation of several companies, in separate areas and at unrelated skirmishes."

"As to the second rumour, I can say that I neither saw, nor heard of any evidence of dragons. It would be a first, I believe, for them to concern themselves with the politics of men. Though, if you believe the stories of the ancient Sudarans and the southern Elvish clans, who reportedly communed with the Golden Race, anything is possible.

"As to the Elvish and Sudaran forces, I would not say that they fought side by side. There were no fighting divisions which contained both Elvish and Human forces. There were Elvish brigades, and human brigades, which seemed to have some sort of coordinated strategy."

"Interesting. That may suggest a temporary alliance, rather than any permanent peace between the Elvish and the Sudarans. Tell me, were you there when King Jerold and King Erhmenyr declared the truce? I understand that the negotiations were exceedingly tense, unlike Jerold's initial meeting with our neighbours to the north."

"I was not there, unfortunately. But I am acquainted with several officers who were. I'm told that both Kings stood nearly toe to toe at the mid-point of the border bridge at the River South's crossing from Loria to Sudara, while they presented each other their terms. Unfortunately, no one is able to accurately report what was said between the two, as forces for both sides were not permitted on the bridge.

"Those who were there gave accounts that King Erhmenyr's initial disposition was highly agitated and combative, but that after half an hour, King Jerold had somehow coaxed a smile out of him."

"Yes, I had the pleasure of attending court at Whiterock on only one occasion before the good King passed to the next life. I must say that he was the most charismatic man whose presence I have had the honour of experiencing. Though I was not able to converse with him myself, I did enjoy hearing his conversations with the Lords and Ladies of Loria. Quite an engaging man. It is interesting that after only a year of peace, Erhmenyr was mysteriously murdered in his own bed. And not having an heir to the throne, the rule of the Kingdom is still contested between its clans. Chaos reigns in the south, and many expect war with Loria once more, should a clear winner emerge in the struggle for its throne."

"I try not to speculate about politics, especially those in

foreign lands. Though I will say, that from a military perspective, there is no clear favourite in the civil conflict to the south. Jerold was a very charismatic and patient man. I can not say the same for his successor."

"Ah, sadly that is true for me also. Though the young boy King is no tyrant, neither is he seasoned, nor a schooled leader of men. One may hope that he improves with time."

"I doubt it will happen as you hope."

"Is that what lead you to request you post here? Far from the capital?"

"Well spotted again Mr. Var Toran. You are perceptive. Though maybe not perceptive enough to leave a man's personal decisions alone."

"My apologies Commander. I meant no offense. I often find that sharing one's personal story with those one serves with can make the time pass more pleasantly."

Tollison stepped toward the bounty hunter and raised a finger as his tone took a decidedly authoritarian note.

"We do not serve together, bounty hunter. I serve the King, and if serving the King means that I must obey an order from him to join your search, so be it. Do not forget that you are a private contractor, not a servant of the crown. You would do well to remember the distinction." Having made his point, the commander stepped back to the porch rail and leaned against it once more.

"Well, Commander" responded the bounty hunter "this will certainly be entertaining."

Several moments passed silently as the two men scanned the road under the setting sun. After a short time, a pair of garrison troops approached the coach house.

"Commander," the first soldier addressed Tollison, "she may have been spotted on the far side of the main road."

"Lead the way men," replied the commander.

"Exciting!" chimed Var Toran. "Exciting, indeed."

dGerrie froze. This was unusual for him. The last time someone had gotten the drop on him with enough agility and quickness to bring a blade to his throat was well before he grew into a man. Even the boy he was then would not have been beaten to the punch, or the draw in this case, by just anyone. As his eyes traced the angle of the blade, which was oddly upward, indicating that it's wielder was taller than he was, dGerrie's jaw suddenly dropped and he let out a gasp in surprise.

"Sprout?"

"Stilt!"

dGerrie lowered his blade as he registered the delicate yet calloused hand, slender arms, and long red hair which framed the soft featured face of the girl he recognized as his friend, Hollyglade.

With a look of surprised recognition, she dropped her sword and grabbed him by the shoulders, pulling him in and embracing him tightly.

"By the gods dGerrie, what are you doing here?"

dGerrie was overcome by shock at first. He had spent a great deal of time in the last week wondering if the girl he was hunting was indeed his friend. He had been torn between hoping that it would indeed turn out to be her, in which case he could hope to aide her in escaping her pursuers, and the hope that it was just someone who looked like her, in which case he could fulfill his contract and still be sure his friend was in no danger.

Now, as she embraced him, while he was still full of the stress, anxiety and the hype he had worked up to come through the barn door and capture his prey, he felt overwhelmed by emotion. Then, releasing the pent-up emotion and intensity that was coiled up in him like a spring, dGerrie dropped his sword and returned her embrace.

As he buried his face in her hair, the smell of animals, dirt, and hay filled his nostrils, and he smiled at the familiar scent of his nature loving friend. Her thin frame, though taller than his, sank into his embrace. He had grown up without siblings, yet having spent many years on the streets of Magnaville, looking out for the skinny little red-haired Elvish girl, watching her

119

grow by leaps and bounds in both height and aptitude, he could only think of her as his little sister.

"Holly, I can't believe it's you. I've been hired to find a tall red-haired girl, but I didn't know it was you." Putting his hands on her shoulders and stepping back, dGerrie's expression changed to a mix of worry and determination. "Sprout, we have to get out of here now. It's not safe. They'll find us."

"What do you mean, we? Are you being hunted too? I could swear it was you I saw at that farm this morning. I don't remember you having a beard. And what's with the garrison's uniform?" She stood back and looked him up and down, taking in his shaggy blonde hair, light brown beard, and his still somewhat skinny frame which carried a great variety of weapons.

"Yes Holly, it was me. It's a long story. I was with The Dancer. He conscripted me out of the Magnaville garrison."

She recoiled at the confirmation of her fears.

"You've been hunting me? You killed that poor old woman!?" She began to cry as her voice grew louder.

"No, Holly. Sshhhhh. The Dancer did that. I had no choice in it. It was either I go along with him, or risk being the next one he turned his sword to. Now that I know it is you that he seeks, I'm done with him. Contract be damned." He took her hand and met her eyes with his. "Holly, you'll always be my little Sprout. Even if you've somehow grown beyond my stature."

She couldn't help but smile in response to his grinning reassurance. Her smile quickly turned back to concern.

"dGerrie, I'm scared. This is too much for me."

"I don't blame you. This bounty hunter is no slouch. Holly…" His expression and tone grew gravely serious "we really need to get out of here. I will be just as much a fugitive as you now. And as good as I am in a fight, Trenon Var Toran is not a man I'd like to cross swords with."

"Trenon what? Is that his real name? His men only referred to him as The Dancer."

dGerrie leant over and picked up both swords, handing the one Hollyglade had dropped back to her and sheathing his own.

"Yes. Var Toran. He's a uniquely vicious man." Pointing to the sword, he asked "Do you know how to use that? I don't recall you ever handling a blade. Though I have a feeling you've learned a thing or two, based on how we found Tom and Hern."

"Not really. I know that the pointy end hurts more. And that was mostly luck. I surprised them in their sleep, though I didn't get away without some scrapes and bruises," she replied with a look of acknowledged naivete. She had not thought she would ever actually have to use a sword, and that she could get away with another good bluff, should any more difficult situations arise.

"Well, you may have to use it eventually if we are going to get out of here." He drew his sword and motioned for her to do the same. "Quickly. We don't have much time." He moved to face her.

"Most men are going to try one of a few things. A stab, like this" He slowly moved his sword toward her in a demonstrated stabbing motion. "Or a slash like this, or this." He motioned both a forehand and backhand downward slash.

"You have to let them make the first move. They don't know that you haven't swung a sword before, so don't let them know. When they stab, or slash, you step to the side, while using your blade to guard yourself like this, or this" he showed both an upward and downward parry "and then you swing back. Not hard, but with delicate control. You don't have to hack anything off. Just try to touch them. Your blade looks good and sharp. Usually a little cut feels like a big cut, in a fight. And if you're lucky enough to hit them in the neck, where the blood will flow fast, you've done the job. Use that Elvish speed of yours, and the length of your arms to keep your distance. Anything more than that is too much to think about." He resheathed his sword and turned to peer through the door. "There's some light left, but we've got to move."

"dGerrie" she replied, still with tears trickling down her cheek. "I don't think I can kill anyone. It's not me. I can't"

"Sprout," he replied, looking her in the eye while placing a hand on her shoulder, and letting out a breath through his nose. "It may come down to either you or them. Make it them. Stay behind me if it comes to a fight. Hopefully, this is all moot, and we can just sneak out of town." He leaned his head out the door and then back in quickly. "Come on. Let's go."

She sheathed her sword, wiped her cheeks, picked up the saddlebag, and followed him through the door. Fear welled up within her at the thought of a confrontation. So far, she had always had somewhere to run and hide, and had not had to stand and fight. Even the two men in the woods did not add up to a real fight. Though she had not come through it unscathed, her surprise attack had been effective enough to give her the advantage.

As the pair crept out of the stable and into the space between the buildings, dGerrie approached the edge of the house opposite the stables and chanced a quick glance along the alleyway in each direction. He flinched slightly, cursed under his breath and took a couple of careful steps back.

"There are groups of garrison troops in both directions. I'm pretty sure Var Toran has them working for him now. I believe that's where he headed when we came to town about an hour ago. We can't be seen by them. I'm not going to try to talk my way past them either. I can't risk being separated from you now. It's better they think I disappeared."

"Let's head back this way" she suggested, indicating a direction further away from the main road "Maybe we can get out of town and into the trees, or something like that."

"It's going to have to do. But let's be quick about it."

Taking the lead, Hollyglade moved with a dexterity and silence that amazed dGerrie. She seemed to him to have grown incredibly capable in several different ways in the short two years since he had seen her last. He followed closely, noticing her limp as they snuck between the buildings and headed to the next alley.

"Sprout, are you going to be able to run, if we have to?" he asked, glancing to her injured leg.

"I out ran you, didn't I, Stilt? Besides, I plan on us using a little stealth, rather than speed. Remember the Central Market? It'll just have to be like old times, stealing coin purses and loaves of bread."

"Sprout, this is different. Neither of us know this town, so there won't be any familiar doors or corners to disappear through. You may have to run, and I doubt I can carry you."

"We'll have to do what we can do. If we can make it to the trees by sundown, then I can lead us through in the dark. It's only a few days until the new moon, so there won't be a lot of light. For me, that's going to be our advantage. No lantern for them to home in on, and their lanterns will be easy to spot and avoid. Once we get to the trees, it's going to be better than doors and corners." She turned and leaned her head out from the edge of the building to check the next alleyway. Seeing no sign of troops, she waved for dGerrie to follow, and stepped into the back street. Taking her cue, he followed quickly, glancing along the alley in each direction to make sure they could make the crossing unnoticed.

As Hollyglade made her way to the edge of the buildings on the far side of the alleyway, she turned to look for acknowledgement from dGerrie before continuing between the houses. He was looking down the street, when something appeared to catch his eye. He looked at Hollyglade and pushed her forward as he whispered

"Move. Now".

She didn't wait to find out what he saw. A moment later, she didn't have to, as shouts could be heard coming from down the alley.

"Oi! You! Stop there".

"Gods Dammit!" hissed dGerrie as they began to run between the buildings. "How did they see us so quickly?"

Hollyglade did not respond, but moved as fast as she could through the narrow gaps between the houses. Looking ahead, she could see that there was an end to the buildings after a few more streets.

"We've got to get out of these streets. We're too slow in here." breathed Hollyglade.

"You're right. It looks like we don't have many more alleys to cross, so let's pick up the pace," replied dGerrie as he looked back over his shoulder to see the two garrison troops turn into the gap between the buildings where he and Hollyglade has stood moments earlier.

Crossing the next alley, more shouts came for either direction. With a quick glance to one another, Hollyglade and dGerrie rushed across the alley and between the next set of buildings. The distance between the edge of this building and the next road was greater than the previous two, but the pair made it to the edge of the buildings as quickly as the confined space would allow them to. As they approached the alley, dGerrie put a hand on Hollyglade's back and urged her onward.

"We can't slow now."

She looked out from the edge of the alley to see a pair of troops coming from each direction.

"They're going to block us!"

"Run Holly," he urged her as he drew both swords.

She sprang across the alleyway with surprising speed despite the limping caused by her injured leg and damaged feet. As he followed, dGerrie gauged the approach of the men on either side, and determined that he would not make it across the alley in time to put them behind him. He made his decision with dispassionate efficiency.

Moving with near lightning quickness, dGerrie made for the gap between the building where Hollyglade had gone. Keeping an eye on the men to his left, who were slightly closer than the two coming from the right, he made for the buildings as though he expected to outrun them. Watching carefully out of the corner of his eye, dGerrie slowed slightly as the nearest man raised his sword to deliver a slash from above.

With all the dexterity he could direct into the maneuver,

dGerrie planted his right foot, stopped and bent backward letting the slash sail past him and into the ground. With his left hand he brought his short sword around from back to front, in a delicate move that took no more than the flick of his wrist, aiming the tip of the blade for the man's throat.

The strike found its mark with immaculate precision, as only the first inch of the blade swept through the flesh below the trooper's chin. As the man stumbled past dGerrie, he made a quick half pirouette to dodge the stabbing thrust aimed at him from the second man. With a graceful follow through, dGerrie made a backhanded slash with the long sword in his right hand as the man passed him, slicing the calf muscle to the bone. The man fell on top of his partner as dGerrie looked up to see the second set of troops close to a within couple of paces.

With a quick glance to his right, dGerrie noted that the two men following the path he had taken with Hollyglade were still a minute away. With another split-second decision, dGerrie decided there was not enough time to allow the two men next to him to make the first move.

With a half step backward, dGerrie lowered his left hand and swung his right hand behind his head to make a backhand slash from the left at the closer man's head. The soldier moved his two-handed sword up to easily block the relatively simple attack, and as he did so, felt the end of dGerrie's short sword pierce his neck from front to back.

With a swift kick, the man was sent to the ground as dGerrie lunged forward over the falling soldier, into a full pirouette. One sword went high, and one went low. Both found flesh, and the last soldier stepped backward, dropping his sword and clutching both his left thigh and his forehead.

dGerrie resheathed both swords and bolted into the gap between the houses in pursuit of Hollyglade. Upon reaching the now dark space separating one house from the next, he stopped in the shadows, and turned back toward the alley, pulling his bow over his head and into his left hand. With one fluid motion, he drew two arrows simultaneously, knocked them, and fired at the men who were almost into the alley. The man in front saw the flight of the arrows just in time to duck. The second was not so lucky, as one arrow lodged in his shoulder. The first man turned for a moment, in an instinctive response to his comrade's scream of pain. As he turned back, the next arrow found its mark in his chest.

"dGerrie!" rasped Hollyglade from several paces behind him. He turned and continued to run, seeing her with her hand over her mouth in a look of shock.

"It's us or them. And I want it to be them. I'm not in the mood to die today, Sprout. Get moving." His tone was demanding, but carried a certain level of assurance that Hollyglade could not deny. Maybe it was that it came from her friend, and maybe it was that it came from a man who obviously knew how to instantly calculate his odds. Either way, Hollyglade knew that now was not the time to debate the moral implications of the violence that had just been apportioned to their would-be captors.

She turned back in the direction of the outskirts of town and moved to the edge of the gap. There she halted abruptly, and held her hand up behind her to stop dGerrie from running into her. She crept backward in fear at what her eyes beheld, turning to look past dGerrie and into the alley from which they had come. She stopped again. Both exits were blocked, and there was no other direction to turn.

dGerrie put his hand on Hollyglade's arm, looked her in the eye

"Stay behind me, Sprout. And let them make the first move." Then, he nodded as he stepped past her and out into the alley.

"Mr. Theurbeault! How exciting this is! I must admit, I have yet seen you fire but one arrow with my own eyes, but the demonstration was so inspiring, I must say that I secretly hoped that you and I may have the chance to spar. I see, that tonight, in this lovely setting sun, that my wish shall indeed be granted" Var Toran dropped from his horse, and stepped forward to face dGerrie. Both men drew their swords.

V : COMBAT

Lord Renald Birk preferred to attend to his own equipment. While other officers, knights, and even some regular infantry would leave their swords, pikes, lances, and sometimes even daggers with the smiths for cleaning and sharpening, Lord Birk took pride in maintaining an expert and elite level of sharpness to his blades. He gained a certain focus through the routine of polishing his armour and weapons. The ritual was something he had performed on the morning of every battle he had ever taken part in since he had first held a blade.

This morning would hold great significance in his military career, and more importantly, the future of the kingdoms of Demaria and Loria. His troops had marched for five days to reach the narrowest point of the Narrowlands and were now assembled and prepared for battle, only a mile from the Lorian border.

The previous day, Lord Birk had sent several of his most accomplished scouts to infiltrate the far side of the border with the mission of covertly gaining intelligence on the state of the Lorian army's readiness for battle. The reports had returned an hour ago. They had stated that there was only a small force stationed at the fork of the Capital trail, which ran from Magnaville across the border and all the way to Rivershore, and the Coast to Coast road, which forked off from the Capital trail near where the border began at the eastern sea, and travelled all the way to Westport. There the Western mountains of Loria met the south side of the Western Sea's Bay of Cliffs, directly south across that bay from Rivershore.

Lord Birk finished his ritual preparations, donned the last few pieces of his armour, and headed for the assembly of commanders. Once there, the seasoned and battle tested leader bowed to the King, and gave nods to his commanders.

"Your Grace, your forces are ready to begin the march into war. We await your command, and yearn to find honour in battle with our enemies," declared Lord Birk, giving the traditional proclamation of readiness for battle.

"Thank you, Lord Birk. I am confident much glory shall be gained in the triumph that awaits us." The King replied with an air of surety befitting such an accomplished ruler and soldier as he was. "Friends. We have ridden long and hard to reach this battlefield with the element of surprise in our favour. Our scouts report only a small detachment of soldiers at the Capital and Coast roads fork. Yet we must not be overconfident, as this new King, or perhaps his Sorcerer, may have some surprises of their own.

"We come with a force of over twenty thousand men, and expect to meet only five hundred, so let us execute our plans carefully, and to the letter so that we may swiftly move to our full objective in Magnaville and Whiterock. Lord Birk, have you chosen which battalion shall lead the charge once we arrive at the fork?"

"Yes, your Grace. I have given the honour to War Marshall Yerin Greln. He is most experienced and first fought in battle with your Grace as an infantryman in the early days of the Ellendor conflicts."

The War Marshall stepped forward, brought his right fist to his chest in the soldier's hail, and bowed.

"Your Grace, I hunger for the moment that I may bring glory to our Kingdom and to your name."

"Very good" replied the king with a nod of acknowledgement to the War Marshall. "Let us move. I tire of the waiting and riding. I too hunger to wet my blade." With that, the King turned and waved to his squire to bring his horse.

Lord Birk nodded to each of the assembled commanders, and the War Marshall, and left to join the King.

"Your Grace, may I ride into battle at your side? You would do me much honour to allow me to fight next to you."

The King looked at the Lord, and smiled.

"If you can keep up, my friend." With the energy and dexterity of a man half his age, the King swung himself into the saddle and spurred his horse to a canter. Renald Birk grinned widely, climbed quickly into the saddle and triggered his mount to a run.

To have called what happened at the Coast and Capital fork a battle would have been a gross overstatement. The Demarian army barely slowed its pace as the small contingent of Lorian forces were wiped out in less than twenty minutes. Though a few riders had managed to escape, the battle hungry Demarian army rode over their enemies mercilessly, leaving no other survivors. Now, the three-day march to Magnaville would begin with the army having lost but a dozen men, spurred on by the ease of an overwhelming victory.

Demaria had a long history of greatness in battle. All Demarian men must serve at least a year in the Royal Army, once they come of age. There were no men in the whole of the kingdom who could not be called upon to fight, and the Lord of the King's Royal Armies, could count on them knowing their role, and craving to earn honour in battle.

War was entrenched in the Demarian culture. From a young age, boys learned to fight with fists, sticks used like swords, staffs like spears, and anything else they put in their hands. There was not a person in the kingdom, neither man nor woman, who could not use a bow to hunt, and therefore, also to fight. A Demarian soldier, earned his rank and colours only after proving proficient in at least three disciplines of weaponry. A Demarian soldier was a fighter to be feared, and respected. A Demarian army, was a force to be reckoned with.

"Lord Birk," called the King, "send dispatches via war pigeons now. Prince Dertron and Prince Dornian will want to know that we are ahead of schedule. Our plans rely heavily on timing, and I do not want any part of our coordinated strategy to miss the hour of our strike. Let them know that we start the siege of Magnaville on the morning of the eve of the new moon. I wish to strike before dawn while the lazy slouches slumber in their beds."

"As you wish, Your Grace. Shall we also give the order to

send the second legion toward Westport? Their commander is set to depart."

"Yes, my Lord. Now is the time. Send them onward, and let us endeavour to reach and make camp within a league of the fork of the Capital road and the West road this evening."

"As you command, Your Grace"

Lord Birk called several pages, and issued the orders to be distributed among the commanders, and then resumed the march toward Magnaville. The day was unseasonably hot, and without there having been any rain for nearly ten days, the road was extremely dry and dusty. He was looking forward to making camp, and enjoying a fireside meal with his troops. This was what he lived for. Battle was what he trained for. Now, he was truly in his element.

"Holly, step back and stay close to the buildings. That way they can't get at you from behind" dGerrie said in as hushed a voice as he could manage, while still being heard. "Remember what I told you. Let them make the first move, use your speed and length. We'll get through this."

She bit her bottom lip and nodded, drawing her sword and taking a couple of steps back toward one of the houses they had come between moments earlier. She scanned the area to see a few more men arrive and take up positions around dGerrie and The Dancer. She took a moment to count them. Nine soldiers, one of which appeared to be their commander, and the bounty hunter. As she counted, the bounty hunter spoke up again.

"My dear," he said, looking directly at Hollyglade, "I have no desire to see you injured in any way. My contract is to deliver you intact and unharmed to my contractor in Whiterock. These men are instructed not to hurt you, and I assure you that once your friend and I have finished our bout of calisthenics, I shall be glad to escort you to Magnaville in comfort and with respect and dignity." He bowed to her as he finished speaking, watched as she made no hint of a reply, and then turned his attention back to dGerrie.

"Now, Mr. Theurbeault, as I must maintain my moral code, I am compelled to offer us both a little exercise to balance our playing field. As you recall, when I dealt with our friends Mr. Brooker and Mr. Webb, I gained a warm up, and you gained some insight. So, in order that you gain a warm up and I gain some insight, I will allow our good troops here the chance to make a name for themselves by capturing the talented Mr. dGerrie Theurbeault. But, first I have a curiosity I must satisfy, Mr. Theurbeault. Tell me, when was it that you decided that my good graces and high wages were something to toss aside?"

dGerrie's eyes had been scanning the circle of men, gauging distances, finding gaps in armour, evaluating stances, and calculating strategy. As he did so, another pair of soldiers arrived, and joined the others. It was clear to dGerrie that the notion that he would be someone the soldiers would have to deal with was a surprise to them. Now he turned his attention to the bounty hunter, and made the same observations as he delivered his response.

"The Dancer. That's what they call you. A bit misleading, I must say. Something more sinister would be more apt. Say, The Slicer, perhaps. But really, I think The Bore, or Mister Overly Verbose, might do better. You do love the sound of your own voice. You take pleasure in the fluster you evoke from those you interrogate, giving your overly elaborate homilies the credit for the work your knife, and my presence have done. Your blatant disregard for the sanctity of innocent life does create a reputation of ruthlessness that many fear, but it has also served to entrench those who do not fear you, and who do hold respect for the life of the innocent, against you." dGerrie stepped back and raised a sword to one soldier who had taken a step closer from his right.

"How very eloquent, my dear Mr. Theurbeault, yet you avoid the central question. When did you throw away your honour, honour that would have been deepened by fulfilling commitments, to side with our quarry?" he asked again as he pointed to Hollyglade with the tip of his sword, and his voice gave hint of a budding annoyance.

"If you must know, it was your own fault. You are so proud of the effectiveness of your methods. So self-gratified by the brutishness with which you extract information. Yet you are blind to how sadly ineffective your methods truly are. You had several chances to find her. You were in the same village, at the same moment, three times including today. Yet you could not find her. And I, with one simple line of polite questioning, found her in less than an hour of being in the same town." dGerrie noticed the smile, usually so deeply fixed to the bounty hunter's face, was beginning to decrease as his eyes narrowed and hardened, and his mouth began to form a hard line. As he watched the slight change in the bounty hunter's expression, dGerrie noticed another pair of soldiers round a corner and join their troop.

"Listen boy!" scoffed the bounty hunter, raising his voice, "Do not think you can dance around the question forever. You speak of my reputation, yet you seem to ignore what it is. You forget that I never fail to fulfill my contract, and that I never fail to get the information I desire. So save yourself the humiliation of becoming the subject of my less than polite techniques, and answer the question posed. When did you betray me?"

dGerrie raised an eyebrow as one corner of his mouth lifted ever so slightly, observing the bounty hunter's change in demeanor.

"You thrive on utter control, don't you Var Toran? It must be frustrating that you do not currently have it. Yes, you outnumber us now fourteen to two, but that is all you have. The assumption that the odds, such as they are, favour you. Nothing else. You don't know how this will turn out. You don't know whether or not you are the superior combatant here, or even if you are my equal, and that frustrates you.

"You aren't as confident as you would like us all to think, and as your reputation depends upon you appearing. And the fact that you can not force me to give you an answer infuriates you." dGerrie could see the anger brimming within the cream white clad and self-proud bounty hunter.

"But, I will give you an answer. I will fill you in on when you sickened me to the point of feeling nausea at the sight of you. It was when you showed yourself to be a small man. Base, even. A feeble-minded fool who can not succeed without brute force weakly disguised as refinement. Without knowing who this girl was, I was contemplating undermining your search for her. I weighed your value against the value of an innocent girl, and the collateral damage you leave in your wake as you pursue the objective of your contract. Without even knowing who she was specifically, I found you lacking the value you place so highly on yourself. I found you wanting.

"Upon finding her, and discovering who she truly was, there was no contest. Her life and freedom outweigh all that you are, all that you have ever done, and all that you ever will be. So, give me your best, Dancer, for I could use some entertainment before I take my leave of you." He snarled the moniker, savoring the effect his taunting appeared to have upon the proud bounty hunter.

Var Toran's face was now completely void of his usual masking smile. His brow tightened, and his eyes flared with rage as he glanced at Commander Tollison and nodded, motioning with his sword for the order to be given.

The Commander waved for four of his men to move in on dGerrie, who was now almost entirely encircled by troops, but for a small angle at his back where Hollyglade stood holding her sword as menacingly as she could pretend to.

dGerrie shifted slightly to allow the men to the western edge of the circle a line to his back. He was predicting that men who were used to fighting in groups generally allowed the man who had the opponent at the greatest disadvantage, the chance to strike first. dGerrie trusted his hearing, and the fact that the sun was now casting long shadows.

Lowering his head slightly, dGerrie shifted weight to his front foot. The strike came as expected, and dGerrie stepped to his left, turning and swinging his long sword at one of the men on the north edge of the circle to force their guard up, and allowing the attacker's slash to pass him. With a neat and agile flick of the short sword's tip, he caught the first man in the armpit of his sword hand, continued with the momentum of his turn, and slashed behind the knee of the man ducking his initial feint. Both men dropped to the ground as the onlookers momentarily focused on them.

Taking advantage of the distraction, dGerrie employed the same spinning double slash he had used in the alleyway earlier, and caught the third man just above his belt, opening his abdomen. The fourth man moved to step over one of his fallen comrades, attempting to thrust his sword simultaneously. dGerrie read the clumsy move, slapped the blade away with his short sword, and with skillful precision, slid the tip of his long sword beneath the wrist guard of the attacking soldier, slicing his arm open and causing the sword to drop from his hand.

Returning to his initial position, to put Hollyglade at his back once more, dGerrie glared at the bounty hunter. The four injured men backed away, holding their wounds, as the commander whistled, calling for a medic.

"Impressive" sneered the bounty hunter. "There are eight of you. Get him!" he snarled.

What came next was unorganised and chaotic, which was exactly what dGerrie had hoped for. The first two men that came close enough, dGerrie sidestepped, sending them toward Hollyglade, but not without sticking a foot out to trip the second, as he spun to slash at the men that followed.

Seeing the man coming for her, Hollyglade took a step back, held her sword with both hands, and focused on his eyes. Her heart began to race, and the tension in her muscles began to increase. Her senses heightened, as she forced out a breath through clenched teeth. In his eyes she saw a moment's hesitation, what must have been him calculating how he might arrest her without doing any physical harm, as he reached to his belt to grab a club with his off hand, glancing down for a moment to find his grip.

In the split second his eyes flitted downward, she lunged forward with all the speed she had. Her length was much more than he had calculated, and his reaction to the lunge was too slow. The tip of her blade slipped between the layers of his brigandine and spaulder. He cried out in pain, dropped his sword, and jumped away, heading after the other injured men. As he cleared himself out, Hollyglade targeted the tripped man, who was now almost on his feet.

As he looked down to pick up the sword which had bounced out of his hand in the fall, she placed a swift kick to the side of his head. Though she was slight of build, her legs were long enough, and her boots were hard enough, to generate a significant impact. The man's eyes rolled back, and he was unconscious before he hit the ground. Hollyglade added another kick to the back of his head for surety, before looking up to see dGerrie engaged with the rest of the soldiers.

As she looked on, two more armed soldiers came into view, and joined the fray. She began to shake, feeling anxiety and fear begin to swell within her chest. As she watched her friend continue to battle the eight men that surrounded him, she could sense the power within her vibrating as it begged for release. She took two deep breaths as she watched dGerrie cut down a pair of men with a baffling whir of flying steel. As two more men dropped to the ground and fell back from him, dGerrie continued his spinning style of attack.

This was his best hope for dealing with so many men, as he believed he could constantly update himself on positions, stance, and the movement of his foes by being able to reacquire sight of them on each consecutive rotation, when they may be lost from his view during an attack or dodge. Seeing a shadow raise a sword above its head, dGerrie stepped further to his left with this rotation, and let the swing pass by him to the ground as he delivered a kick to the man to the attacker's left, stabbed another in the leg opposite that one, and followed through with a slash across the arms of the man whose sword was now hitting the dirt after his missed downward swing.

Another man slashed for his head, and dGerrie ducked under the attack, letting the man's momentum carry him toward Hollyglade. He extended both arms as he swung both swords in opposite directions to catch one man in the gut, and another in the thigh, with the tip of either sword, following through by striking the man he had kicked, with the butt of his longsword. Three men remained on the offensive, while dGerrie registered The Dancer out of the corner of his eye, standing back from the fray. The men stopped for a moment to glance at each other and then back at dGerrie. dGerrie kept his gaze on the three men as he called back over his shoulder

"Sprout?"

As the man slipped past dGerrie, he had to hop over his fallen troop mate in mid rotation as his missed slash carried him toward her. In order not to trip, the man glanced down at the soldier lying beneath him. As he did so, he took an uncontrolled swing at Hollyglade. Seeing his attack come as he was midair over the unconscious man on the ground, Hollyglade stepped to her right as she made a crude but effective parry of the slash.

The midair, yet slight redirection of the man's attack sent him marginally off target, just enough for Hollyglade to bring up her sword and swipe it down on his back. The blow only barely cut through his brigandine, but was enough to knock him down. Seeing him hit the ground, Hollyglade reacted by stabbing him in the buttock, which resulted in a scream of pain. She then placed a firm boot to the side of his head, sending him into unconsciousness. Turning back to the road, she answered her friend's call.

"I'm still here. Not hurt, so far."

"Stay where you are, then."

Turning his attention fully to the three remaining troops, dGerrie took a deep breath and widened his stance, pointing the tip of each blade at the two men on the outside. The middle one moved first, lunging forward with a two-handed stab. dGerrie stepped left, spun right to deflect the stab with his longsword, letting the attack pass him by. With the follow through of his pirouette, he swung his short sword on the backhand toward the man who had been on his right.

The slash was parried, but dGerrie made another half turn and swung at the man's calf. That slash was also knocked aside, but the second attack dGerrie made with his short sword found its mark at the man's elbow. It was enough to cause his sword to fall, as dGerrie turned back to see the third man bringing a downward diagonal slash straight for his head. dGerrie leaned back as he brought the long sword up with his right hand, hilt first, to deflect the blow with the base of his blade.

With his left leg, he stepped back to regain his balance, used the momentum of the parry to swing the long sword around his own head, and then swung over the third man's head to connect with the neck of the one who had attacked first. Without a pause and with a flick of his wrist, dGerrie flipped his short sword into the air, catching it in a backhanded grip and stabbing the last man through the back. As he did so, a sudden shooting pain leapt up from his right thigh, and he stumbled to the ground.

Looking down, he registered the fletching of a crossbow bolt sticking out of his upper leg. He dropped the longsword to place a hand on the ground to steady himself, as he looked up to see Trenon Var Toran pulling back the string of a crossbow, and raising it to fire once more. dGerrie raised his short sword, pointing it at the bounty hunter, as he tried to stand. Looking at Var Toran, dGerrie clenched his jaw, snarled with his lips, and pressed himself upward.

Just as he lifted his right hand from the ground and placed it on his right thigh to push himself to stand, another searing pain leapt from his left shoulder. The strike of the bolt spun him sideways as he dropped the shortsword.

"Coward!" he spat as he glared at the bounty hunter. Then, everything went black as the last thing dGerrie heard was a wooden thud.

Seeing her friend go limp and fall to the ground, Hollyglade could not contain herself. She ran to his side, ignoring the commander who stood over him with the spear in his hand, the back of which had just rendered dGerrie unconscious. She shoved the commander out of her way, as he seemed unthreatened by her, and rolled dGerrie over to look at him. She could not see whether or not he was breathing. She began to vibrate with power, as rage began to push what control she had left, out from the forefront of her focused concentration.

Her hold on the immense power within her began to slip, as her thoughts began to shift away from containing it. She lifted her head toward the bounty hunter, the man who had been the architect of her flight, her fears, the death of too many innocent bystanders. It had been men like him who had pushed her to the breaking point ten years ago when she last released an outpouring of power, when they had killed her parents and tried to capture her. Now once again she faced the death of someone she cared about, whom she had seen as family, loved, and who had loved her. She was torn between destroying the man who had caused so much collateral damage in his quest to capture her, and becoming the cause of even more collateral damage in resisting that capture.

As Hollyglade fought the conflict within her, the power began to leak out from her uncontrolled, like the trickle of water from a cracked cup. The air began to get hot, and the ground beneath her began to tremble, waves of vibrating power coursed through her limbs like lightning about to crack the sky. She rose to her feet, clenching her fists, and tightened her jaw as she bared her teeth. With her head slightly lowered, she glared at the man who had hunted her down and slain her adopted brother.

Seeing the display of awesome force begin to rise from the girl, Var Toran knocked another bolt in the crossbow. As he was about to raise it, he paused and took a step back, releasing one hand from the readied weapon and holding it up, pleading with the girl to halt. As he did so, Commander Tollison, who had in the last few seconds stepped back toward the girl as she was rising from her knees, swung the spear.

The butt of the pole weapon connected cleanly to the back of the girl's head, sending red hair flying, as she was knocked forward from the impact. As the shaft of the spear connected with the girl, a burst of energy shot forth from her, knocking the bounty hunter, the Commander, and the few men who were still standing, to the ground.

As he hit the ground, Var Toran's ears began to ring loudly. His vision blurred, yet he remained conscious. After a few seconds, he stood up and tried to regain his balance. He looked over to see where the girl was, to find her slumped over the unconscious body of his now former employee, looking unresponsive. He moved toward her with the intent of checking to make sure she was still alive, when Tollison stepped over her and raised the spear toward him.

"Stop, bounty hunter."

"What are you pretending at Commander? Your job is done here. I have my target, you are relieved."

"Your little misadventure here has cost me either the health or the lives of twenty men. You will not take this girl from here under my watch. She will be processed by the rule of law."

"No, Commander, she will not. My purpose serves the King, and I carry out this contract with his authority. You have the letter to prove it."

"Then you and I shall have that sparring match you were so interested in before you lost your nerve with this one." The Commander looked down at dGerrie's limp body, and then back to the bounty hunter.

"My dear Commander, that is not a fight you can win." The bounty hunter drew his sword, and stepped to one side to begin to circle the Commander. After a couple of steps, he stopped and took a fencing stance. As he did so, the he saw something he did not expect, but that brought him to a halt.

As the Commander began to move forward from his position straddling the two fallen fugitives, one of the men who had been bested, swung his club, and connected with the back of the Commander's head. With a crack, the

Commander's eyes rolled back in his head, he stiffened, and fell to the ground. Var Toran instinctively raised his sword toward the man holding the club.

"There's been enough of that for one day. Take your prize and leave." Said the trooper as he dropped the club and put his hand back in his armpit to try to stop the flow of blood.

"A wise decision, friend," replied Var Toran.

As the medics arrived with a cart to take away the wounded, Var Toran led his horse to where the girl lay sprawled over her defender. Leaning over to check her for breathing, he whispered to her

"The sorcerer will be glad of his prize, and I'll be glad of my gold. Come now girl, it is time for the road."

Tying her hands with rope, he lifted her over his shoulder and draped her over his horse. She let out a groan, but did not seem to wake. He climbed into the saddle, turned his horse northward, and began the three-day journey to Magnaville.

VI : HOSTILITY

It was mid-afternoon, and the young King was enjoying spending time in the main hall of Whiterock socializing with the various Lords, Ladies, and members of noble houses who made up the court. He had found solace in such socialization as of late, and was beginning to truly be able to take some joy in the company of others. It had been more than a few weeks since the disappearance of his brother, the death of his father, and his transition from Prince, to Crown Prince, to King. It had seemed to Harford that he had been unable to sufficiently mourn his losses before having to take responsibility for an entire kingdom. He was thankful for the help and guidance of the Lords of the court, his Vestry, and his closest ally, the Sorcerer Ni'Morstrom.

"Tell me Lord Runde, have your family always been seafarers? I had no idea that fishing could be such a lucrative enterprise" inquired King Harford of the grizzled Lord.

"Yes, my King. For as many generations as my family's history has been written down, the writing has been of the sea. You know, Your Grace, that during my father's, and your Grace's grandfather's time, house Runde was mainly responsible for the training and recruitment of the Royal Navy. In those days there was much need for it, as skirmishes with both Demaria and Ellendor were common, though throughout your father's reign, there were no incidents with Demaria, and our disputes with Ellendor were very rare indeed. It has been a welcome change in our house, to be mainly occupied with casting nets and hauling fish. Has your Grace been at sea often?"

The King looked at his feet for a moment, realising that he did not identify with any aspect of this Lord's house, and chosen life. He yearned for someone to connect with on a personal level, and hoped that there would be someone among the members of the court with whom he might find common ground.

"Sadly no, My Lord. I have never sailed. I get seasick.

Even the small boats my brother would take me for rides in, at the Hot Lake, made me feel ill. I do enjoy the beach though. The warm sand between my toes in the summer is always fun. Maybe I'll have time to go to a beach next summer, and play with some friends. I do like building sand castles. Have you ever built one?"

The venerable Lord, shot a look of chagrin to his companions, but quickly regained his composure as he reminded himself that though he was still a boy, this was the King.

"I can't say that I have done so in many years, your Grace," he replied with a slight bow. "I'm afraid I rarely have time for activities of relaxation. Perhaps when my sons have taken over our family's trade from me, I shall be able to enjoy retirement and open some of the books which gather dust on my shelves."

The young King, realizing that he had just shown the extent of his youth and inexperience, blushed, pursed his lips and tried to sound more mature.

"And tell me, Lord Runde, how has the summer season been for your fleet? Were your catches plentiful?"

"Well, Your Grace, I must say that we have had better years all in all, but this summer was not a total loss for cod, salmon, and mackerel. We begin the crabbing season shortly, and hope that it will provide a bountiful catch."

"Well, My Lord, then that is also my hope for your house." Seeing his personal page indicate that he had a message for the him, the King nodded and excused himself "It appears I must attend to matters elsewhere. Good day, My Lord." He stepped to an empty corner of the hall to receive the message.

"Your Grace," the page began, "Lord Wendal calls the Vestry to assemble, saying it is of utmost and immediate importance."

"Thank you, Tedd. I shall attend. Please have the Vestry hall prepared properly."

The page nodded and left to execute the King's instructions.

The King felt a sense of nervousness. There was something odd about the urgency with which the assembly had been called. Vestry meetings had always been scheduled, and so this was a new experience for the young ruler. Not knowing what to expect, he left the main hall and headed to the Vestry hall to see what Lord Wendal had to tell them.

Entering the Vestry hall, King Harford knew he would be arriving first, yet he did not know where else to wait. Once inside, he was greeted by the Sorcerer Ni'Morstrom.

"Your Grace, I am glad to have found you here before the rest of our assembly arrives. I have heard some of what makes this meeting most urgent. I'm told that a Demerian force has crossed our border and attacked the contingent stationed at the fork of the Capital road and the Coast to Coast road. They tell me that our forces were wiped out, but for a handful of riders who managed to escape and bring word of the attack here. This is war, my King."

"Why have they attacked us? Is it because we executed their Lord? That should have made us even, right?" The young King's reply was filled with insecurity and anxiety.

"Your Grace, we can not know for sure what drives them to invasion, but I can assure you that I shall have a sufficient response. To explain the details would take more time than we have at the moment, but you must trust me when I tell you that soon I shall have power sufficient to repel this invasion with my own hand."

"What do you mean? You can fight a whole army by yourself? Is there some spell for that?"

"In a way, Your Grace, yes. But I have not completed my work as of yet. In order for me to wield the power necessary for such a feat, there are still some preparations I must make, and rites I must perform in private. But, Your Grace, I am certain that once my work is completed I shall be able to win this war for you, and bring this Kingdom the glory it deserves."

"How long will it take you to be ready?"

"I shall be ready at sundown on the day after tomorrow,

Your Grace. I have been waiting for the one last element which is on its way to me now. Once it is here, I shall be able complete my work, and I shall have the power necessary to repel any incursion made against you. However, my King, I must ask you not to share any of this with anyone else. My work depends on having privacy, and the questions that the other lords would pose to me would serve only as a distraction, and a delay." As the sorcerer assured the young King of his capabilities, the other members of the Vestry began to arrive. The King looked at the sorcerer and nodded his consent.

The King's Secretary, Mr. Bevin Sant, called the meeting to order.

"Your Grace, Lords, Advisors, I call to order this emergency meeting of the King's Vestry. In the presence of His Grace King Harford the first, Incumbent of Whiterock, Master of the Realm, High Lord of Loria; I am Bevin Sant, Secretary to the King and His Vestry.

"Present also, are Lord Quentin Wendal, Master of The Royal Forces; Lord Shand Ventrent, Master of Trade; Lord Erndale Marnon, Master of information; The Sorcerer Ni'Morstrom, Advisor to the King.

"I call this meeting to order. Lord Wendal, you have requested this assemblage. Yours is the floor." The secretary sat down at a table along the side of the hall, and picked up his quill to begin recording minutes.

"Thank you, Secretary. Your Grace, My Lords. The Demarian army has crossed the border, attacked and defeated the small cohort stationed at the Capital Coast fork. Only a few men escaped the onslaught with their lives and rode to carry their report here.

"They report that King Dermond rides with a force of twenty thousand. Upon receipt of this news, I dispatched messages by air to recall our forces to the city to form a defense here. Due to the service of the mission to expel the Elder Folk, our forces are spread thinly across the area around the Capitol, and some cohorts and legions may not make it back to the city before the Demarians reach our gates.

"I have sent word to the Fifth and Second Legions, who were assembled three leagues west of the Capital for training exercises, to fall back and prepare to engage the Demarians here. But, I must inform this Vestry that unless the other cohorts return from the south and east in time, which seems unlikely, we shall be outnumbered at least two to one on the battlefield. Therefore, I recommend that we prepare the city for siege immediately."

Lord Wendal bowed as he finished his report, and then took his seat. The young King did not respond immediately, looking first at Bevin Sant, and then at the sorcerer.

"What do the rest of you say?" he asked with a hint of trepidation.

Lord Erndale Marnon, Master of information replied first.

"Your Grace, Lord Wendal and I had a few moments to share our knowledge of the Demarian advancement, and one important detail of the troop movements came with the return of the soldiers who managed to escape the battle at the fork. That is, that they did not see any siege engines amongst the Demarian forces. No catapults, towers, ladders, or the like. While it may be that such armaments shall come along after the initial force arrives, it seems that their plan is not to attack the city immediately.

"This may give us time to prepare for a battle outside the walls while the Demarians await their siege weapons. We are sure that even with such weapons at our gates, that months may pass while the invaders attempt to gain entrance to the city. We are well supplied here, and winter arrives as we speak. I believe that patience is our best strategy, as I agree with Lord Wendal that a prolonged battle upon the field is likely unmanageable now." Taking his seat, Lord Marnon looked confident in his assessment.

"Lord Ventrent, what say you?" asked King Harford.

"Your Grace," he replied, rising from his chair, "I am Lord of Trade, and know little of the matters of war. But, as a learned man who served both your father and grandfather, I can say that I have seen war. It does seem that we have little choice in the matter. A siege seems imminent. Just how imminent it is, is the only question."

The King opened his mouth to speak, but halted as the sorcerer leaned over to whisper something to him. After hearing the sorcerer's secretive counsel, he offered his thoughts.

"My Lords, I agree that we must eventually withdraw our troops to within the city walls. Prepare what must be prepared to withstand a long siege. I am confident that we will not see a long siege, nor a battle on the field. My Lords, I leave the war plans in your hands, and ask only that you keep me informed."

"As you wish, Your Grace." replied Lord Wendal. "With your leave, I shall begin at once." He stood and waited for the King's acknowledgement. Upon receiving a nod, he departed.

With a look to the King, the sorcerer also excused himself.

"Shall we adjourn, Your Grace?" asked the Secretary.

"I suppose. Yes," replied the King.

With that, the remaining lords, along with Bevin Sant, bowed and exited the chambers.

The young King looked around at the empty chamber, and felt distinctly isolated. He turned to head back out to the main hall and stopped after a couple of steps. He was not sure if he wanted to be with the members of the court who were milling about. They all seemed so much grander to him than he did to himself. He enjoyed the company of others, but these people seemed completely uninteresting, boring, and allergic to fun.

He turned back from the direction of the main hall and began to head for his personal chambers, thinking that he would call his page and have him bring some books about war and the histories of the sieges of Magnaville. Once again, he stopped after a couple of steps, realizing that he did not want to be alone in his chambers with dusty old books.

He turned from the direction of his personal chambers and began to head for the stables. He thought he would go and see if the stable master's son, Lyowen was there. He was the same age as the young King, and the two had often played together over the last few years.

Then, the King stopped once more. He lowered his head, pouted, and bit his lower lip. He remembered that Lyowen was no longer in Whiterock, nor in Magnaville. He remembered that Lyowen's Father was human, but that his mother was Dwarvish.

The young King stepped back to his seat at the head of the Vestry hall, sank into the ornate throne, into his loneliness, and began to cry softly.

The pressure on her stomach was intense, and combined with the nausea, dizziness and ringing in her ears, Hollyglade felt a strong urge to vomit. As she slowly opened her eyes, she saw the underside of a horse's belly cinched with a saddle girth, a set of stirrups with boots in them, and her own legs hanging from the far side of the horse. She realised that she was draped over the horse as it walked slowly.

With some effort, she tried to slide off the horse's back, and onto the ground, but when she did so she found that her wrists were bound. In response to her movements, she felt a hand on her back.

"Not so fast girl. You must not try to run or escape me. That would be terribly bothersome, and completely off-putting. And we are just about to get you your own mount, once we have a quick bite to break the fast." The man brought the horse to a stop, and grabbed her arm below the shoulder. "Now my dear, slide off slowly and sit on the ground."

As she slid off the back of the mount, she began to see stars whirling about her. She tried to take a few steps to gain her balance, but found that her feet would not move apart from one another. She fell to the ground only barely able to block the road from meeting her face by bringing her bound hands up in front of her, landing hard on her elbows. The pain of the fall was too much, the fatigue was too great, and the nausea was unrelenting. Hollyglade was barely able to roll to one side as her stomach emptied what little it contained in several vomitous heaves.

"Oh dear, sweet girl. We must get you settled before we ride further. This just won't do."

She looked up at the man as he dismounted, and her face twisted into a grimace as she realized with disgust who it was that had carried her here. Seeing the malevolent bounty hunter standing above her, she once again tried to get to her feet, fighting the searing acidity in her throat and mouth. Anger rose within her, and began to compete with the feelings of illness she suffered, for foremost place in her conscious mind.

She pulled at her restraints as hard as she could, but found that the effort only caused the rope to cut into her wrist. Feeling around her body in the hope that he had missed taking one of the several sharp objects she had been carrying, she found only disappointment. Her frustration mounted, and she began to seethe internally, wanting desperately to free herself and take some sort of vengeance on this man. Her mind swirled.

Was it her fault that dGerrie had died, her fault the old white-haired woman had died, her fault that the family in the farm had died, her fault that all the soldiers had been injured or killed? Maybe it was her fault in some way. There's always another choice, she thought. She had killed no one by her own hand, and it had been this bounty hunter's choice to use the methods he had. It was his fault, and she swore to herself that she would make him pay somehow, if only she could fight the nausea and dizziness long enough to bring things into focus.

He responded to her attempt to stand by pushing her down into a sitting position with a disapproving wag of his finger.

"Now, now. If you wish to ride, rather than walk all the way to our destination, you will sit and be patient as I procure another animal."

"Water. Please." she managed to rasp. If she was going to do something about her situation, she needed strength.

"I suppose I must bring you to my contractor in good condition," he acquiesced, as he handed her the water skin.

"Stay seated while I chat with this fine purveyor of transport." The bounty hunter stepped away to speak with a rather rotund man.

Hollyglade took a moment to try to get her bearings. She recognised the area having passed through it, and the farm where they were now stopped, sometime in the last month. She had approached the farmer about work, but had been turned away, being told that he was not comfortable hiring Elder Folk given the state of affairs in the region.

Her head was pounding, and she reached around to the back of it to feel where the pain was coming from. The cold had made her hands and feet numb again, yet she tried her best to assess her injuries. Her hand felt the roughness of crusted and dried blood which had matted itself into her hair at the base of her skull. It did not feel wet, but the lump felt significant. Looking to the sky in an attempt to gauge the position of the sun, she felt the dizziness intensify as the world began to spin around her. She slumped to one side, fighting with everything she had to stay conscious and upright. It was no use. She collapsed to the road and felt everything go dark.

The sound of hoofbeats and creaking wood roused her from her insensate numbness. As she opened her eyes, the light seemed incredibly intense and painful. The brightness caused her head to swell with pain as she squeezed her eyes shut to fight the profound discomfort. In trying to bring a hand up to shade her head, she felt a tug at her wrists. She opened one eye a crack to see that her hands were now tied to the edge of a small wagon. She tried to sit up, but could not pull her legs under her, finding them bound to the opposite end of the cart. She let out a groan as the wheel struck a rock in the road.

"Well, well. I see you have decided to join the land of the living once more. That's a good thing, as having to procure this wagon, and get you into it, were both costly endeavours. I wish to recuperate that cost, which requires you to regain some haleness."

"Water. Please"

A water skin landed in her lap, and Hollyglade reached it with her fingertips, pulling it into her hand. To drink, she shifted herself toward her feet in order to bring her mouth to the water skin in her hands. Taking several long drafts, she felt a small measure of the restoration of her senses. Peering upward through the small slit she opened between her eyelids, she determined the sun to be at its zenith. She had been unconscious for nearly a full day, and was feeling the effects. She turned her head to see the cream white clothing on the back of the man whom she had been running from for what seemed like an eon.

Her thoughts returned to dGerrie, and to his body lying slain in the street back in Greenfield. Her eyes began to well with tears. She had felt so close to getting free of the relentless pursuit of her captor, and had felt nearly sure of it once dGerrie had found her. She had been so confident in the skill and dedication he had shown. Such friendship is rare and precious. Upon their discovery of each other in the stable, Hollyglade had been sure that together, they would manage an escape. She was wrong, and it had cost him his life, and her closest friend. Her bereavement turned to enmity, her sadness to anger, her hurt to furor.

Yet again, she felt the swelling of power within her. Like the rise of waves before their crash upon a rocky shore, she felt the intense buildup loom over her, ready to crush her resolve on the stone of her loss. This resolve had grown in her mind as she had weighed the consequences of action and inaction, the value of release and restraint, against each other.

Her thoughts moved to the day she had first met dGerrie, ten years ago outside a tavern in the Red Lanes of Magnaville. The man that had carted her from where she had been found, on the road through western plains just days after the great destruction, was trying to take his payment from her. Payment not previously mentioned while the man had still been sober. Payment of flesh.

She remembered feeling then what she felt now, growing

inside her, and the moment it dissipated when the young boy had clubbed the suddenly predatory farmer unconscious in the street. She remembered the relief she felt when the boy had taken her hand and led her away into the safety of obscurity. She remembered telling him that she wanted the farmer to die, and that the boy had told that five-year-old girl, "There is always another way."

Sitting up as much as she could while tied to the cart, Hollyglade slowly began to open her eyes to try to adjust to the light. It was a struggle, and the pain in her head was not lessening. However, she was determined to get her bearings and assess her current situation. After several minutes, she was finally able to see clearly.

She was the only passenger in the wagon pulled by a two-horse team moving at a quick pace, and driven by Trenon Var Toran, The Dancer, her captor and her friend's murderer.

"Where are we going?" she inquired bitterly, hoping that she may learn something that may help her escape, or at least know what to expect.

"Ah, she speaks!" exclaimed the bounty hunter. "So nice that you and I shall be able to share some conversation on our journey. Well, to answer your question, we head for the capital. You are to be delivered by tomorrow evening, at the latest, though I would prefer to make it there by this evening, or sometime in the night, if I can keep these beasts moving at this pace."

Hollyglade opened her perception to the horses, gently prodding their minds for an indication of their level of fatigue and stamina. They were tired, and a sense of frustration with their unfamiliar driver was at the forefront of their minds. Hollyglade began to open her mouth to say something about giving them rest, but thought better of it. Letting on that she had that particular gift may prevent her from gaining some advantage later, though she lamented not being able to do something to aide the animals.

"To whom are you contracted to deliver me?" she asked, hoping to gain some knowledge she might be able to use to get away, or at least defend herself from whatever awaited her.

"Ah, that I can not reveal." replied the bounty hunter apologetically. "But let me assure you, it is with the blessing of the King, that the contract was made. You should be comforted by the fact that your presence at the capital shall serve a greater purpose. Or so I am told."

His tone and demeanor exuded self satisfaction, and though she could not see his face, Hollyglade could hear the disconcerting smile cemented there.

"Tell me girl, what is your name? In all this time, and after all the trouble I have gone through looking for you, no one has been able to tell me your name."

Her initial reaction was to spit out her name at him, but she stopped short of doing so when she recalled how agitated he had become at dGerrie's refusal to answer his questions.

"It doesn't matter," she grunted, determined not to satisfy him in any way.

"Oh, but it does, my dear. In polite conversation it is expected that one should introduce one's self to the person one plans on conversing with. You must tell me your name, for I wish to properly address you."

"I have no plans to converse with you politely. Therefore, you do not need my name. And, if you aren't willing to answer my questions, why should I answer yours?" she retorted.

"My dear girl, I did not say that I would not tell you who desires your presence, but that I could not tell you. My contract forbids it, and I never break the terms of a contract. Shall I just call you by what you have been nicknamed by some of my men? I do not find the terms flattering, but I must address you somehow."

"I do not particularly care, but I'm curious what name they utter." Her curiosity was based solely on finding out whether or not she had been successful in convincing them that she was dangerous. She did not feel like a dangerous person, or that there was anything about her, besides her hidden power, to be feared, but the illusion could come in handy again.

"Well, you may not like what name came out of their

stammering. I believe it was something along the lines of giant elvish fire-haired naked devil, and I believe also you were referred to as The Red Witch. That first title seems a bit long. It does not roll off the tongue very well, however the Red Witch sounds rather catching, don't you think?" He asked, with a playful grin.

She did her best to hide her expression as she heard the names. It gave her a small amount of pleasure to hear that her bluff, designed to cause the necessary dread to allow her to effectively interrogate his men, had worked to such effect.

"Well, they are certainly descriptive," she replied with a hint of sass.

"Yes. I was very intrigued by their account of you in the night. Tell me, was it true that you managed to get the better of both of them while naked? And you must tell me what magic you used, if any, for I wager that you used none."

"What makes you think I used no magic?"

"You must answer my question first, my dear, for it is rude to redirect a conversation without answering a question posed to you."

She hesitated, but decided this was not the issue to evade him on.

"Well, if you must know…"

"I must."

"Your men were lazy, and like you, cowards. I let them fall to sleep in their own time, and then simply smacked them on their fat ugly heads."

"Tisk tisk, my dear witch. It is impolite to call someone a coward in polite conversation."

"It describes you aptly, does it not? Your unwillingness to fight dGerrie demonstrated as much. Anyway, what happened to the two of them? I left them partially naked, but well enough."

Looking up at him over her shoulder, she could see enough of the side of his face to perceive a slight waver in the smile he so proudly tried to maintain.

"Well, dear girl, I had to teach them a lesson about keeping their guard up, and not allowing teenaged girls to get the better of them. They failed the lesson, and thus, I relieved them of their duties. As to your suggestion that I acted cowardly, my dear witch, my act was not one of cowardice, but one designed for your preservation.

"My contract stated clearly that I must retrieve and deliver you intact and unharmed. It was evident that any further prolongation of the altercation in the street would likely have resulted in you suffering greater harm. Thus, my decision to shoot my traitorous employee was one of mercy."

She fought to contain the mixture of remorse for dGerrie, whom she had tried to preserve, and was now sure she must add to the growing list of people who had died at this man's hand, and anger at this man for his part in their demise. She wanted so badly to tear free of her restraints and fight this bounty hunter, even if she couldn't see any way in which she might be able to get the better of him. Her outrage and grief both swelled, and combined with her dizziness and nausea, to overwhelm her faculties. She took a deep breath to try to centre herself and regain her mental balance. After a moment, she continued to try to dig into his thinking, hoping to expose something useful.

"Interesting." she replied, bitingly. "Perhaps your reputation is somewhat inflated. The notoriety that precedes you is of uncompromising efficiency and effectiveness, but also that you leave a trail of blood. I imagine that you encourage the dissemination of this fallacy to inspire fear, and therefore encourage capitulation from those you target for capture or interrogation. That reputation really needs updating to include 'runs from a fight when he's not the clearly superior combatant,' and also, 'leaves a trail of the blood, but only of the helpless and innocent'" She made her suggestions with a thick helping of mocking sarcasm.

"My dear Red Witch, you speak with a wonderful eloquence, one I quite enjoy, yet rather over-confidently for someone tied up in the back of a wagon. You speak quite assuredly of yourself for someone who was unable to evade the capture of the one she now attempts to provoke. I assure you, I am quite comfortable with the accuracy, and effectiveness of my reputation. It is your small reputation that may need updating. For I am convinced that you are no witch, for if you were, you would have used some form of magic to either prevent your capture, or facilitate your escape, neither of which you have accomplished, let alone attempted.

"No, I believe that if you have any magical capabilities at all, you are unschooled in their use, and therefore no threat. So, let us dispense with the barbed jabs at each other's reputation, and simply enjoy some enlightening conversation. Please, tell me when it was that you and Mr. Theurbeault realized that you knew each other."

A great deal of her wanted to show him just how much power she had, to blast him into oblivion in a triumphantly vengeant outpouring of power. She could not let herself slip down that path, and add more weight to the already unbearable burden of lost life she carried, knowing that such vengeance would most certainly not be restricted to this one man. She considered giving in to his prodding, and telling him that it was only when they came face to face in the stables in Greenfield that her friend had turned from pursuer to rescuer, but decided to stay the course, dGerrie's course, of denying him his desire.

"Why does it interest you so much?" she deflected "You killed him. You are done with the chase, a chase that he managed to end by simply asking the right questions, by the way. Why bother with what's behind you?"

"Ah, a good couple of questions. I'll concede, and tell you the reason my curiosity piques so, in regard to Mr. Theurbeault's betrayal. As a bounty hunter, it is the main focus of my trade to capture fugitives from justice. Often, the fugitives whose contracts for capture are offered to me have some skill and intelligence, for most of the simpler minded outlaws are caught by the army, garrison, or some less accomplished bounty hunter. When your line of work involves catching intelligent fugitives, it is helpful to have an understanding of the mind of those you seek to apprehend.

"Though Mr. Theurbeault was not the fugitive I was contracted to catch, he put himself in that category when he sided with my prey. So being able to compare the observations I made of him during the time he appeared to remain faithful in his service, with the inner thoughts he harboured that lead to his duplicity, would serve to be educational. The profit from one's continuing education can never be overvalued. And therefore, my dear Red Witch, I politely ask that you tell me what you know of his thinking, if only to pass the time. And if the conversation manages to facilitate your grieving for him, I encourage it, as I endorse such motivation."

He was almost convincing, and she was almost convinced. She was starting to feel the pain in the back of her head, along with the nausea and dizziness, increase again, and decided that dragging out this annular verbal sparring match was becoming taxing. So she lied.

"I don't know. He didn't tell me when it was that he decided that he would rescue me instead of capturing me. There wasn't time to discuss it. You heard as much about it as I did, before you got cold feet and realized you were no match for him with a blade."

"Well, that is disappointing. I suppose your bounty will have to be my consolation." The bounty hunter sighed, and reached into a bag, pulling out a strip of dried beef and offered it to Hollyglade. "You'll need to eat, if you're going to expect to have any salubrity about you when I deliver you."

She took the food hesitantly, still feeling nauseated, but began to eat it after convincing herself that the benefits it would lend to her haleness would outweigh the unknown value of the annoyance her refusal might provoke.

"Maybe there is something else you will tell me," he continued. "Another rumour about you is that you are a survivor of the Great Destruction. That you were found near its centre, only days after the event, by a farmer travelling to the capital. Is that true?"

"It is as you say. I was found there days later, but that does not make me a survivor." Her thoughts were of the personal loss that had come from the event. She did not feel like a survivor, but a victim.

"I'm told you lost your family in the event as well, and that your father had been schooled in the arts of magic. Is that true as well?"

"I don't remember my father practicing any magic, but I can say that it was not the Great Destruction that killed my parents. It was a bounty hunter and his thugs. They were after me as well, for what reason I do not know, but my parents fought them, and were killed for it." *And I killed those men in response, and everyone for leagues around, and I'll find a way to kill you too.* She held herself from saying the last part, as she realized she may be saying too much already.

Her head was still pounding, and the neither the dizziness nor the nausea had subsided. Her mental focus was declining, and she was finding the verbal sparring too taxing to continue. She took another bite of the salt beef, forcing herself to chew it despite the nausea.

"Well my dear, I must say that I do pity you somewhat. Had your parents, and not the street dwellers of the capital, been able to raise you, you would likely be skilled in your magic. Such a waste."

After another hour, they came to a bridge, which Hollyglade recognized as the bridge over the Green River, on the South Road. She realized that this meant she had been unconscious when they crossed the South River, and it was now only a half day's travel to Magnaville's southern edge. Anxiety built at the realization that soon things were likely to get worse. She was not looking forward to whatever awaited her in the capital.

As night fell, the silhouette of Magnaville's skyline in the last rays of twilight would have been a beautiful sight in Hollyglade's eyes, were it not for the nature of her arrival there. The central tower of Whiterock, the castle which had long been home to the Kings of Loria, loomed above her as the wagon approached the southern gates to the city. Looking up at the sliver of the moon, Hollyglade determined, at least as best she could tell, that they had arrived one evening prior to the new moon.

The bounty hunter stopped the wagon at the gate, as it was now closed, and was approached by several garrison troops.

"Halt there," called one of the guards. "Identify yourself and state your business"

It was customary for the city gates to be closed at sundown, but Hollyglade could detect a hint of seriousness and apprehension in the voice of the guard.

"I am about the King's business," replied the bounty hunter "I come to complete a contract for the capture and return of this fugitive. I must enter the city to deliver her promptly. Here you are, friends." He produced a small paper from his tunic and handed it to the guard. "I think you'll find everything in order. Though I must ask, what causes so many of you to be stationed at the gate this night. Is it not the usual practice for there to be but two or three men here?"

There were indeed far more than the usual number of troops at the gate. Hollyglade estimated fifty in all.

Looking over the paper, and giving a nod of approval before handing it back, the guard answered the bounty hunter's inquiry.

"You are lucky to have reached the walls when you did. The Demarian army marches this way, and they are estimated to be at our gates by the day after tomorrow, if not tomorrow. Lord Wendal has sent dispatches to recall all army and garrison units to the city to aid in its defense. All medical units have been recalled as well. We are informed that once the Demarian force has been sighted from the wall's towers, the city shall be sealed, and final siege preparations shall be made.

"It is fortunate for you that you arrived before that. Otherwise you would not have had the safety of Magnaville's walls. Most of the garrison and army units who are expected to outpace the Demarians to the city have arrived, and we expect the gates shall be barricaded soon."

The bounty hunter looked back at Hollyglade and then to

the guard.

"Well, my good man, I am thankful that we have fine men such as yourself protecting the good people of Loria. Now, I must attend to my obligations, and allow you to return to your duties."

The guard nodded and waved him through as the gates were opened before them. The bounty hunter urged the horses forward, and they moved through the entrance as the gates closed quickly behind them. Upon entering the city, The Dancer stopped the cart again, and turned around to face Hollyglade.

"Now, my dear, I'm going to have to insist that from here on out, you not be able to cause me any distress or delay. So, I am going to place upon you this gag and blindfold. I apologize for the discomfort this may cause, but it is necessary since I am required by my contract to lead you to the point of delivery in secrecy."

He climbed into the back of the wagon and knelt beside her to apply the gag. Hollyglade struggled for a moment, and then decided that it was not the time to fight. She needed to conserve her energy. She was also relying on the fact that she knew this city better than her captor, and was confident that since they had entered the city from the south, near the Red Lanes where she had grown up, that she could deduce her whereabouts no matter where he led her from here. A rope was tied into the binding on her wrists, a blindfold applied, and her feet were freed

"Come now, my dear," purred the bounty hunter. She was too diminished to resist.

Their path lead through the narrow back alleys and side streets, all of which Hollyglade felt she could remember, until they stopped somewhere along the wall to the castle, just below the tower. Hollyglade was sure she knew where each of its entrances lay, but when the bounty hunter knocked on a door at the base of the wall, she was surprised that there had been a door there at all. Was this something new, or had she lost track of where they had gone? Some anxiety began to develop in her mind.

After a moment, the door opened, and she was lead inside, the bounty hunter guiding her head under the low opening of the doorframe. Once through the door, she heard it close behind her as she was pulled along what sounded like a tunnel made of stone or brick. After only a short distance, they stopped as she heard someone approach.

"You have returned rather close to your deadline."

She did not recognise the voice which seemed to be implying some level of disapproval. He did not speak like the Lords of the land, nor like the rich gentry, nor like the poorer folk either. Hollyglade detected an accent, one she could not place precisely, though she had prided herself on being able to deduce a person's region of birth by their accent while living in the diversity of the capital.

"Ah, yes. Within the time allotted, I have returned. You are correct," replied Var Toran.

Hollyglade detected a hint of indignation in the bounty hunter's voice.

"She is intact and unharmed, as requested and agreed to. Though I must say that she did not come quietly, and not without great collateral cost."

"Your payment was sufficient, Mr. Var Toran, to cover such costs. Do not mention your difficulty to me now. The state of her wellbeing is my only concern. The rest has been covered with gold. Take your payment, and your leave. Your contract is complete."

She heard a certain level of impatience in the stranger's voice, and shuddered at the thought of what might be awaiting her. She tried to back away from where the sound of the stranger was coming from, but felt a strong tug on her wrists. Hearing the sound of a large sack of coin, she felt some relief at the notion that she would be free of the company of the bounty hunter, yet fear and dread over what may come next in the grasp of the stranger.

"I thank you for your business, and take my leave of you," she heard the bounty hunter say as the bag of coin clinked in his hands. From closer to her, she heard him whisper "It's been a pleasure, my dear." She listened as his footsteps could be heard heading back along the direction they had come.

After she heard the sound of a doorway open and close at the end of the tunnel, there was only silence. She took a step backwards, and flinched as she met the wall at the edge of the passage. Feeling the cold stone, she tried to move along the wall and away from where the stranger's voice had been.

"Where do think you'll go?" came the voice again. "You are now my guest, and I insist you stay a while." His voice changed its tone, and now conveyed a sinister malice mixed with vindictive satisfaction. Hollyglade tried to feel the wall for anything she could grab hold of, a torch or some other implement she could use as a weapon. Nothing met her searching hands. She stopped and tried to reach out with her mental perception hoping that something would register, even though she knew that this stranger was no animal, her instinct was to try to use her ability.

As she did so, she felt her blindfold loosen, though she did not feel hands upon her face. When it dropped, the person she saw standing before her was draped in dark robes which allowed only the lower half of his face to catch the dim light. The scarred and wrinkled visage stretched into a grotesque smile as a hand reached up toward her. Her mind registered something it had not felt so intensely in a decade. Something she had only previously registered as coming from within.

Power.

Hollyglade tried to back away as everything went dark.

The Sun was not quite visible on the horizon as the first few rays of light illuminated the assembled forces. Lord Birk reined his horse to a halt as he arrived at the King's side. The Demarian army had marched at a brutal pace, taking only short stops to rest and eat, all the way from the Capital and Coast fork, in order to gain a day and hopefully take their target by surprise. Though the forces were tired from the march, the thrill of their easy victory over the Lorian cohort had wet the appetites for war of the men making that march. As dawn broke, the Demarian soldiers were fervently anticipating the battle to come. A battle that all of them expected to win in impressive fashion.

"Your Grace, our scouts have returned from the night's reconnoiter, and I have received word that both Princes' fleets have reached their destinations on the updated schedule."

"Good. Let's hear your report," commanded the King with eager expectation.

"Scouts report that seven to ten thousand troops are assembled in formation outside the walls of the city. A force half to two thirds our size, but one that could pose some difficulty with the wall to guard their back," reported Lord Birk.

"Then a true test of Demarian mettle awaits us. I have confidence that our plans shall compensate for any trouble they cause. What of my sons?"

"Prince Dornian's forces should be starting their assault on Westport as we speak, and Prince Dertron was able to land five thousand men two leagues south of the city during the night, and his fleet should make it within range of the Lorian fleet's last known positions outside the Magnaville harbour within this hour. Our siege engines are behind us by less than one league now, and will be here in at most two hours, Your Grace. We await your signal." His report was delivered with a matter of fact resolution that seemed to please the King.

"Thank you, Lord Birk. Send the envoy with our terms for surrender, to the gate under the white flag. I will give this boy one chance to save his people from the hardship of siege warfare."

"At once, Your Grace."

Lord Birk bowed slightly, and left to go dispatch the envoy with the King's demands, as orders to begin the march to the battle lines were announced.

Word returned from the Lorian Commander within the hour, stating that Lord Quentin Wendal desired a parlance with his Demarian counterpart. Renald Birk bore the reply to King Dermond.

"Your Grace, the Commander of the Lorian Royal Forces asks for a parlance."

"Good. I like meeting face to face with the man I am to battle against. Let us ride out to meet him. Lord Birk, War Marshall Greln, you shall accompany me to meet Lord Wendal, and see what kind of man he is on the battlefield. Though I have met him under circumstances of peace, I am curious to see his demeanor in a suit of armour."

"Very good, Your Grace. We are ready to depart at your leisure."

"Then let us ride. I tire of the anticipation."

With that, the three men mounted and headed for the front line.

"Your Grace," Lord Wendal addressed the Demarian King, "I am surprised and honoured to receive you in the Kingdom of Loria. Though I must say that your entourage is rather large on this occasion, much more so than the last time Your Grace visited Whiterock, but I am sure we can arrange suitable accommodation if Your Grace would be so kind as to allow us time to prepare properly for this welcome, yet unexpected, visit. How may I be of service to you?" The Master of The Royal forces bowed deeply as he greeted the king with playful sarcasm.

"Lord Quentin Wendal," replied the King, with a raised eyebrow "I recall your sense of humour, and I must say you are bold to employ it while facing the odds you do." The King watched as the Lords' smiles wavered. "And I respect you for it" smiled King Dermond.

"Thank you, Your Grace," replied Lord Wendal, with some measure of relief.

"Now, My Lord, you have requested this parlance. I note that my counterpart is absent, do you speak with your King's full authority?"

"I do, Your Grace."

"What wish you to say for him?"

The Master of the Royal Forces took a deep breath, letting it out slowly as his eyes narrowed slightly, while he chose his words.

"Your Grace, both our kingdoms have reason to be offended at the recent actions of the other, and it is the hope of our King, that some peaceful solution or resolution to our discord may be found. We would ask that you agree not to engage in siege hostilities until negotiations have been given full chance."

"You wish to talk now, do you?" replied the King in a suddenly severe tone. "Where was the desire to talk when you held Lord Casterin of Downwater in your dungeons? Our request for his return was unanswered. Do you forget that our two Kingdoms have shared traditions concerning the handling of hostages? Do you forget the treaty which brought the counties of Shoreford and Clearvale under Lorian rule? A treaty signed to secure the return of the Princes of Demaria? Speak not of bargains when it suits you unless you can speak of them when it does not." The King chided the lord.

"Your Grace, with the utmost respect, there was no offer of terms of release made for the King's brother either. The just execution of his abductor was seen as fair and lawful due process."

"Ah, there it is. Finally, you come out with it. You blame my Kingdom for the disappearance of your Crown Prince, after you take misdirected revenge for it. Does the boy King truly believe Demaria would throw away a generation of brotherly relations between our Kingdoms for no reason? Believe you that we are barbarians who rape and kill purely to slake our lust for battle? Your King's so-called vengeance was directed errantly. No Lord of mine would act against another sovereignty without my direction, and I would give no such order."

"Your Grace denies that the Prince was executed at

Downwater and floated out to sea, as our reports confirm?"

"It is denied. No such event took place. Were I to discover that one of my Lords had abducted and murdered the Crown Prince of Loria, I would have taken his head and planted it firmly on a spike myself. I tolerate no such incitements from those I rule. War for the sake of war, or for no reason at all, carries no honour. I mourned the loss of your Prince. His father was a great man, and it was our fervent desire that the young Prince should succeed his father and continue our good, peaceful, brotherly, and profitable relationship. You look to place blame where none belongs."

Both men stood silently for a moment, as the King's denial and admonishment hung in the air, and Lord Wendal was unsure where to proceed next. He had expected an explanation, a blame for some wrong or offense, but not a denial. The King was the first to break the silence.

"I'm told that your new King has resurrected the old ways, and has a Sorcerer in his inner circle. Tell me, how long after this practitioner of the arcane came into the King's service, did the King begin to break with the tradition of his father and the advice of his Vestry?"

The Master of the Royal Forces looked at the King for a moment, and then lowered his gaze as his expression began to show embarrassment. He was here representing his King, yet even he believed that his King was now representing someone else. But to admit that here and now, would be folly. A Kingdom with a puppet for a King could not legitimately come to a negotiating table, and therefore Quentin Wendal could not acknowledge what he believed to be true.

"Your Grace, I know nothing of the details of their relationship, other than that the King seeks advice from the Sorcerer in the same manner as the rest of His Vestry. We advise him, and he rules. Such is the way it has always been."

The King looked to Lord Birk momentarily before turning back to his adversary.

"Lord Wendal, I reject your King's request for negotiation. Instead, I offer terms for surrender," declared the King, watching as Lord Wendal's look of surprise broke through his seasoned restraint. "They are thus: Your King must vacate his throne and titles to me. Your Royal Forces must clear the field and pledge fealty to me. Your Lords and their houses must pledge the same, and in exchange I shall allow your boy King to retire to his summer home on the Hot Lake and retain the status of Lordship over the Southern Plains. If these terms are not agreed to, I shall bring my army to your gates, including the five thousand that landed not but two leagues south of your city. Including the armada which approaches the harbour as we speak, and including the armada and legion which now invade Westport."

The King stopped and watched as the colour left the face of the Lorian Master of the Royal Forces upon hearing that the situation was much direr than he had known. Lord Wendal said nothing, and King Dermond did not wait for him to find the words.

"You have the hour to reply," the King declared as he took the reins of his horse and placed a foot in the stirrup, pulling himself into the saddle.

He did not want a reply, and did not expect the acceptance of his terms. Now, it was war he desired. The thirst for battle had grown during the march, and he was not to be denied. The King turned without giving Lord Wendal time to respond, and spurred his horse back to the Demarian line. Lord Birk and War Marshall Greln followed closely behind.

Lord Wendal returned with his commanders to the city gates to deliver the Demarian King's terms knowing that a siege was imminent.

VII : SIEGE

Hollyglade awoke in the dark, finding herself on a floor of stone. Though her eyes were not covered, and her mouth was no longer bound, she could not see anything. She tried moving and found that her wrists and ankles were now free. Feeling around herself with her fingertips, the stone felt rough-hewn and irregular. She moved in one direction trying to gain some sense of the shape and size of the room she was in. Slowly and gently, she explored the space around her until she came to one wall, which she used to steady herself as she began to stand up. With a crack, her head found the ceiling and she let out restrained yelp. Reaching up to feel the top of her head, and measure the ceiling, she heard someone take in a gasp of air.

"Hello? Who's there?" someone called to her, with a tremulous voice.

Hollyglade's first reaction was to take up a defensive stance. She tried her best to force her giantish low light vision to adjust to the darkness and show her who had spoken. It was a fruitless effort. Her vision would work in low light, but not the complete absence of it.

"Hello? Can you hear me? Are you alright? My name's Jeron. Are you hurt?"

Jeron. Where have I heard that name before? She wondered to herself. He sounded harmless enough.

"I'm ok, I think," she replied. "Where am I? What is this place?" The sound of their voices echoed slightly, giving Hollyglade a sense of the size of the room she was in. It did not seem large, though she could tell now that the person speaking to her was a short distance away.

"I wish I could tell you exactly where we are, but I honestly do not know. I have seen our captor only once, and did not recognize him. I can tell you that he is some sort of sorcerer, but that is all. I don't even know where in the country this prison lies. Can you tell me your name? You're only the second person who has shared a part of this confinement with me, and the first who speaks the common language."

"Hollyglade," she replied, "and we are somewhere within the walls of Whiterock, or underneath it. I can't be entirely sure."

He inhaled audibly

"You're sure we are in Whiterock? In Magnaville? You're certain?"

"Yes. You seem surprised. How did you get here?"

"I was ambushed on the road to Westport quite some time ago, though I can't tell you exactly how long ago, as I have lost track of time while confined in here. I awoke in this cell and saw no one at all for what seemed like days. How did you get here?"

She recognized some of the story as one she had heard gossiped about in various taverns and inns within the villages and towns she had visited over the last month or so. But, she was sure that the stories had ended with the death of the subject.

"Wait, what did you say your name was, again?" she asked.

"Jeron"

"THE Jeron? Crown prince who disappeared and was declared dead a month ago?" she questioned with exclamation.

"The. Wait, dead?" He replied

"Wow. You have no idea what has gone on above you, do you?"

"Correct. No Idea, whatsoever. I don't even know what day it is."

"Well, when I came into the capital, it was at night, and I feel like I can't have been out for too long. The moon was but a sliver, and will be a new moon when it rises next. I was brought here by a bounty hunter and delivered to a man in dark robes with a voice like the grave. I did not recognize him, but I have heard that there was a sorcerer in the capital advising the King, so I must assume that was him. If he put me in here, and you saw him in here, that must mean we have something in common, though I can't imagine what. Also, the guards at the gate told the bounty hunter that the Demarian army marches here. I'm not surprised, as I heard that King Harford had one of their lords executed not very long ago. Supposedly as a retaliation for your death. It was said that you were abducted by some Demarian Lord and killed."

"Did you say the King? Have they crowned my baby brother already? And the Sorcerer is advising him? And war is at the gate! This is not good."

"Yes. They crowned him not long after you died, er, disappeared. And the Sorcerer showed up in court about a month ago, I hear. I'm surprised you did not see him yourself."

"He must have arrived after I set out to mourn my father in the mountains above Westport. I am surprised he was able to persuade the Vestry to accept him."

"I don't think they really did. The talk is that he wedged himself in to the King's, to your brother's, confidence against the advice of the Vestry. Many blame him for the odd decrees that followed shortly after."

"Odd decrees?"

"Yes, I guess you would not have heard. First, the Elder Folk were sent out of Magnaville. There was no explanation for it. Some suggested that it was us Harford blamed for your death, but there was no evidence of that being a fact, nor of Harford believing it. Then the decree was expanded to include everywhere from the Demarian border to along the High Trail and all the way along the Low Road to the coast. Of course, there was no hope of enforcing it above the foothills. The Elvish houses would not budge now, having defied all four kingdoms for generations, from Ellendor to Sudara, all along the Western Ranges. It was under the guise of that decree that the bounty hunter who captured me conscripted army and garrison troops to complete the job."

Jeron was having difficulty assimilating so much information all at once, that he felt some of it pass him by.

"I'm sorry, I must ask you to slow down a bit. This is a lot to take in."

"It's alright. I understand."

"There is a war on?"

"Not yet, I don't think. What was said at the gates was the first thing I'd heard about it, but it sounds like there will be one. That's all I know."

"This is bad," Jeron fretted. "Did you see any sign of the Demarians?"

"No. There was no indication of them from where we were. But we did approach the city from the south. There's really nothing else I can tell you about it."

"Alright, let me ask you something else. You're of the Elder Races?" he asked.

"Yes. My Mother was Giantish, and my Father Elvish."

"Wait, what? You are half-each of two Elder Races? Is that even possible?"

"It must be. Here I am."

"I take your word for it that you are here, and that you are real. Do you possess the gifts of either of your parents?"

"I do. Some of each, but I don't like to talk about it."

"I thought half-breeds lost their gifts. How is it you did not?"

"I don't know. I've never had anyone to ask. My parents died when I was five."

"Oh, Hollyglade, I'm so sorry to hear that. Please forgive me."

"There's nothing to forgive. It's been ten years. I had a sort of family here in the city. We made the best of it."

"You sound so strong minded, sure of yourself. I'm amazed that someone who went through that is as well adjusted as you seem to be. You say that the decree was originally just for Magnaville, and then expanded. How long ago was the expanded decree made?"

"I wouldn't say I'm entirely sure of myself. Sure of some things, less of others. I don't know exactly when the decrees were made, but I started getting turned away from public houses and being passed over for work, around two weeks ago. I was headed south. I have never left Loria, and thought I'd visit Sudara."

"You do not fear to enter Sudara in it's chaos?"

"Precisely. No one to issue decrees."

Jeron remained silent for a while, and Hollyglade did not interrupt him, instead taking the time to feel about her cell some more. She discovered that there was a set of steel bars at the side facing where the sound of Jeron's voice came from. She felt each bar, looking for the door, and the lock, hoping to find a way to pick it and escape. She was puzzled when she found no hinges, lock, handle, or any other type of variation in the bars at all. In her confusion over the lack of a door, she felt each of the bars again, and found herself perplexed with the construction of the cell.

"Jeron?"

"Yes?"

"There is no door to this cell. How did I get in here?"

"That I have not seen. When the last girl I shared this space with was brought in, as with you, I was rendered unconscious and did not witness either of you being placed in, or removed from the cell. I would hazard a guess that it is some work of the Sorcerer's magic. He worked some sort of magic upon me also. He forced me to move from the back of my cell, and walk to him at the bars. He then compelled me to place my hands upon the bars while he took some of my blood."

"He took some of your blood? Did he drink it? I have heard of creatures that look like men, that feed on the blood of men, but I just assumed they were stories made up to scare children into staying in bed at night."

"He did not drink it. He poured it into a vial of some kind, wherein there was a dark liquid. When the two combined, the result turned white. This seemed to give him some sort of satisfaction. It gave me a dreadful disquietude."

"He obviously wants you for something. And me also. I just wish that I knew what, so that I could at least try to conceive a way to fight it."

"Well then, we must educate each other about who we are. Maybe then we will find some commonality."

There was something about Jeron that put Hollyglade at ease. Perhaps it was because he was a person she had heard about, and therefore felt she knew in some way. Maybe it was that they now shared a common ordeal. Perhaps it was that he seemed much like his father, a King who was loved by everyone for his just and benevolent rule. Maybe all of that, and more. She did not care. He was in this with her, and she decided to put faith in his apparent honesty.

They spoke for hours. Each telling each other of their upbringing, family history and the events that led them to their present confinement. Each asking questions to follow lines of thought around theories developing from the stories they shared. They agreed not to give up, and were both energized by the pursuit of a common goal, even if the goal was unclear. Though it was difficult, she told him about dGerrie, his brotherly love for her, his attempt to rescue her, and his death at the hands of The Dancer.

"Alright, so let me recap this, from now backwards," Jeron offered. "You were brought here sometime in the last day, or what feels to us like a day. You were captured by a bounty hunter who was hired by the sorcerer and backed by Harford. This bounty hunter had hired your friend, dGerrie, who did not know it was you they hunted, and you did not know it was he who was among the bounty hunter's men.

"In the pursuit, this bounty hunter caused a fair amount of collateral damage, including taking the life of your adoptive brother. Prior to that, you had been working for the past several years training beasts of burden and otherwise working with animals, in the general area of north-eastern Loria. This was fine until you were forced to head south by Harford's decrees.

"Before that you had grown up in Magnaville, in the Red Lanes, with dGerrie and some other orphans, making the best go of it you could. You arrived in Magnaville as a refugee of the Great Destruction, as many children did at that time.

"Prior to the Great Destruction, until the age of five, you

lived with your parents in a farming village along the West Way, which was destroyed in the event. Your parents were an Elvish man, and a Giantish woman, both of whom bore the gifts of their race. Have I recalled it all correctly?

"Yes. I think you've managed to get it all."

"But I feel something has been left out." He paused to choose his words and phrase his question delicately. "You haven't spoken of your gifts, other than to say that you have them. As the Crown Prince, I was educated from the time I could speak, and part of that education was the histories of the Elder Folk, which included studying the rare mixing of races. I remember quite clearly, that there is a well studied, though infrequently documented rule of nature in such breedings.

"And that is, that a child born of a pairing between Elder Folk and humans results in a healthy child, but one that does not possess the gifts of the Elder Folk. The child's subsequent descendants would also be void of the gifts of the Elder Folk. It is also well established that pairings of two Elder Folk from different races produce offspring that are unable to thrive once born, if born at all.

"So Hollyglade, how did you survive to, and beyond your birth? And how did you survive the Great Destruction? I believe if we know the answer to these questions, we may know why the sorcerer wants you, which may give clues to why he wants me, and therefore some clues as to how we may fight him."

She sat for a moment to contemplate how to answer. Her father had explained some things to her, but only at a level that a five-year-old girl could understand, and so the answers she could offer now, parts of which she was sure she had forgotten, were vague at best. She decided to offer them anyway.

"Well, listen, you must understand that the only explanations I was given were from my father, who though he possessed the Elvish gifts, was still but a farmer. And the only reason I was given any explanations to anything, was because I was being teased by other children. So, what I was told was meant to cheer up a five-year-old girl, and not to enlighten a scholar."

"It's alright Hollyglade, it's what we have."

"Well then," She took a deep breath to gather her thoughts and bring forth the memories. "my father told me that I was a miracle. I occasionally asked him what that meant, and he usually told me that the gods blessed us by keeping me alive, but when I was five, he did tell me that what he meant by that was that the gods gave him the ability to keep me healthy.

"He explained it something like this: He said that all creatures are made of the elements. Made of Earth, Air, Fire, and Water. He said that people are incomplete until they are born, because while we are in our mother's womb, we have only the water in the womb, the fire of her warmth, and the dust of the earth we were constructed from. The fire and water begin to combine with us to make us whole while we grow in the womb, and the air finishes the job when we are born, making us whole.

"He said that when two different Elder Folk try to have children, the children grow too fast in their mother's wombs, and the air doesn't come soon enough to finish the job, so the children fall apart before they are completed. When I asked him why I was different, he told me that he had used the gifts the gods had given him to hold me together, until I met the air and it finished the job of building me. He told me that doing so had made me strong, and that I would have many gifts. He told me to always use them to help people and to be a good person."

She stopped for a moment as a tear began to roll down her cheek as the memories of her parents became vivid once more. "But I did not use the gift to help others. I did not know how. I only used it to kill. And so, I have sworn off that power. I have only used a touch of it for warmth from time to time."

Jeron sat pondering all he had heard. Having studied some of the laws of magic, and the science of the world, what she had said about her birth, and formation in the womb made sense to him. He could see why none of the Elder Folk had been successful at producing children in the past.

"Hollyglade," he began, "I believe I know what makes you special, but first I must ask you what you meant when you said you used your power to kill. Trust me, when I say that I do not judge you. I only wish to gain knowledge to help us."

"I have never told anyone what I did. No one. Not even my closest friend."

"You must share it. You must unburden yourself."

She sat silently for a moment contemplating what to say, how to say it. It was a secret kept for most of her life, words she had never uttered aloud to anyone. Keeping that secret, and hiding the power within her, had been such an integral piece of her core identity for incredibly long. She knew that sharing the truth could likely serve a purpose, one that may lead to her salvation, and that of the Crown Prince of Loria, a seemingly good and honest man. She fought to convince herself that this was finally the time to unburden herself of that dark secret, to share with someone who she truly was, the good and the terrible. Without fully deciding to do so, she spoke.

"Alright," she sighed "It was me. I caused it. In my anger, I released my power."

"Caused what?"

"I caused the Great Destruction."

Jeron's jaw dropped and he let out a quiet gasp of disbelief.

"How? Why? Wh...?"

"Some men came to the village looking for me. I mean I didn't realize they were looking for me at the time, but they were. They killed my parents and tried to take me. In my fear, anguish, and anger, I lashed out emotionally. I thought I was just screaming and trying to struggle away from them, but the power just came out. It just came out. I could not control it, I could not focus it. I was a five-year-old girl who was just overcome with grief, despair and ferocious rage.

"The power just went everywhere, and in a fraction of a moment, everything was gone, burnt, destroyed. I just sat there, next to the burned bodies of my parents, of our whole village. I sat there just sobbing in anguish for days until a trader came through and took me to the capital. I was so exhausted, thirsty and hungry, that I didn't even say a word. I was delirious, and incoherent. My clothes had been burned away, and I was cold and confused."

Jeron waited and organized his thoughts before replying.

"Hollyglade, I am sorry that you had to endure so much pain, loss, and hardship in your life. No one deserves that. My heart breaks for you." He paused and sat under the weight of his empathy for her, wishing there was some way he could change her past and take away her hurt.

"Thank you," she said after a moment.

"I think I know why the sorcerer wants you. I think it's obvious, now. He wants your power. There can't be any other explanation. I'm not sure what he plans to do with you or how he plans to use your power, but he wants you for that."

"I can't see how it's of any use to him. It's my power, and I can't use it. Or at least, I don't know how, and so I won't"

"I don't know either, but he must have some plan. Maybe he's going to try to coerce you, or control you. We both know that he can do that to us on some level. Maybe he has a way to do it on a deeper level also. The old tales about the sorcerers who lived before my grandfather's time say that the sorcerers craved power, and that it was the undoing of their kind. They were once plentiful in the known land, and most of them served their Kingdoms much the same way as priests serve in the Temples now. But the culture of their order changed when some of them began to crave greater power, and they departed from service, and sought instead to rule.

"The books say that it was their infighting that lead to the downfall of their sorcerer society, as many of them killed each other trying to control the world's sources of power. This one must be one of the few survivors believed to have escaped the infighting. Or, at least, he is from their line."

"Maybe it's true. But I won't let him have my power," she maintained.

"Good. Don't let go of that determination. You said something else about using your power for warmth. What did you mean by that?"

"Oh, well the one thing I can control is heating up rocks. I can hold them and push some power into them to make them warm. I very rarely do it, and only to have a hot rock to sleep with on a cold night, or to cook on stone when there is no firewood."

"Hollyglade!" he exclaimed "That's it! You can get us out!"

"What? How?"

"The floors and walls are stone, and the bars are metal. You can melt the bars!"

"No, I can't. I have tried heating metal. It doesn't work that way. I'm not putting heat into the stones, I am putting in power, and then the heat comes out. If I do it to metal, I get burned. Hot rocks don't burn you like hot metal."

"No. Don't touch the bars, touch the rock. Heat up the metal by heating up the rock that it touches. That way you won't get burned!"

She thought about it for a moment, and then decided that it made sense.

"Alright. I'm going to try, it's not like I have anything else to do."

She felt the bars again, and traced them down to the floor. Placing a hand on either side of one of the bars and closing her eyes, she focused on the stone. Power began to rise in her, and she began to breathe deeply, trying to relax in order to focus her mind on the stone. She concentrated on her fingers and palms, on the texture of the stone, and on her contact with it. She could feel the power flow out from within her, down her arms and out through her hands. The stone began to get warm.

"Woah!" gasped Jeron.

As she continued to let the power flow from her, she opened her eyes to see the stone had begun to glow. In the low light she could see around the stone prison where she was confined, and she could now see Jeron across from her in a cell much like hers. His face was lit with amazement, as much as the by glow of the stone. She could see his disheveled black hair, which flopped over a face that appeared gaunt from malnutrition. His face was covered by his coarse and bedraggled beard, and his eyes were slightly sunken though they stared at her, widened with amazement. He wore travelling attire, though it appeared timeworn and threadbare, and his feet bore no footwear.

She looked back down to the point where the metal bar entered the stone, and saw the metal had begun to glow slightly as well. Just then, a loud thunderous boom, accompanied by the shaking of the floor resonated around them. In shock and surprise, Hollyglade lifted her hands from the floor.

"What was that? What did I do?" she gasped.

Another boom hit, and the walls shook ever so slightly.

"That was not you," replied Jeron as he stood up. "The siege has begun."

The pounding continued with regularity, and both Jeron and Hollyglade felt a sense of urgency growing.

"Hollyglade, you must keep trying, if you can. The siege may be the distraction we need to make our escape," pleaded Jeron, his voice growing disquieted.

"I'll try," she agreed, as she placed her hands back upon the stone. The continuing sounds of the bombardment unsettled Hollyglade and rattled her concentration with every shake of the walls. Again, she closed her eyes and tried to block out everything but the feel of the stone, and her connection to it. Once more, she felt the power begin to flow into the rock and create heat. As she opened her eyes, Hollyglade saw that the stone and the metal of the steel bar were both glowing even more hotly now. Watching the metal closely to see if it would begin to melt, she tried to push her power into the stone faster. The heat of the rock was beginning to hurt her hands, yet she persisted, knowing that this was her best, and likely only, chance to free herself.

As the metal bar began to glow more brightly, Hollyglade's

confidence returned.

"I think I can do it!" she exclaimed.

"Good! Try pushing on the bar above where it is hot to see of it will bend." responded Jeron, encouragingly.

She stood up, paying attention to the ceiling, and pressed a foot against the bar, pushing as hard as she could. To her surprise, the bar began to stretch where it was glowing with heat as it bent outward.

"It's working!" Jeron cheered. As he let out his excitement, they both heard the latch on the door to their prison open. As the door swung in, Hollyglade stepped back from the bars of her cell in fear of what might come through.

With black robes covering him from head to toe, the sorcerer stepped into the room, and turned to Hollyglade's cell.

"Well, well, what have we here?" marveled the Sorcerer with a disturbing timbre. "So, you can use your power. Impressive, for someone unschooled in the thaumaturgical arts. I would be quite interested to see what else you know, but I'm afraid we do not have the time for such indulgences. Come."

He raised his hand to her, and Jeron saw her eyes roll back in her head as she collapsed on to the stone. Jeron was filled with a mix of dismay and fury as he grabbed hold of the bars on his cell shouted at the sorcerer,

"Leave her alone! What do you want with her? She's done nothing to you!"

The Sorcerer did not turn as he spoke.

"My dear prince, you shall find out soon enough, for you shall join us shortly. Be patient, and all shall be revealed."

With a snap of his fingers, the sorcerer signalled for the guard to enter the room. Once the guard was present, the sorcerer raised his hand toward Hollyglade's cell and chanted something quietly. As Jeron watched, the bars of the cell stretched and bowed to form an entryway through which the guard stepped into the cell. Once in the cell, the man picked Hollyglade up off of the floor, and hoisted her onto his shoulder. Turning and stepping back out of the cell, the guard exited the room.

Once the guard was clear, the sorcerer ceased his chanting, and the steel bars of the cell returned to their original shape. The sorcerer turned to leave and cocked his head slightly toward Jeron as he grinned.

"Sit tight my prince, I shall return for you shortly," and then left, closing the door behind him.

Jeron awoke to find himself outside of his stone cell for the first time in what seemed like months. To his dismay, one type of prison had been traded for another. Though the room was dark, there was some light coming from an open window partially blocked by a heavy curtain across the room. There was also some candlelight coming from a table on the other side of the room. The table was covered in vials, tubes, bowls, and various other instruments of alchemy. The room appeared to be some type of laboratory.

Standing with his back to Jeron was the sorcerer, focused on something that Jeron could not see. Feeling his body for restraints, Jeron could find none, but discovered a fresh wound on the inside of his forearm, oozing still. He peered around to examine his enclosure, and found himself confined to a steel barred cage roughly the length, width and height of a man. As he examined his cage, he saw that Hollyglade lay in an identical enclosure next to his. He looked to see if she was conscious, and found her eyes to be closed, yet he was able to observe her chest rising and falling.

After taking a quick look back to the sorcerer, and hearing the loud sounds of battle coming through one of the open windows, Jeron whispered to her,

"Hollyglade. Hey. Hollyglade. Wake up."

Her eyelids fluttered, and she let out a slight groan as she brought a hand to her head. Opening her eyes, she turned to look at Jeron, and then at her surroundings, stopping to focus on the sorcerer.

"Jeron, where are we?" she whispered nervously.

With a quick glance at the sorcerer, and then back to

Hollyglade, he replied in a hushed tone,

"I believe we are somewhere in the central tower, though I do not recognise this apartment, per se."

Hearing the conversation behind him, the sorcerer turned to see his captives awake.

"Well, you two, I'm glad to see you are awake to take part in this most auspicious night. I must thank you both, for this evening you shall contribute to a night that shall become legend among the Kingdoms of the land. You shall be instrumental in bringing peace and prosperity to not only Loria, but its neighbours as well."

"What in the gods' names could you possibly be hinting at?" shot Jeron, clearly no longer caring about raising the ire of their captor.

"Ah, my Prince, I am so glad you asked. But it is you, my dear," he said as he turned his attention to Hollyglade, "who should have the greater curiosity about your role here. For it is you who shall give me the greatest power ever imagined by our kind."

She sat up, and faced him, holding the bars of her cage with one hand to steady herself. She looked him in the face, though she could not see his eyes, and did her best to seem confidently defiant.

"I'll give you nothing. What I have can not be harnessed or controlled. It's of no use to you."

"Oh ho! My dear girl! How wrong you are!" he exclaimed. "You are indeed special, and your power is great, but I shall take if from you. In a certain way I find it disheartening that you never learned to wield it for yourself, nor do you seem to know just how special you are."

"I am not special," she retorted, "and I will not let you take this from me. You'll have to kill me trying, and then there will be nothing for you to take." Her defiance was genuine. Her furious anger real. She had seen her power cause enough death and destruction by her own hand, and was not going to willingly allow someone else to use her power to cause even more suffering.

"Oh, how wrong you are, dear girl. Since we must wait to begin, let me enlighten you." The sorcerer stepped to the curtain and opened it to allow some light into the laboratory. "You see, dear girl, if you had been educated in the magical arts, you would know that there are several kinds of power, and several ways to wield it. The two main streams of thaumaturgical practice are the Wizard's chosen practise of Magery, and the practice of Sorcery.

"There also exist lesser streams of magic, like the gifts of the Elder Folk, who have various innate magical abilities, and can wield power in various ways. But, in all cases, the wielders of power are just that: wielders of it. We all must find sources of power, draw upon those sources, and then use that power through the lens of our specialities, spells, incantations, potions, or other forms of magic.

"You could think of it like taking a water jar, filling it with water, and pouring it into a potted plant. The water is the power, the jar is the part of the user where the power is held, and the hand holding the jar belongs to the wielder of that magic, and the plant is the target of the magic. I myself was trained in the stream of Sorcery, yet have expanded my learning to include all disciplines of the arcane."

"What does any of that have to do with me?" Hollyglade interrupted.

"Ah, yes. Well dear girl, as I said, you are special. You are the first known example of a surviving offspring of two different Elder races. And as such, you are quite unique. Having studied many examples of the failed attempts to produce offspring from pairings such as that of your parents, I have discovered why the offspring fail to survive their birth.

"As I mentioned, users of magic must draw power from various sources in order to then wield it. Wielding that magic is an expenditure of power. Once a user of magic has cast his spell, he empties his proverbial jar, and thus his power is limited. But when two of the Elder races join with each other to produce a child of the blend of their races, that child is in and of themselves, a source of power." He paused for a moment as the revelation hung in the air. Hollyglade was puzzled, and did not have the words to respond to the sorcerer's divulgement.

He continued

"The reason all other children with mixed heritage such as yours die in the womb, is that the power that resides within them is too much for their infantile bodies to contain. Thus, the power tears their being apart and their essence is lost, resulting in stillbirth and a dissipation of the source created by their conception. You were saved from such a fate by the courage of your father, whose decision to try to hold together your essence within the womb kept you from succumbing to the power within.

"As a result, you lived, and your mortal shell was made strong enough to contain the vast power which originates from your being. As you may be able to imagine, someone with the knowledge of how to wield such power, would be able to accomplish much, once the need to draw power from outside sources is no longer a concern."

"What makes you think you can take another person's power? And even if you do, what makes you think you can become a source of it yourself?" She asked, still hoping to learn something that might help her fight.

"Ah, there we have it, dear girl. It is not your power I desire, but the part of you that creates it. That, is what I shall add to myself, once I have taken it from you."

"What good will it be to you anyway? As I can see from looking at you, you are not Elder Folk, your body would reject anything you try to take from me." She was just guessing with her theory, and hoped that his confirmation or rejection of it would tell her something.

"Again, you are more informed than you seem. Yes, as I am now I would not be able to take that which you have, and add it to myself. I must either change what you have, which would devalue it, or change myself. Knowing that I do not want to alter your source of power, I am left with altering myself. That is where the good Prince will aide me, in my transformation."

"How could I possibly have anything that would make any difference to this?" Jeron challenged. "I am no Elder Folk, and have no magical heritage."

"Ah," the Sorcerer purred eerily, "now we come to what makes you special, my dear Prince. You have very special blood, that of the Nartakish race once thought extinct. Such blood is the key to bridging the gap between the Elder Folk, and humans."

"I am no such thing. My blood may be Royal, but that only makes my station within society special, nothing more," Jeron denied, though only doing so out of a principal of resistance to the Sorcerer's claims.

"Oh, but it is true, Prince. You have the blood. My tests have proven it, confirming my research into your lineage. You see, it was not a blind guess that led me to take you captive. I spent years looking for the descendants of the last known members of the Nartakish clans. The Nartakish were a very rare sub-race of humans who possessed the ability to wield power and practice magic with but a thought. They were gifted with the fortitude to draw tremendous amounts of power from any source they found, and hold it for indefinite amounts of time.

"Their downfall was in believing that they could make themselves live forever, being sustained with nothing more than the power they drew into themselves, and therefore they decided not to bother breeding to continue their line. But this proved folly, as they eventually learned that though they could sustain themselves for incredible lengths of time on the power alone, they could not do it indefinitely. Those who committed themselves to that doomed path eventually succumbed to the deterioration of their flesh which the lack of normal sustenance brought upon them.

"However, I discovered that there were a few who decided to marry into the lines of humans, outside of the Nartakish clans, and thus their line would continue on, even if the blood was diluted, and the gifts no longer manifest. Your family line is well documented, but the connection to the Nartakish was removed from the records kept here in the Royal Library. No, it was only among the ancient ruins of the once grand and proud house of The Distorted, that I found a small section of their once great library. And in that ancient library of the old Sorcerers, the Tome of the Elder Houses, a detailed documentation of the proud clan lineage of the Elvish, Dwarvish, Gnomish, Giantish, and Nartakish peoples. And in that, a reference to a marriage between house Blacksky of the Nartakish, and house Peaksoul."

Jeron's face transformed to a look of awe and terror, for he knew that the sorcerer did not lie. He had studied the history of his house, House Peaksoul, and had noted that there were some vagaries in the details of his ancestry during the time of the Arcane Upheaval.

"Jeron," Hollyglade interjected "Why should that matter?"

"He can not tell you why it matters, girl," replied the sorcerer, "but I shall inform you. You see, the Nartakish blood has one special property that is unique among all the races. It is able survive any sickness, and any malady that would normally affect any of the other races. I have found through my research, that this is because it is unchanged by the blood of anything that it mixes with. However, I have found a way to alter the Nartakish blood, human blood, Elvish and Giantish blood, to blend with each other to make a wholly new blood.

"When this blood flows in my veins, I shall be able assimilate any part of any other being into myself. So, there you see where you shall contribute to a new era. I have taken blood from each of you, altered it and have mixed it with my own. All we wait for now, is the dark of night, and the presence of the new moon whose tidal pull shall make the blending permanent. Once the blending is permanent, I shall pull from within you the essence which makes you whole and allows you to create your power, and I shall consume it, adding it to the fabric of my own being, and thus becoming my own source of unlimited power." He began to smile with a sinister grin as he revelled in the approaching hour of his planned self-exultance.

"Now, enough schooling. There is still some work of preparation to be done. Dusk is nigh." The sorcerer turned back to his work table, picked up a couple of bowls, and moved into an adjoining room.

Hollyglade and Jeron looked at each other with shared fear and concern. Neither could see a way to fight what was taking place, yet both knew an attempt had to be made. Shifting closer to the edge of his cage, Jeron spoke first.

"Hollyglade, you have to fight him."

"I don't know how" she fretted. "You've seen the extent of my knowledge of power and magic."

"No. He's made a mistake."

"What do you mean? We are who he said we are."

"That's not what I mean," he whispered. "He has schooled us. We know more now than we did before. We know that you have unlimited power, and that's what he wants. We know you have more power than he does, otherwise he wouldn't need yours. So, we know it's possible to defeat him."

"But Jeron, I don't know how!" she whispered strongly.

"You can figure it out. I know you can. You are obviously a very intelligent girl, and I'm going to help you."

"Alright, but what can I do?"

"Think about what he said about the water jug. The person pouring a water jug could pour it anywhere they want, but they choose to hold it over the potted plant. For you, it's not a jug, it's more like a barrel, or a lake, or even the whole ocean. You have just have to learn to pour it where you want it to go."

"How to I do that?"

"I believe he told us. He said that the body is the wielder of the magic, you just have to pick a target."

Hollyglade gazed into nothing for a moment while running over the possibilities in her mind. She understood that she had immense power, and that she could choose to wield or withhold it. It was clear to her that touching stone was a form of targeting, and that there may be a way to target something without touching it.

"Maybe I understand a little. It's what I'm doing when I touch the stone, I'm thinking about it. But I have to be touching it."

"No. You don't Hollyglade. Think about it. The power only came out through your hands in that cell down there. It didn't come through your legs, or your back, or where you sat on the stone. So, you already told it the path to travel. You just have to tell it a path that goes beyond your fingertips."

"Jeron, I am no student of magic, nor wizardry, or sorcery. I do not know how." She sniffed, putting her face in her hands.

"No," he agreed "you are not a wizard or a sorcerer, nor an archmage or a shaman, nor an elementalist or enchanter. You are Hollyglade, first of your kind, and source of power. Wielder of power. You are the one some called the Wayrender, Firebrand of the Western plains. Your father and mother gave their lives to preserve you, and your incredible gift. Do not be ashamed to use it. You have said that they raised you to be a person who uses your strengths for good. I believe that you are good, and thus I have faith in you. Now is the time. Destroy this evil, and be the good that triumphs over it."

She looked up at him in surprise and amazement, wondering how someone who had just met her could have faith in her when she had so little in herself. Then, her amazement became her determination. The Crown Prince of Loria, a man, though young, known to be learned and wise, who had followed closely in the footsteps of his father Jerold the Just, the greatest King Loria had ever known, was placing his faith in her. If he made the choice to have such faith, then she must choose it also.

"I'll do it. I'll fight him. But you must help me figure out how."

With a smile of invigorated determination and focus, Jeron clenched his fist and met her gaze.

"Yes, Hollyglade, let us share our knowledge once more."

The pounding was deafening, and his ears were ringing as he awoke to find himself on a hard, flat surface. Feeling around, his hands found the edges of a wooden table. Forcing his eyes open, the failing light of late afternoon poured through the window of the infirmary. He struggled to sit up and found several wounds about him, including a nastily throbbing lump on the back of his head. As he became more or less seated upon the table, a man moved over to him and grabbed ahold of his arms to steady him.

"Woah there trooper, slow down. You've been through a lot the last few days, I wasn't sure you'd ever wake. You've had a rough time of it," said the man, dressed as a medic.

"Where am I? How did I get here?"

"Well, you're in the garrison infirmary. I'm Yoric, the garrison medic. You, and a few others were brought here when the army and the garrisons were all recalled to reinforce the legions already stationed in the capital."

"Recalled? Reinforce them for what?"

"Wow, you must have been out of it for a while, soldier. The Demarians are at our walls, that's who you hear trying to knock a hole in them. Two of our legions showed their force by presenting themselves on the field to the north, but they were ordered to retreat behind the walls when the Demarians showed up from the south also. I am told there is a battle at sea beyond the harbour, too. It's good you're up. Every able body has been ordered to the wall to take up a bow. I noticed you came in with one across your back, and I'm sure they could use you up on top of that wall."

The soldier brought his hand to his head, and then felt his other wounds. His leg felt sore, and he was not sure if he could stand on it.

"Do you have water?"

"Here trooper," replied the medic, handing him a jug. "You had a few holes in you when you came in, but I sewed you up correctly. I'd not try to run on that leg, but you may be able to pull a bowstring." The medic turned back to the unconscious trooper he had been working on earlier, and continued his treatment.

The soldier felt his shoulder, and disagreed with the medic's assessment. But, being in no mood to argue, he looked around for his boots.

"Where are the rest of my things?" he asked, hoping that at least some of what he had carried about him made it to the infirmary.

"Over there" pointed the medic. "You're sure fond of blades my friend. I believe there were several times I'd thought I'd found them all on you, only to discover more and more. 'Twas quite the treasure hunt," he chuckled.

Sliding off the table, the soldier nearly fell all the way to the floor as his wounded leg did not hold him as he expected. Pulling himself up against the table, he regained his balance and limped over to the pile of clothing and weapons the medic had pointed to. Taking his boots, he pulled on one at a time, using a stool to prevent having to bend all the way to the ground. One by one, he placed each of the blades in its customary position on his body, though some of his hiding spots remained empty of their usual blade. He took the bow and quiver of arrows from the table, slinging them across his back.

"Yoric," the soldier called to the medic, "I had two swords. Do you know where they might be?"

"Ah, friend. I do not. But look there, behind that crate of bandages. There I place weapons belonging to soldiers who do not regain their verticality, in order for the garrison to reclaim and reassign them. I believe you may find a few blades there still."

Limping over to the crate, the soldier slid it along the workbench, and found several blades in sheaths lying wrapped in their scabbards. Taking a look through them, he found two that he felt comfortable with, one longer and one shorter, and tied them to his waist. Wincing with discomfort, he turned back to the medic, to see him begin the process of amputating a leg. With reluctance, he moved closer to the medic to make an inquiry.

"Yoric, can you tell me if the King's new Sorcerer's guard detail remains with him? I was assigned to him before I left for a short expedition, and would like to resume those duties now that I have returned." He did not tell the medic that in fact it was something like a dream that had run through his mind while he had been unconscious, that lead him to want to find the sorcerer, and that he had never been assigned to any part of Whiterock itself.

"I can't say. I'm not up to speed on who is doing what now that the siege is on. I've got plenty of men out that door there that need some kind of work done, so best you find a commanding officer and ask him."

"Right, sorry to bother you," he apologised. "Mine should be with his detail. I thank you for your care, Master Yoric."

"Hey," the soldier continued hesitantly, feigning embarrassment "I'm a bit turned around, which way to his quarters from here?"

"Out the door, through the triage room, up the stairs at the back, across the soldiers' mess, and then through the courtyard into the tower. You should know your way from there." The medic did not look up as he began to saw through bone. Not wanting to see any more of the inside of the poor man's leg, the soldier turned and let the room.

Outside the Medic's operating room, the soldier found the triage room full of wounded men being tended to by women volunteering as nurses. The sounds of pain and suffering, accompanied by the smells of blood, urine, and the contents of men's bowels and stomachs inspired an instantly nauseated reaction as he waded through the casualties. Seeing the stairway at the far end of the hall, he made his way through the mess of injured men, limping around the suffering troops while trying not to jostle anyone along the way.

The stairway seemed imposing now, with the injury to his

leg, but the soldier pulled himself up it with one hand on the railing, wincing with every step. He pressed on through the pain, as he was now determined to find whom he was looking for. His duty and allegiance were no longer to the crown, no longer to his temporary assignment, no longer to just himself. For the first time in a long time, he felt compelled to protect and care for someone who needed him, someone who would not survive on their own. This renewed sense of singular purpose drove him to push past the injury and pain, to block it out of his mind, and forge ahead in search of his friend.

Upon reaching the top of the stairs, he turned toward the door to the mess hall, and shuffled his way over to it. Pushing the door open with both hands, he entered the hall and found it empty. Seeing the door at the far side, which led to the courtyard at the base of the Tower of Whiterock, he began to weave his way through the tables and benches that had been left in disarray by the troops rushing to the defense of the city.

He wanted so badly to stop and rest at one of the tables, but his goal drove him onward. About halfway through the jumble of dining tables, he heard a voice call after him.

"Mr. Theurbeault! What a surprise this is! Oh, what fun!"

Stopping to turn and see where the voice called from, he spotted the bounty hunter entering the mess hall from the same door he had used.

"Var Toran," dGerrie cursed as he looked the bounty hunter over. "You're still here. I thought you would have crawled into a cave somewhere, what with all those skilled men out there holding swords."

"Oh, I do enjoy a good jest, Mr. Theurbeault. I'm glad to see you are well. I was disappointed that you and I did not have the proper chance to spar while we were both in Greenfield."

"Spar?" dGerrie spat, as his eyes narrowed. "Crossbow bolts are not a tool with which honest men spar. You are a coward, who now comes ready to spar with a man whom he has hobbled with arrows."

dGerrie gingerly stepped out into the centre of hall, where

there was a space free of tables, and stared at the bounty hunter, narrowing his eyes and clenching his jaw in a silent snarl.

"Yes, it was unfortunate that I had to expedite things so rapidly, but you must remember that I was on a tight schedule, and I felt that further conflict would have endangered the health of the girl. If you recall, she was to be delivered free of injury, and I did not wish to jeopardize the contract further by playing with you, Mr. Theurbeault."

"What did you do with her?" snapped dGerrie.

"I did as I was contracted to do," replied the bounty hunter flatly. "I delivered her to the Sorcerer Ni'Morstrom, as promised," he explained, obviously no longer concerned with keeping the contractor's identity a secret. "I assure you, if anything untoward has happened to her, it is not of my doing."

"It will be on your head," dGerrie sneered as he drew his swords. "Come, coward. Let us dance." Feeling the burning in his shoulder, it took dGerrie all the effort he could muster to keep from showing on his face what he felt in his arm. With a smile, and a slight bow, the bounty hunter stepped into the centre of the mess hall, and drew his sword and dagger.

"Tell me," inquired the bounty hunter "with whom did you train at sword play? I must say, that the style you employed in Greenfield was quite interesting."

"I'll tell you what, bounty hunter, if you kill me, you can ask me all the questions you want. But until then, you'll just have to communicate with your blade."

Trenon Var Toran sighed.

"So be it." He took several steps toward dGerrie, raising the tip of his sword. In response, dGerrie began to circle to his right while facing his right side toward his opponent, effectively walking backwards, in order to keep his injured shoulder protected. Raising his right arm to shoulder height, and pointing the tip of his longsword at the bounty hunter, dGerrie's thin yet towering frame presented an imposing form.

The bounty hunter moved first, throwing a high lunging feint which was easily parried, and then following up with a swipe at dGerrie's lead leg. Having kept most of his weight on his back leg, a simple back step was enough to avoid the slash, though dGerrie felt the deep twinge of pain that came from flexing his injured right thigh. His counter to the slash was quick, yet direct as he spun the tip of his longsword downward from left to right. The bounty hunter managed to bring his blade back around from the follow through of his attack to parry the blow. dGerrie continued to circle as he noted the speed with which his opponent recovered.

Feeling a shooting pain with each step of his circling, dGerrie stopped and faced the bounty hunter head on. Seeing the change in tack, Var Toran altered his stance to present his left side, and brought his sword high. Again, the bounty hunter made the first move, stabbing at dGerrie's right shoulder, allowing the stab to be parried outward, and spinning with the force of the deflection. He continued the pirouette and came about with a slash at waist level. dGerrie moved his left hand to bring the short sword around to block the slash, but his shoulder did not respond well to the command, and only caught the blade partially, resulting in a cut just above his left hip. With a rasp, he stepped back to protect his left side again.

Seeing the successful touch, the bounty hunter pressed his attack, this time making a swipe for dGerrie's lead leg. Seeing dGerrie make the same step back counter, the bounty hunter then returned with a slash toward the right shoulder. Grunting with the strain of the effort, dGerrie brought his longsword up to block the slash, but having only one leg planted, he was only able to partially arrest the force of the strike, resulting in the bounty hunter's blade impacting his bicep. The thick leather of his jerkin prevented the sword from cutting deeply, but the impact was painful, and broke the skin slightly.

dGerrie could feel blood trickling from both fresh wounds, but did not let them take his attention from the fight. He could see that he was a step slower than his opponent, due to his deteriorated condition, and knew that he would have to adjust his tactics. His usual speed and precision were not available to him now, and some other strategy would have to take their place. He pivoted his body, to show his left side, and aimed his short sword at the bounty hunter.

When his opponent made his next move, an outside-in slash at his left shoulder, dGerrie flicked the tip of his short sword upward, using only his forearm and wrist. The blow pushed his sword inward and allowed the slash, although diminished in strength, to connect to his injured shoulder. As the blow was coming, dGerrie loaded up on his good front leg and countered with a half turn forward and a neat stab at chest level. The bounty hunter moved with his dagger to parry, but was not able to completely deflect the thrust. The tip of the longsword found the flesh of the bounty hunter's ribcage, beneath his right shoulder. With a yelp of pain, the bounty hunter sprang back and grabbed the hole in his cream white tunic as the blood began to flow and stain it red.

"Ah, a clean touch, Mr. Theurbeault!" exclaimed the bounty hunter. "I am indeed scratched."

dGerrie did not press his attack, instead resetting his stance to continue to show his left side. Waiting for his opponent to make the first move again, dGerrie felt the third wound seep under his sleeve. His left arm was screaming in pain, yet he knew he could not allow it a reprieve. Saying nothing, dGerrie watched the bounty hunter set himself for the attack. It came quickly.

With a step forward, Var Toran thrust at dGerrie's left shoulder again, and this time the stab was parried with the short sword. With a quick recall of the blade over his head, the bounty hunter shifted his back leg forward and then brought his weight to his front leg again as his blade whirled over his head. In a fraction of a second, dGerrie recognised the move as one the bounty hunter had used in the clearing in the woods to cut down one of his men.

With both legs, dGerrie hopped to his left and simultaneously leaned back, brought his longsword around behind his head from right to left. As the bounty hunter's blow angled down to dGerrie's right, where his leg had been a moment earlier, he watched the sword whip by within a fraction of an inch of his face, as he continued to bring his longsword around past his left shoulder and down toward the bounty hunter's torso.

Var Toran reacted quickly enough to step back and evade the shaft of the longsword, but dGerrie's length made up the difference, as the tip of the blade dug into his chest below the collarbone and sliced diagonally to his belt. The leather of his tunic decreased the depth of the cut, but did not stop it completely, as a gash was opened up along the length of the swipe.

Seeing the success of the counter, dGerrie followed up with a stab from his left with the short sword. The stab was not accurate, nor firm, as the bounty hunter stepped back with a half turn and slapped the thrust downward with his sword. With the feeling leaving his left arm, his grip failed, and dGerrie dropped the blade. Feeling it fall away, he cringed and stepped back, not wanting to expose himself in an attempt to regain the weapon. Placing both hands on his longsword, he took a stance with his right side slightly forward.

Kicking the short sword aside and under a table, the bounty hunter sheathed his dagger and placed both hands on his sword, leveling it toward dGerrie.

"Now, Mr. Theurbeault, we move into uncharted territory. I have noticed that you are fond of carrying a multitude of blades, and I desire to find out how you handle yourself with but one," quipped the bounty hunter with a smirk.

Watching him carefully, dGerrie could see the slightest hitch in the bounty hunter's movements now that he was dealing with two fresh wounds. Though neither wound was on one of his limbs, the bounty hunter seemed affected by them. dGerrie suspected that he too was hiding the seriousness of his injury. With a quick flick of the tip of his blade, dGerrie shifted both feet forward, and let the bounty hunter parry his feint. Observing with which technique, and how quickly his opponent responded, dGerrie contemplated his strategy. Though he still felt slower than his opponent, dGerrie was sure that the gap in speed had narrowed. Hearing the sound of the battle raging outside, dGerrie felt some urgency to get on with his search for Hollyglade.

With a slight upturn of the corner of his mouth, dGerrie stepped forward and flicked the tip of his blade in a small circle, tapping Var Toran's sword, and making him adjust his stance. Again, he tapped his sword downward and shuffled both feet a half step forward. Again, and once more he provoked the bounty hunter with the obviously non-threatening move.

Then, the fifth time he made the move, the bounty hunter put more force into his parry, and sneered in annoyance as he did so. Seeing the added effort, dGerrie knew that he had received the counter he was looking to provoke. With an added flick in the opposite direction, dGerrie reacted to the bounty hunter's parry with a counter of his own, siding his blade along that of his opponents until it hit the cross guard of the bounty hunter's weapon. Then, with a roll of both wrists, dGerrie popped the tip of his blade over the handle of the bounty hunter's cross guard and drove his blade beneath the sleeve of his tunic. His blade found flesh, and dGerrie forced it forward into the bounty hunter's arm.

With a scream of agony, the bounty hunter dropped his sword, recoiled while grabbing the wounded arm, and reached for a dagger. Holding the dagger out in front of him while retreating out of dGerrie's reach, he cursed violently.

"What kind of cheap street tactic is that, you filthy gutter rat?" spat the bounty hunter.

"The effective kind," dGerrie smirked. "I must say, your eloquent and aristocratic demeanor vanishes quickly under duress, coward."

"You have no honour. I take my leave of you, plebeian cheat."

The bounty hunter backed several steps away, and then turned and made quickly for the door. Watching him go, dGerrie felt a righteous indignation swell in his chest, feeling that this was too little retribution. Sheathing his sword, he took his bow from his back, plucked an arrow from his quiver, knocked it and fired as the bounty hunter put one foot through the opening of the doorway.

With the weakness in his left arm, the shot was not his best, and the missile did not find its target. However, it found a mark slightly to the right of its target, and buried itself to the half shaft in the bounty hunter's right shoulder. With a scream, Var Toran slipped around the door frame and out of sight.

Letting out a deep breath, dGerrie retrieved his dropped weapon, sheathed it, and again headed for the tower.

VIII : CONTEST

"Your Grace, the Demarian forces continue to press their siege of the North gate. Though our archers rain arrows upon them, they are well shielded and seem not to be suffering significant losses as they employ the ram. The enemy has many skilled archers of their own, and a seemingly unending supply of arrows. Many of our archers on the wall have been wounded, and we have begun to rotate infantrymen onto the wall to continue our barrage against the enemy.

"Had we not signalled for the second and fifth legions to retreat to within the city walls, I am sure that they would have been overrun by the enemy. Your Grace, I must inform you that it is likely that the Demarians will enter the city, and if they do so we must be prepared," reported the Master of the Royal forces. He had been, up until now, confident that the walls of Magnaville would withstand any siege for months.

This confidence had been formed from the study of The Histories of the Sieges of Magnaville, and several other texts on siege warfare. But nowhere in his reading had he come across a siege anywhere near the magnitude of the one taking place outside the walls where he now addressed his King. The largest siege ever undertaken against the city of Magnaville, was done so by a force less than half this size, and with a mere handful of catapults. Quentin Wendal was now feeling the consequences of overconfidence.

"My L..L..Lord," began the young King with a stammer "I thought you said we could withstand a siege for months. Why are we losing?" Confusion and despair flooded Harford's face as he tried to grasp the gravity of the situation.

"Your Grace, there was no way for us to know that we would face such a force, until they were seen on the march some days ago. It was our belief that the second and fifth legions would outnumber our enemy, and would defeat them on the field, or at least turn them back, preventing a siege altogether. In all the history of war in our Kingdoms, theirs is the largest assembled force to have set out to war," quavered

Lord Wendal as he desperately tried to think of some way to salvage at least a stalemate with the Demarians.

"Are they going to get in?" asked the King directly.

"It now appears likely, Your Grace. They employ some new kind of device with which to ram our gate. It appears that they shall eventually break the gate, though our builders try their best to reinforce it. I suggest that we make preparations to evacuate you from the city, in the hopes we might regroup."

"Regroup?"

"Yes, Your Grace. I feel now that our best strategy is to signal our forces to assemble between the South and Green rivers and make plans to engage the enemy outside the city walls. I also believe it would be safest to spirit Your Grace away to Stonehome, on the High Trail within the Western Mountains. There you would be safe with only the need of a small force to keep an enemy at bay, as the High Pass is too narrow, and its cliffs too steep for the Demarians to reach you there."

"You want me to leave the city? What makes you think we can get past the Demarian army that now lays siege to our walls?"

"Your Grace, there are secret tunnels beneath the city which could provide a means to slip past the Demarian line. But we will have to wait until the sun has set, that we might use the cover of darkness to slip away unseen."

"And whom would you propose accompany us to Stonehome?"

"Your Grace, Lords Ventrent and Marnon would take two cohorts and ride the High Trail to Stonehome with you, staying until word arrives that our victory is secure."

"Lord Wendal, are you sure that such a victory can be won?"

"I am Your Grace. Between the garrisons and your Royal Army, we at least equal the forces of our enemy. Once the recall is complete, we will have a force assembled large enough to face the Demarians. Our only test will be time. That is why I wish to evacuate you from the city, so that the enemy has no chance to seize the crown."

"Lord Wendal, these matters are not within my scope of expertise. I defer to you in this time of war. Make your preparations."

"At once, Your Grace."

The Master of The Royal Forces exited the King's personal chambers with haste. Turning to his personal page, the young King tried his best to contain his anxiety.

"Tedd, will you stay close to me?"

"Until my last breath, Your Grace."

The King looked with trepidation out his window at the battle which raged against the city walls, as the sun neared the horizon.

"Tedd," the King called to his page, who looked up and stood to attention. "Go to the Sorcerer's Laboratory and tell him I must speak with him. He prepares some sort of magical counterattack to this siege. Tell him that his time is running out, and that I need to know that he can repel the enemy. Go, and report to me how long it will be before he is able to give response to the siege."

"Yes, Your Grace." The page hurried out of the chambers to carry out the King's orders.

"Your Grace, we have begun to ram the gates and I am confident that it is but a short matter of time before we are through," reported Lord Birk. He had been near the front line most of the day, organizing the offensive and coordinating each wave of the attack with his commanders. The Lorian forces had given a show of strength upon the battlefield outside the city walls initially, but retreated to within its gates once the bulk of King Dermond's army had presented itself on the ridge above Magnaville's outlying fields. Lord Birk had ordered the start of siege tactics shortly before the noon sun, and though the city's walls were strong, the overwhelming number of siege engines he had employed were beginning to break cracks in its structure.

"Good, Lord Birk. Make ready a cohort of your best fighters, for once the gates have been breached, I shall lead them into the city. I want to find this boy King myself and put fear in his heart by my own hand," announced the King as he stood and readied himself to continue the battle.

"Your Grace, I advise that you allow some of our forces through the breach ahead of you, as I do not wish you to risk yourself to such an extent as the initial breach would create," replied Lord Birk, thinking to himself that the King's advanced age put him at excessive risk.

The King raised an eyebrow and smirked in response.

"My dear Renald," the King chortled as he placed a hand on the lord's shoulder, "I did not ride this far to hide behind other men. My blade has felt the inside of more men than any ten of these good warriors put together. It will not remain dry now. Have your cohort assembled quickly, that I may ride for the front line."

The King's resolve was unshakeable, and Lord Birk had learned long ago that once the King had made up his mind, there was no changing it. With a bow, Lord Birk excused himself to assemble the men to ride with the King.

Ten minutes later, Lord Birk returned to the King with a cohort of one hundred men, presenting them in formation, ready to advance on the wall.

"Your Grace, these good men are honoured to ride with you."

"With us, My Lord. I will not deny you the honour" grinned the King.

"You Honour me indeed, Your Grace," smiled Lord Birk.

As they mounted their horses, the shouts of hundreds of men came from the front line. Shouts of triumph.

"Your Grace, the gates are opened!" declared War Marshall Greln, riding into the midst of the gathered cohort.

The King responded by drawing his sword and raising it over his head.

"Let us ride!"

The light coming through the window was beginning to change as the sun neared the horizon. Hollyglade and Jeron had shared every thought that entered each of their minds on the matter of how to resist the Sorcerer. Neither was completely confident of anything, but they agreed that both of them would do all they could to refuse him.

"Jeron, once he starts whatever it is that he's going to start, the biggest fear I still have is that if I resist him too hard, and that causes me to release too much power, you'll be as much the victim as he is."

"Hollyglade, don't worry about that. Whatever it takes to defeat him, that is what you must do. Do not hold back for my sake. I believe in you, and if I have to suffer to save this kingdom, then so be it. I would be unworthy of my Royal blood if I were not willing to risk it to save the innocent."

"But I'm not…." She stopped as the Sorcerer returned to the laboratory. He was carrying two vials of liquid, and dragging what looked like a coat stand, with tubes running from a jar hanging on one of its pegs into the sleeve of his robe.

"Now my friends," the Sorcerer commanded "you will join me in a drink. Think of it as a toast to your contribution to my greatness." His tone was spectral and macabre in its timbre, as he moved first toward Jeron. With a motion of his hand, he forced Jeron to his feet.

"What are you doing to him?" Hollyglade demanded through gritted teeth. Though she had been rendered unconscious by the Sorcerer's power, she had not witnessed the him employ this level of manipulation. She was shocked at the power she perceived being used upon Jeron. She reacted with a sudden upheaval of her own power, but fought it down instinctively, as she had done so many times before. She cursed herself silently as she did, admonishing herself for not controlling her emotions. She knew that the time to use her power was at hand, but she wanted to be the one to make the decision, she had to be. This could not be allowed to be a reaction, it had to be a function of her intent. She gripped the bars of her cage as she clenched her jaw in frustration.

Seeing her reaction out of the corner of his eye, the Sorcerer responded to her question.

"Bridging the gap, dear girl. Don't worry, you shall understand fully in a few moments."

Jeron stiffly moved to the front of his cage, and grabbed hold of the bars. Pressing his chin to the bars and tilting his head back, Jeron's eyes widened in fear as the Sorcerer poured the contents of one of the vials into Jeron's open mouth. Grinning widely, the Sorcerer stepped away as Jeron swallowed involuntarily, and then fell back from the bars and wiped his face.

Hollyglade watched as Jeron spit out whatever he could of the remains of the liquid that sat in his mouth before he looked at her and shook his head. Before she could process what she was seeing, the Sorcerer moved to Hollyglade's cage and made the same motion to her. She felt a deep pull at the core of her being, urging her to stand. She fought the urge to get up with all her will, yet her arms still pushed her off the floor, and her legs still moved her to the front of the cage. The sensation was painful, yet not entirely unfamiliar. As she struggled to make every effort she could think of to fight the power that manipulated her, she began to understand what she felt.

This was power working on her, not unlike the power that she worked from within her when she had tried to melt the metal bars of the cell in the stone prison. But this was different, backward somehow. Instead of feeling it flow from within her, she felt it bind itself to her, surround her, move her like hands upon her shoulders might restrain her. But she could not overcome it, and she was at the front of the cage with her mouth open, her mind screaming curses of contention.

As the liquid hit the inside of her mouth, her tongue seared with sensations of bitter and sour so strong that she felt nausea instantly. She wanted so badly to spit it out, but could not make herself do so. Fighting hard not to swallow, her mouth closed over the vile concoction, and she unwillingly pushed the liquid into her stomach. As the repugnant potion left her mouth, she felt the power that had encased her depart. Falling to the floor, she spat what remained of the liquid as far as she could.

She began to heave, and hoped that she might bring up the contents of her stomach, but could not coax it forth. As she turned her head, she watched as the Sorcerer consumed the contents of the last vial. Then, he began to laugh in a manner that caused the hair to rise on the back of Hollyglade's neck.

"Ahhhh," crowed the Sorcerer, "the time is nearly here. Under the dark pull of the new moon, I shall take ultimate power, and make it mine. Your gift shall become my strength, and with it I shall place all those who oppose me under my feet. There is no power that shall stop me, no force that will be able to stand against me. The name, Ni'Morstrom the Almighty, shall dominate the histories of this world!"

Hollyglade shrank back from the front of her cage as she watched the sinister diabolist walk to the window and fully open the curtains and shutter to stand in the light of the fading sun. As she observed him, she heard him begin to chant, and could feel the room begin to resonate with the rhythm of his incantation. Her attention was pulled away as Jeron called to her, whispering harshly.

"Hollyglade, you must fight him, you must. I am impotent in this contest, but you have a way to combat him."

"I tried, Jeron. But I couldn't do it. He's too strong, too skilled."

"He is not stronger than you, I am sure of it. If he were, he wouldn't need you. You can overpower him. Please, tell me what you felt when he controlled your movements."

She dropped her head, closed her eyes, took a deep breath to regain her composure and confidence, and then looked to Jeron.

"It felt, in some ways like when I use power to heat stone. It was different, though."

"How?" he whispered as he looked over his shoulder at the chanting sorcerer.

"It wasn't inside me, it was around me, like hundreds of hands grabbing me and moving me, but like water too. Water that moved and became solid as it pushed and pulled me against my will."

Jeron, brought his hand to his chin thoughtfully for a moment, as he stared unfocused to the floor while working the information over in his mind. Then with a look of understanding, he raised his head and met Hollyglade's eyes with his.

"That's it. I think that's it."

"What?" she asked with urgency.

"Water. It's like water."

She looked at him puzzlingly, and waited with anticipation as he worked to express the thought.

"Think of the jug pouring water, or like a waterfall. If you were pouring a jug of water, one that can never go empty because it has a source of more water within in somehow, like you have the source of your power within, and then I come along and start to pour wine into your jug of water. Think of what would happen. The flow of water from your jug would just wash the wine out, push it out, because it can't go up the stream of water coming from the jug.

"Imagine trying to pour a barrel of wine at the base of a waterfall and hoping to stain the riverbed red. The water would just dilute the wine and carry it away. You must become that waterfall. You have to overflow!" He grabbed the bars of his cage in the accentuation of his declaration.

Hollyglade's breathing increased as she tried to translate the analogy into something she could use, something she could do. This made sense to her, yet contradicted everything she had taught herself to do concerning her power. So many years had been spent clamping down on the swell of power, holding back the flow of it, tightening the lid on that proverbial jar. To stop employing those preventative measures would be difficult. To reverse them, and thrust forth the power she had constantly fought to contain, felt like it would be pure folly. But she knew that the thing within her that she must now fight, was no longer the power itself, but her fear of it.

"But Jeron, if I pour out my power at him, won't he just take it?"

"Some of it, probably, but he can't handle all of it. We have to believe that. Think of him like a wine or water skin. Fill him so full of power that he bursts! His plan trusts in the fact that you haven't used your power, and he's banking on you not using it against him. You have to take him by surprise, you have to overwhelm him. You have to try."

She looked at him with a sudden ferocity that told him that she finally believed, that she was ready to fight for something. She clenched her fists and jaw, gritted her teeth, and stood up. The room began to vibrate more intensely, and as Jeron looked between Hollyglade and the Sorcerer, the air began to warp like heat rising from sun-baked rock.

The Sorcerer turned from the window, appearing to sense the change in Hollyglade's mien. He stopped his incantation, and thrust a finger at her as he roared with an otherworldly booming fury,

"You desire to contest with me? I invite you to try!"

He stepped to face her, held both hands out toward her and began to utter a ritual that neither Hollyglade nor Jeron could comprehend. As he did so, the room began to vibrate.

IX : OVERTHROW

As they neared the now demolished gate which lay fragmented under the crippled walls of the great city of Magnaville, King Dermond, Lord Birk, War Marshall Greln, and their accompaniment of more than one hundred soldiers on horseback charged through the fighting which was still taking place on both sides of the opening. When the gate had fallen, Lorian forces had pressed through the opening and taken the fighting to the Demarians outside the wall. There was no clear battle line as men fought intensely both in and outside the entrance to the city.

Many of the Lorian forces had not been able to retreat to within the safety of the city walls when the signal was given, and had been caught facing the whole of the Demarian army in the initial charge. None of those men still survived. Those who had retreated into the city numbered in the thousands still.

Having also lost many troops in the opening offensive, the Demarians were eager to take the fight to the Lorians inside the walls. The fighting was loud, intense, bloody, and severe. Neither side gave any sign of breaking, and the Demarian King's cohort were forced to fight their way to the gate, and through it.

The gate was not wide, and when it had been fully functional and in working order, no more than four horses could ride abreast through its opening. Now that the remnants of the destroyed doors took up much of the space within the frame of the gateway, the debris made it quite narrow.

War Marshall Greln spurred his horse to the front of the attack, and swung his longsword with vicious intent, taking out several Lorian troops in a matter of half a minute. Closely following behind him were several more of the cohort, who joined the attack in close proximity. They were the first mounted fighters to the gate, and cleared the way as the King and the rest of the cohort pressed forward behind them. The battle continued to intensify as the full cohort of mounted soldiers poured through the gate. Once through, more

Demarian forces followed immediately behind.

Then, progress halted. This was Magnaville, and the Lorian forces knew it well. Though the Demarians had managed to get through the gate, they were now essentially boxed in, and at the mercy of the Lorian Spearmen and Archers. Arrows rained down upon the Demarian soldiers as they entered the interior of the city. The Lorian commanders had organised their forces into walls of men, whose spears were twice as long as one man.

King Dermond shouted instructions to his men as the advance ground to a halt.

"Form up behind me! Make a wedge!" came the King's booming voice.

In response, half the cohort moved behind the battle hardy warrior, and pressed forward as one. The King directed the advance toward the main avenue which lead to the centre of the city, and to the castle.

"We push for Whiterock!"

"Lord Wendal, the Demarians have breached the North Gates and are entering the city!" shouted a page who came running into the Vestry Hall, where King Harford was being prepared for evacuation.

"How can that be? How did they get in so quickly?" exclaimed the Lord as a look of shock overcame his visage. "Your Grace, we must make haste, for there may still be time for you to escape unharmed," pleaded Lord Wendal.

The young King did not respond. Hanging his head, he appeared frozen in thought. Overwhelmed by all that swirled about him. His thoughts went to his father. What would he have done? What would my brother have done? Why am I here, instead of him? Without giving a reply, the young King slumped into his throne and dropped his head into his hands.

"Your Grace," pleaded Lord Wendal, "we must act. If we stay here and do nothing, we shall surely be overrun. A fight throughout the castle would be too costly, and likely not one that results in your escape."

Harford then raised his head, and for the first time he bore a look of anger and determination. He had lost everything he truly valued, his father, brother, mother, friends, and even the freedom and innocence of childhood. He felt something within him break, and lost the desire to hold back. He stood and held a finger out toward Quentin Wendal.

"We shall not flee," he asserted "I do not have faith that we shall get beyond the Demarian line. It seems clear to me that you have underestimated them at almost every turn, and I can not assume that this plan of yours shall suddenly be the exception to that trend." He stood and addressed Lord Wendal, and the other commanders assembled there. "You say that the Demarians are within our walls. Well, is this not our city? Do we not have the advantage here? You told me of secret passages. Can we not use these, or some other aspect of our city's construction to confound the enemy? Lord Wendal, you must press that advantage and hold them off, keep them out of Whiterock as long as possible. You must have faith that another opportunity will present itself."

Lord Wendal was taken aback by the King's sudden change in demeanor, and had to take a moment to return his lower jaw back to where it had fallen from. Then, looking to his commanders he issued his orders.

"Men, we must show faith in ourselves and our King. This city has never fallen to an invader, never been broken under siege, and today shall not be the day that changes. Pass the order out to the men fighting everywhere, that they are to use the city's infrastructure to their advantage. Keep the Demarians boxed in at every opportunity and rain arrows on them from above for as long as there are arrows to fire. This is Loria, and we must defend her to the last!"

The assembled men responded with salutes of fist to chest, and looks of renewed determination. Each bowed and hurried off to push their forces to strengthen their resolve to continue the fight. Upon their exit, Lord Wendal turned to the King.

"Your Grace, we must still make some kind of arrangement to ensure that you are protected. Will you not allow me to escort you away in secrecy?"

The young King looked at the Master of The Royal Forces and shook his head.

"No, my Lord. I will not run. I still believe there is hope for our victory. Go now, and put your knowledge to some use in organising the fight."

"Yes, Your Grace". Lord Wendal bowed and exited the hall, leaving the King alone.

"Tedd, where are you?" the King fretted to himself under his breath. When will that Sorcerer make good on his promises?

"Birk! Get those men and fall to me!" shouted Dermond Riaghlad over the din of clashing swords and the buzz of arrows whipping by and slamming into armour and earth. Lord Birk shot the King a look of acknowledgement, and shouted for the two dozen mounted soldiers still fighting together with him to follow. Of the one hundred men who had entered the city with the King, there now remained less than half, and both the King and Lord Birk were determined not to give an inch in their quest to gain access to the castle at the centre of the city.

"Your Grace, this is a stalemate. We are at the advantage on the ground, yet their archers pick us off almost at will. We must not remain here," panted Lord Birk upon reaching the King's side.

"You're right Birk, we must press the advance. We can not play in the streets any longer. Let us make a hard push for the castle gates. How many men have we who still carry axes and warhammers?"

Lord Birk took a quick survey of the men as they continued to fight while keeping himself and the King encircled within their ranks. The Demarian soldiers around them were fighting doggedly, but with a clearly superior skill set. As Lord Birk surveyed the battle taking place around them in the small intersection of two streets within the city walls, not a single Demarian soldier was outmatched on the ground. Surrounded by Lorian army and garrison fighters, the Demarians held their own. The only casualties during the few moments it took for the King and Lord Birk to confer, were a pair of men who were hit by arrows from above.

Though there were a considerable number of archers on the rooftops, they were unable to fire completely at will, as the fighting was in such close quarters, that the risk of hitting their own men was incredibly great. So great, in fact, that a significant number of Lorian casualties came from arrows gone astray.

Lord Birk finished his count and turned to report to the King.

"It appears we have three with warhammers, and two with axes, Your Grace."

"Good. Then now is the time to use these horses for what we've trained them for. We charge for the gate!" Without waiting for acknowledgement, the King raised his sword and shouted to the men surrounding him, "Men! With me! For Glory!"

The Demarian charge was dynamically forceful. As the King lead his thirty men toward the castle gate, more followed on foot. The fighting had been rather stationary up until that point, with soldiers on both sides doing battle in the streets along lines drawn within the first few avenues inside the city walls. When King Dermond broke through the Lorian line at nearly a gallop, it sent men crashing into each other, and a ripple effect went though the Lorian lines, sending them staggering backward just enough to change the momentum of the battle.

Seeing the shift in momentum, the Demarians pressed forward and put the Lorians on their heels. Instead of the Lorian troops holding fast in the narrow streets and alleyways, they were now being pushed back down them by the sheer weight of the advancing Demarian troops. As the front line of the battle spread out and away from the main city gate, more Demarian troops began to pour in through the opening. As the invaders began to flood into the city, ladders were erected on the inside of the city walls and Demarian troops began to fight their way up stairways and onto the elevated positions where the Lorian archers had been raining death down upon the battle below. The shift in momentum was as sudden as it was dramatic.

Swinging his sword from side to side with a force and accuracy unmatched by anyone within the battle, King Dermond broke a pathway toward the castle gate. In the two hundred yards from the intersection to the gate, Dermond Riaghlad slew more than a dozen enemy soldiers from the saddle. Upon reaching the gate, he turned and fought left and right to allow his cohort to form up around the heavy doors.

"Bring the axes and warhammers!" he cried as he struck down another Lorian soldier.

"To the door!" Lord Birk shouted. In response, the four men who made it to the gate moved their way through the fighting and began to attack the heavy steel reinforced doors to the courtyard which surrounded the tower of Whiterock. The fighting grew fierce around the gate as the Lorians tried to rally to defend the entrance to Whiterock. Forces from both sides poured into the square and the sounds of the clash of metal on metal became cacophonous.

King Dermond's horse became pressed against the wall to the left of the door, as the crushing mob began to run out of room to fight.

"Birk! Get that door open!" he cried as he switched his longsword to his left hand to fight off a spearman who had managed to get past several Demarian fighters. Hacking through the shaft of the spear, Dermond was forced off his horse as his right leg was nearly crushed against the wall. Once on the ground, he pulled his shield from the horn of his saddle as he whirled a slash at the Lorian soldier coming to the attack, and switched his sword back to his right.

With sword and shield at the ready, he set his back toward the gate and unleashed a frenzied attack on several Lorian soldiers who had managed to squeeze through the line. Taking down one with a simple shield block and counter strike, the King was unable to stop all three, and a single soldier managed to stab through the back of one of the Demarian soldiers hammering away at the castle gate. Seeing the man fall, Lord Birk leapt from his horse to join his King on the ground, and cut the Lorian soldier from shoulder to crotch in a massively powerful strike.

Standing side by side with King Dermond, Lord Birk yelled over his shoulder to the soldiers trying to hold a circle around the gate.

"You there, come pick up that hammer and move to the gate!" In response, one of the soldiers stepped back from the line, parried a stab from the Lorian he was engaged with, and stuck a fatal counter blow to the neck. Turning and picking up the fallen soldier's warhammer, he then began to join the others beating on the gate.

"Just the way I like it!" exclaimed the King as he cut down another Lorian soldier. "Bloody and desperate!"

"Glorious, indeed!" replied Lord Birk as he blocked a slash, leaned back to deliver a kick to the gut, and then brought his sword down on the back of the neck of the tall and well built Lorian trooper.

As the slain soldier hit the stone of the street concourse outside the gate, Lord Birk heard a sudden and powerful crack. Turning to look at the gate, he could now see that it was bent inward, and nearly open.

"Men, to the gate! Push with all your might!" he bellowed.

In response, the Demarian soldiers who were close by turned and thrust for the gate, pressing all their collective weight against it. Hearing the cry, the Demarians who had been slowly fighting their way toward the castle from the city gate, moved with renewed vigor and formed a wedge behind their King and Lord Birk. After a few short moments, the gate gave way, and the Demarians burst through the gate and into the castle's tower courtyard to be greeted by a shower of arrows and crossbow bolts. With shields held overhead, the Demarian force pushed toward the doors to the main castle keep, fighting for every yard of ground they covered.

Hollyglade stood facing the Sorcerer as his chanting reached full volume. She could feel the power surge forth from him as he countered her initial offering. This was new to her, and the sensations were overwhelming. She had felt what it is like to be punched, kicked, shoved, stepped on, and thrown to the ground, but this kind of attack was wholly different. She felt physical pain like burning, crawling across her skin, yet also the pain of something she could not describe penetrating her to the core. She imagined this must be what being struck by lightning would feel like. As the Sorcerer cackled his delight at the sight of her wincing in pain, she felt like she might pass out from the torment.

"Hollyglade!" Jeron shouted to her. "fight back!"

Her eyes darted toward Jeron for a split second to see him holding the bars of his cage to keep himself from falling to the ground, and then back to the Sorcerer. She knew that if she was to avoid being consumed and destroyed by this struggle, she would have to fight back, would have to win. She gritted her teeth, lowered her head, and narrowed her eyes as she focused her concentration inward, fighting through the pain of the attack surging upon her. With a determination of her will, she forced her power upward from within her, and directed it against the flow of magic that cascaded over her.

Slowly, she began to feel the pain within her recede as her own power forced back the incursion of the Sorcerer's barrage. Feeling the success of the effort, Hollyglade intensified the force of her power, drawing strength from it, calling it up from deep within her, and thrusting it outward in all directions to push away the offensive intrusion. She stared down the Sorcerer as she clenched her fists, flexing her arms and shoulders as she pressed back against him with the power she called forth. She could feel the tide turn in her favour as the last of the effects of his attack were forced out of her by the exudation of her inwardly formed defense.

Seeing the change in the her, the Sorcerer howled in anger and began to shout his incantations at her, stepping forward and leaning into his efforts to overcome her strength. As he did so, Hollyglade responded with greater focus and force, and the air in the room began to swirl about them. The curtains that had been covering the windows began to flap erratically, like flags flying in a thunderstorm. The shutters began to open and close with the push and pull of the vibrating torrent of wind and power that thrashed about the laboratory. Several of them tore from their hinges and flew out to the courtyard below. The air warped around the Sorcerer in concentric circles of thaumaturgical rippling, creating vibrations in the floor and walls, knocking over vials, jars, bowls, plates, candle holders, and almost everything else that was set upon the tables and shelves in the room.

Hollyglade felt the increase in his attack once more, and responded with a re-intensification of her own production and wielding of power. The result forced the Sorcerer backward from her as the pressure of sustaining his magical onslaught created a repulsive wave between them.

As the battle raged between them, Jeron watched in fear and amazement at the astonishing and brutal unleashing of power from each of them. He did his best to dodge the flying debris that made its way between the bars of his cage, but now the waves of power themselves were beginning to reach him as they expanded outward from between the two combatants. He moved to the far edge of his cage and pressed against the bars to try to separate himself from the battle raging between Hollyglade and the Sorcerer.

Their contest intensified as he looked on, and he could now smell the air becoming hot, and could see the distortion waves emanating from each of them. Hollyglade appeared to be holding her own, but Jeron could not tell if she was able to affect the Sorcerer, or if she was simply keeping him from invading her. As he watched, he began to feel heat and pain pressing against him, forcing him up against the bars of the cage. He did his best not to cry out, for fear of distracting Hollyglade. He was determined to allow her to battle this evil manipulator unabated, but was now suffering from the radiating waves of energetic force that bombarded his body. He could not hold back the cry, as he was driven to the ground, and yelped in pain.

Hollyglade's attention wavered as she heard a howl from beside her coming from Jeron's cage. She quickly glanced away from the Sorcerer to see Jeron lying on the floor in a ball holding himself and shaking in pain. Her heart jumped into her throat in response and she stopped the flow of her power as she saw what the battle she waged had done.

Her mind shrank from her counterattack as she felt the guilt of all the collateral damage she had caused in her lifetime, and all the collateral damage that had been caused in the last weeks' pursuit of her, come to a head in her mind.

"Jeron! No!" She yelled as she jumped to the edge of her cage to grab the bars, trying to will herself through them to go to him. As she did so, she felt a blast of energy knock her from where she stood. She was instantly thrown back to the far end of her cage, where she slammed into the bars and slid to the floor.

With a roaring and bloodcurdling laugh, the Sorcerer howled at her

"You are no match for me, girl!" He dropped hands and stepped closer to her cage. "You have no skill. No discipline. You throw power about with no chance to see it land where you desire. You wish to oppose me, yet all you manage is to batter the precious Prince while giving me an entertaining yet paltry display of emotional conjury." He took in a long breath, and looked to the window to see the sun hitting the horizon.

Then, the Sorcerer turned back to Hollyglade.

"You have but a few precious minutes left girl. Make your pleas to whatever gods you believe in, for I shall not spare you now." He turned from her momentarily to examine the bottle which was still hanging next to him, feeding its contents through the tubes that disappeared into his robes.

Hollyglade looked at Jeron and winced under the pain of guilt she felt over having caused him harm.

"Jeron, I can't fight him. It'll kill you. I just can't do it," she sobbed apologetically.

"Hollyglade, you can, and you must. And if I die as a bystander in the battle, then I go to the grave as a proud man. I willingly lay down my life as a sacrifice to preserve the triumph of good over evil." He grabbed the bars of his cage and pulled himself up, walking over to Hollyglade. He did not care to whisper now, as he knew that no matter what he said, no matter who heard him, that he must convince this girl, this half Elvish, half Giantish possessor of unlimited power, to use her gifts for the good of all kind. He knew that if this Sorcerer were to prevail against this innocent girl here, that he would destroy the innocent everywhere.

"Hollyglade, I believe in you. I trust you. You must believe in and trust yourself. It is he who is no match for you. You are the possessor of unlimited power. You are the one called Wayrender, and Firebrand of the Western plains. You are the one who can save the people of this land. You must focus your power on him, and drive it into him until he is rent. Outside these walls, men are fighting and dying for what they believe in. I am ready to do the same. Had I a sword, I would slay this manipulator, tear him asunder for faking my death, manipulating my innocent brother, and setting two Kingdoms against each other and causing the deaths of thousands. Hollyglade," he bored his stare into her eyes as he paused to grab her attention fully, "defeat him."

Tears rolled down her cheeks as she grabbed the bars of her cage and pulled herself up. Turning to face the Sorcerer once more, she clenched her fists and held them in front of her chest, looking at her knuckles as she began to gather the power within her.

Sensing her change in demeanor, Ni'Morstrom turned from

the glass jar that was now empty, and pulled the tubes out from within his robes, causing a trail of blood to run down his arm and drip from his fingertips.

"You still think you have something to oppose me with, girl?" he snapped, seething with anger and violence. "You overestimate your chances with me, for you have none! I am no mere charmer, plying cheap tricks and prestidigitation. I am no simple enchanter performing silly spectacles for the amusement of the crowd. I am Ni'Morstrom! Hereafter I shall be known as the all powerful! I am no young wizard, and I am not merely from the line of Sorcerers, not simply one of the House of The Distorted, I am the last and greatest of their kind!

"I am the triumphant one who slew all those who opposed me in the great fall of my order. I have defied the decline of age, I have defied the diminishing of my flesh, and I shall defy you, girl! You have no strength, no control, no finesse, and certainly not the stamina to measure yourself against me. I have stood the test of generations of men, and not been swayed from my goal. Now that it is within my grasp, I shall endure no contention from such as you.

"Try your hand. Test yourself again, if you dare. This time, I shall not release you from the contest with breath in your lungs." He raised his hands once more, and thrust them toward Hollyglade as he began to recite his incantations with resonant vehemence.

This time Hollyglade was ready. This time she invited his attack. This time, she did not hold herself back. With all her will, she focused on her enemy, bored into him with her mind and targeted the core of his being. She let out a yell as she poured out her power at him, blocking out all the periphery about her, and narrowing the scope of her vision and concentration on the Sorcerer. She could feel the immense unleashing of power burst forth from within her, and force its way through the space between her and the Sorcerer. She could sense, with an almost tactile surety, the flow of her power drive back the magic of her enemy and plunge into him.

As it did, he surprised her by ceasing his attack.

The Sorcerer stood fully upright and opened his arms wide to push his chest into the stream of Hollyglade's power. He threw his head back, dropping the hood of his robe, and revealing his scarred and wrinkled visage. Laughing maniacally, he brought his red and yellowed eyes down to glare menacingly at her.

"Your eagerness to wage battle with me is your undoing, girl! I welcome your foolish volley! You try to destroy me, yet you fill my vast reservoir! Ha! Do not be shy. I shall take it all!"

She slowed slightly as doubt began to creep into her conscious mind. This was what her father had warned her about, telling her not to use her power to fight, but only to heal. This was more power than she had ever allowed herself to release, and this was more than a release, this was a thrust. She wavered as she began to question her own resolve. Could she see this through? Was this really the strategy? Was there really a limit to how much power this sorcerer could absorb? Then, a voice broke through the sounds of the whirling air, and vibration of her power. It was Jeron's.

"More, Hollyglade! Don't stop! More!"

"Yes! More!" howled the Sorcerer with a perverse enthusiasm.

Hollyglade made up her mind, and drove the doubt away with the force of her power. With a step forward, she leaned toward the target of her thrust, the focus of her onslaught, and unleashed the full force of her power in a stream of anger. With all her emotion, she drove her strength at him, forced her power into him with righteous fury. Anger for the loss of her friend dGerrie, for the loss of those whom The Dancer had slain in his pursuit of her, for the loss of the troops dGerrie had been forced to kill or injure in his upright defense of her, for the countless people who had died when those bounty hunters had tried to kidnap her ten years ago, provoking her to an explosion of grief. For her parents, who had died trying to protect her from those same bounty hunters.

As she continued to drive her power at him, the bars of the cell that were in the path of her strike began to melt, and in a matter of seconds dropped to the floor in pools of molten iron. Seeing the path was now clear, she began to step forward toward the Sorcerer. As she did so, his face slowly started to change from an expression of sinister pleasure, to one of uncertain apprehension. The change was not lost on Hollyglade, and she stayed her course, forcing her power into him. As her attack continued, the Sorcerer's face took on a look of panic, and Hollyglade reached out to him with her mental perception, not knowing if she would be able to read anything. To her surprise, she read him, read that he was starting to break, that he was transitioning from a state of the fullness of power, to one about to burst at the seams. She could almost see it, as he tried to close himself off to the influx of her stream of power, and failed.

She stepped through the opening in the cage created by the battle raging between her and the Sorcerer. As she cleared the pools of liquid metal, which began to catch the wooden floor alight, she could feel some resistance to the flow of her power. Looking the Sorcerer in his sickly and bloodshot eyes, she saw his expression harden again as he once more took up his attack upon her.

The struggle between them became visible, as bolts of blue and azure lightning shot from where the force of each of their wills met and contested to gain the momentum in this battle for supremacy.

"You shall not prevail, girl!" shouted the Sorcerer as he leaned toward her and began to unleash the full breadth of his might. The point at which each of their streams of dynamism met began to move toward Hollyglade, and the bolts of lightning that shot from the centre of their conflict began to curl toward her.

She felt the jolts of vibrating light brush against her, causing heat and pain, as she tried to resist the pressure of his revived attack. It seemed like it was becoming more than she could handle as she fell to one knee and cried out when the injured joint touched down on the floor. Yet she did not yield, did not give in, did not waver in her determination to overcome him. She kept on fighting as her skin began to register the searing heat created by the bolts of dark blue, white, and azure. She fought on as her teeth began to vibrate and the taste of acid filled her mouth, as the tiny hairs on her arms became singed and filled her nostrils with the stench of their burning. She did not give in as he took a step toward her and grinned a sinister and sickly smirk at the sight of her wincing in pain.

The tide had turned, and she needed to turn it back, she needed to stand up and intensify her attack on him, take it to a level that no one could withstand. As she leaned forward to try to stand up, something caught a small part of her attention from the corner of her eye. The door to the laboratory had been blown off its hinges in the fury of the storm created by this contest of power, and now she saw a tall man step through it. She could not make him out clearly through the blinding light of the explosive expression of power converging between her and the Sorcerer.

She could not afford to turn her attention away from the Sorcerer now, and so she chose not to react when she saw the man make a motion to take something out from behind his back. She decided to take the calculated risk that the storm of energy raging between her and the Sorcerer would prevent interference. Ignoring the man, she turned her full attention back to the Sorcerer.

With a yell, she stood up and leaned forward, stretching her arms toward him as she pushed out power with the full concentration of her mind. As she intensified her attack upon the Sorcerer, trying to swing the tide back in her favour, she saw him shift his gaze to the door, to the man who had come through it.

dGerrie moved across the open space between the soldier's mess and the doors at the bottom of the Tower of Whiterock, yet not without leaving a trail of blood droplets across the courtyard. While he traversed the courtyard, he watched as all the men within it had run to the gate at the edge which led to the streets outside the castle walls. He could hear the pounding of warhammers on the outside of the gate, and the raucous clashing of heavy fighting taking place beyond it. Upon reaching the base of the tower, he looked back at the gates to see men trying desperately to find things to reinforce the steel framed wooden doors. He did not expect them to hold out long.

dGerrie limped along the wall at the base of the tower, leaning on it and leaving bloody handprints on the stone as tried to keep his balance. Once he reached the entrance to the tower, he found it locked, as was to be expected. Reaching into his tunic, he pulled out a small knife, one that might serve as a sharp dining implement in the hand of the average citizen, and fed it into the keyhole. With a few delicate movements, he found the tooth he searched for within the keyhole, and rotated the knife carefully until he felt the click of the lock releasing. Holding the knife steady, he lifted the door latch and opened the door no more than a crack and slipped inside, closing it behind him.

Before moving away, he made sure to secure the lock from the inside. Once he was sure that the door was locked again, he looked about the interior of the tower base, and found the stairs leading upward. Limping toward them, he drew his short sword and took a lit torch from its sconce on the wall. He began to climb the stairs slowly, fighting the pain each time he was forced to lift his injured right leg.

As he ascended, he began to hear sounds coming from above. Sounds of glass and pottery breaking, things falling over, and the sound of wind. dGerrie was filled with confusion and apprehension, as it had not been windy outside the tower, and he wondered what sort of magical dangers he might be getting himself into as he made for the apartment of the Sorcerer. He pushed the fear to the back of his mind, as he focused on the fact that any dangers he would face, he must confront in order to get his friend out of them.

Climbing the stairs as quickly as his hobbled frame would let him, dGerrie gained elevation at a slow, but steady pace. At about the halfway point, he reached the guard's lookout to find it empty. This must have been due to the emergent situation at the gate below. He took a moment to look out from the tower's loopholes to see the gate burst open, and a swarm of Demarian troops pour through the smashed courtyard doors. Fighters from both sides shouted, as the Demarians cheered their advance, and the Lorians screamed to each other to regroup. dGerrie knew that this meant his time was running out, and he did his best to increase his pace as he turned from the loophole and resumed his arduous progress upward.

After several more flights of stairs, he could hear voices above, but could not make out what was being said, though the tone was obviously furiously impassioned and sinister. As he climbed another flight of stairs, he heard something frightening, the sound of lightning cracking amidst wind, and the sounds fabric tearing, wood splintering, doors being ripped opened, and furniture being knocked over. He did not know what to make of the mixture of sounds. Was he heading into a tornado contained within the walls of the tower? He pressed on and tried to cover the last few flights of stairs as quickly as he could.

Rounding the corner at the top of the last flight of stairs leading to the Sorcerer's apartment, dGerrie felt the full force of the wind coming from the battered doorway. He stopped with his sword at the ready as he noticed a boot just beyond the curve of the wall leading to the doorway. It appeared as though there was someone sitting on the floor against the wall opposite the door to the apartment. He approached slowly, planning to take the guard by surprise. As he got closer, he could see that the boot belonged to someone lying on the floor in a pool of their own blood. dGerrie crept closer, and found the body of a young man dressed in a page's uniform, with a large fragment of the wooden door lodged in his chest. dGerrie swallowed hard and took a deep breath, as the realization of the variety of perils that lay beyond that door hit him. He looked away from the page and turned his attention back to entering the apartment.

There was no door left in the frame, and dGerrie could see into the room through the sliver of doorway visible around the corner from where he approached. Through it, he could make out some steel bars, and an assortment of debris from the wreckage being caused by the whirling wind. The crackling sounds continued, and flashes of light came from somewhere just out of his line of sight within the room. He could not delay any longer, he knew he must act now, and so he moved toward the door.

As the interior of the room became visible to him, dGerrie could see the furious storm erupting within, and from where it emanated. There before him was Hollyglade, embroiled in some indescribable battle of power with a robed figure, whose head was scarred, eyes yellow and bloodshot. The Sorcerer he had heard about was attacking his friend with some sort of arcane incanted diabolism. He had to help her, had to intervene.

In a split second, dGerrie analyzed his tactical options, and acted. Dropping his sword, he reached for two daggers tucked in the back of his scabbard, and pulled them out. As he did so, the Sorcerer turned toward him with a face twisted into an expression of frenzied rage.

dGerrie did not hesitate. He did not delay to take aim. He did not hold back. With every ounce of strength and accuracy he possessed, dGerrie hurled both daggers at the Sorcerer.

His aim was perfect, the rotation of the daggers was sublime, and the force with which he sent them to their target was ample.

Both daggers buried themselves in the Sorcerer's chest, and as they did, an explosion of power shot out from him, sending him flying away from Hollyglade and into the wall behind. The wall did not hold, as the force of Hollyglade's continued attack tore a massive hole in the side of the tower and sent the Sorcerer flying out from the laboratory.

The blast burst forth from between Hollyglade and the Sorcerer, sending a shockwave in all directions, blowing out the remaining shutters on the windows and flattening to the floor everything that still stood in the laboratory. dGerrie tried to cover his head as the blast erupted, but he was knocked back against the wall, slid to the ground, and everything turned black.

Once through the gate and into the courtyard, King Dermond's cohort were met by a host of Lorian troops. The barrage of arrows from above was immediate, fighting toward the Keep with their shields held above their heads to protect themselves from the threat from above. As a result, many Demarians fell to the swords of the Lorian soldiers on the ground in the initial charge through the gate. Once the second wave of Demarians flooded through into the courtyard and engaged the Lorians in close quarters, the arrows began to hit both sides equally, and ceased after several moments.

King Dermond did not hesitate once through the gate, and engaged with the first Lorain soldier that met him. Parrying a backhanded slash with his sword, he thrust his shield into the attacker's neck, and followed with a slash through the gut. Stepping over the fallen trooper, he was met by a soldier with an axe swinging for his head. The King was quick to react, and brought his shield up to meet the blow, which came with such tremendous force, that it buried the axe head in the shield and split it from top to bottom. Before the attacker could pull his weapon back out from where it had become stuck, the King pulled on the shield, and therefore the axe with it, and yanked the attacker off balance toward himself, thrusting his sword into the man's side. The attacker dropped to the ground, and the King slipped his arm out of the shield's grip, letting it fall while slashing the back of the attacker's neck. Now, with both hands on his sword, he leapt over the downed axeman with a pirouette, and brought his blade down on the shoulder of the next trooper who had stepped toward him, knocking him to the ground and opening a deep crevice below his neck.

"Birk! Greln!" he shouted as he brought his blade up to block an over hand cut. "To the steps!" With a half pirouette, he slammed his shoulder into the soldier whose sword had met his, knocking him backward and turning another half pirouette as he followed up with a swipe across the face of the soldier. Looking back to see both the Lord and War Marshall leading a group of fighters toward him, he heard a loud cracking sound from above. As he turned his attention toward the sound, he saw fragments of wooden window shutters falling from near the top of the Central Tower of Whiterock.

Looking back around him, the Lorian troops had also been distracted by the sound, and the King took advantage, cutting down a spearman whose focus was not on his foe. The distraction did not last long, and the fighting continued at a frenzied pace, though the tide had turned in favour of the invaders. Now the King was joined by the full force of the reinforcements who had finally made it through both gates.

"Your Grace, we have the advantage in numbers within the courtyard," reported Lord Birk as he arrived at the King's side after dropping an enemy with a trip and slash to the back.

"Let us work to gain entry to the keep, My Lord. Our goal is most certainly to be reached somewhere within."

Lord Birk gave a shout to the Demarian soldiers fighting in the courtyard

"To the Keep!" and nodded to the King, as they both turned and began to climb the steps of the entrance to the Keep. As they did so, the bulk of the Demarian forces were directed by the War Marshall to form a wall behind them. With shields raised to create a barrier from the arrows being fired once again by Lorian archers, they moved up the stairs slashing and cutting their way forward. Once halfway up the stairs, the arrows seemed to stop coming, and a shout went up from the melee below. Lord Birk turned to see what had changed, and gave a triumphant yell as he informed the King

"Your Grace, War Marshall, our troops engage the enemy on the battlements! We may advance at full pace!"

Yerin Greln shouted instructions for the men to form a wedge behind the King and Lord Birk, and the cohort began to push forward up the stairs to the door as more Demarian troops continued to enter the courtyard. The fighting upon the stairs was fierce, but the momentum of the Demarian wedge was too much for the castle's defenders. In a matter of a minute, the King was at the door to the keep.

"Hammers!" called King Dermond as he knocked to the ground another valiant yet overmatched Lorian soldier. Two men made their way through the centre of the wedge as the fighting continued along its edge. When they reached the doors, they began the work of breaking them open. It would not take long, as these doors were not meant to be defensive.

Just as the doors gave way, another booming explosive crash came from the tower, and The King looked up, raising his arms to shield himself, expecting some form of attack. To his amazement, he saw a flash of blue and white light accompanied by wood and stone debris erupting from near the top of the tower. Nearly the entirety of the combatants, on both sides looked up in shock and horror as the top of the tower shifted slightly and a began to crumble above the giant, gaping hole in the side of the tower facing the Keep. His attention was quickly called back to the Keep as the sound of the door bursting inward snapped him back to the task at hand. As the doors gave way, the Demarians poured through and into the foyer. The King, Lord Birk, and Yerin Greln were all among the first wave through the door.

Upon entering the foyer, they were met with a handful of garrison troops, who initially made motions to engage the invading Demarians, but quickly dropped their weapons once it was clear they were impossibly outnumbered. King Dermond sheathed his sword, and stepped in front of his men who held the Lorian garrison at the tips of their swords.

"Where is your boy King?" he asked in a surprisingly subdued tone.

Out from the doorway to the main hall of the keep stepped Quentin Wendal.

"His Grace, King Harford will see you, Your Grace," he said as he bowed respectfully and turned to the side, motioning with his hand toward the far end of the hall.

The King nodded to his men, and Lord Birk, War Marshall Greln, and most of the cohort sheathed their weapons and ascended the steps to the hall. Several dozen Demarians stayed behind to guard the Lorian garrison, and the door to the hall.

Entering the Main Hall, his face, grey hair, and ornate armour sprayed with the blood of numerous fallen Lorian soldiers, King Dermond Riaghlad marched across the floor of the main hall to the dais, where the child King, Harford Peaksoul sat upon the throne of Loria.

As King Dermond approached, Harford stood and bowed low,

"Your Grace."

"Your Grace," King Dermond replied from the edge of the dais. "The City of Magnaville, the Castle Whiterock, are mine. Though skirmishes continue as we speak, you are defeated. Though I have not received word on the wing, I am confident that Westport and the harbour of Magnaville have fallen also. Accept your defeat, and I shall sound the horn of detente, so that no more men need die in a battle already lost."

The young King looked to his Master of the Royal Forces, who nodded his reply, and then back to the warrior King before him. Taking his crown from his head, Harford stepped down the stairs of the dais, and held it out with both hands, tears welling in his eyes.

As Dermond Riaghlad took the golden circlet from the now deposed juvenile ruler, Lord Birk whistled to the troops at the entrance to the hall, waving his hand in the sign to cease the fighting. King Dermond carried the crown of Loria up the steps of the dais, turned, and lowered himself into the ornate throne. As he did so, three blasts of a horn could be heard from outside the walls, followed shortly thereafter by ringing of castle bells. As the sun disappeared below the horizon, King Dermond drew a breath of victory, and Loria became subject to his rule.

X : EGRESSION

"dGerrie!" screamed Hollyglade as she turned to see her friend, one she had assumed was dead, now slumped on the floor. She ran across the room cursing herself for not controlling her power, hoping beyond hope that dGerrie was merely unconscious, and had survived the blast. Upon reaching him, she grabbed him around the shoulders and pulled him close. To her amazement and relief, he took a breath, though he did not rouse.

"dGerrie, you have to wake up! Please! I need you!" she cried as she felt the floor begin to shake. Looking around her, she could see cracks in the walls and ceiling, dust falling from above, and could hear the sounds of the structure above her starting to give way.

"Hollyglade!" came the call from behind her. "I need your help to get out. We need to get down from the tower!"

She turned to see Jeron pulling himself to his feet, his face dripping with blood from a wound hidden somewhere in his disheveled hair, his arms and legs covered in scrapes, and his clothes torn to rags.

"The lock. We might be able to break it, then I can help carry him down and out of the tower."

Hollyglade looked at dGerrie's face, which appeared almost peaceful under the fresh scrapes which oozed with blood, and at his arms and legs where she found several fresh bleeding cuts. Her heart pounded with fear and urgency as she lay him down and tore herself away, turning to see how she could help free Jeron.

She moved quickly to the door of the cage, and examined the lock. She looked up from it as Jeron's hand met hers through the bars, touching her for the first time, his eyes welling with tears, and his face bearing the depth of his appreciation.

"Thank you for saving us. I owe you my life."

She nodded, and looked back to the lock.

"I haven't saved us completely, yet. This looks damaged,

so I don't think I can pick it. We'll have to break it somehow." She took a look around her for something strong enough to use to try to smash the lock. Everything was broken and splintered, and there was nothing she could see that would work like a hammer. As she moved away from the cage to dig beneath some of the rubble, the roof let out a loud series of cracking noises, and began to collapse around the hole made by the sorcerer's forced defenestration.

"Hollyglade," shouted Jeron "the sword!" He pointed to the blade that had fallen from dGerrie's hand when he had entered the room. The tip of the blade was showing from beneath a fallen wardrobe. Hollyglade hopped over an assortment of broken furniture, smashed bowls and jars, her still healing knees, calf muscle, and feet screaming at her as she landed. Upon reaching the wardrobe, she tried to pull the sword out from under it, only to have her fingers slip off the end of the blade.

"It's wedged in. I can't pull it out. I'm going to try to lift the cabinet."

She slipped her fingers under the corner of the large and soundly constructed piece of furniture, and began to try to raise it off the sword. It did not move as she let out a long groan while straining against its weight. She looked back to Jeron and shook her head. Looking at dGerrie, she wished he were awake and well enough to help. Then, it struck her. She remembered he usually carried a multitude of blades.

She quickly stepped back over to him, grabbed him around the ribs, and carefully rolled him over.

"I'm sorry, Stilt. Please forgive me. I hope this doesn't hurt too much," she whispered apologetically. To her relief, she found a second sword, strapped to his back, which had slipped down behind him. Pulling the blade from its sheath, she returned to the cage. Looking at Jeron through the bars, she took a step back. "Back up. I'm going to give it a try," she said as she wound up to take a swing at the lock.

With all her strength, Hollyglade brought the sword down on the lock. The vibration that shot through the weapon into her hands and up her arms, caused her to drop the blade. As it hit the ground with a clatter, more of the roof caved in behind her, and she dropped to the floor covering her head instinctively.

"We have to get out of here now!" she yelled as she picked up the weapon and wound up for another strike.

"Wait!" shouted Jeron, "I have an idea. Bring that here." He motioned for her to come to the door of the cage. "Give me that," he said, reaching through the bars for the sword. "We're going to have to do this together." He placed the tip of the blade in the lock's shackle and placed both hands on the hilt of the sword. "Grab ahold with me," he said, holding the blade ready. She nodded, and placed her hands on its crossguard.

"On three, we drive the blade down through the lock. Understand?"

"Yes, let's go," she replied as she tried to gather her strength.

"One, two, three!"

Together, they drove the blade down as hard as they could, each letting out a cry of exertion. As they pushed the blade into the lock's shackle, it gave way and popped out from the slide holding the door in place. Jeron immediately pushed the door open, and stepped through it. With a deep breath, he grabbed Hollyglade, squeezing her in a deep hug, then letting go and meeting her eyes with his. With a nod to each other, they moved quickly to where dGerrie lay, still unconscious by the door to the laboratory.

"Help me get him up, I'll need to stretch him across my back, and we'll need to lighten the load. Grab whatever blades he has, and strap them to yourself, we may need them later," Jeron commanded, serious and focused.

Hollyglade took one of dGerrie's arms and pulled him up as far as she could. To her amazement, Jeron, having the look of a starving orphan himself, pulled all six and a half feet of her friend onto his back, and began to push himself up to stand.

With a tremendous groan, almost a yell, Jeron lifted himself to his feet, holding his slumped payload across his shoulders. He amazed even himself, as he found a burst of strength in the midst of the life-threatening crisis.

"Let's get out of here, fast!" he said, straining under the weight as he headed for the stairwell.

Hollyglade slung the scabbard she had taken from dGerrie over her shoulder, and followed Jeron through what remained of the doorway. Turning right, they headed down the staircase toward the bottom of the tower. Halfway down the first flight of stairs, Hollyglade heard a loud cracking sound, and turned to see the doorway itself begin to slant to one side as the top of the tower started to let go of its attachment.

"Go!" she shouted, placing a hand on Jeron's back to steady him as much as she could while urging him downward. They descended a flight of stairs quickly, as the tower crumbled above them, and fragments of the wood and plaster interior walls rained down upon them.

"The whole tower is going to come down on our heads if we don't get out of here," shouted Hollyglade, the fear and desperation in her voice urging Jeron down.

"If we can make it down before it falls on us, we can get to safety" he shouted in reply as he began to take the stairs two at a time.

"How? The whole army is out there fighting the Demarians."

"Just leave that to me. But we have to get down these stairs quickly."

As they descended, the sounds of the tower breaking apart above them grew louder. Jeron pressed his pace downward, doing his best to balance dGerrie's limp body on his shoulders as he went.

"Hollyglade, watch out for this trip step," he called, indicating one of the defensive features of the tower, designed to give defenders an advantage over attackers who would be unfamiliar with the staircases. She hopped down it, groaning as her injured knee and feet dealt with the extra pressure of the landing. Once down that flight of stairs, they reached the lower defensive ring, and Hollyglade took a half second to look out through one of the archer's loopholes. To her surprise, the fighting had seemed to stop, and some men were directing others to lay down weapons in piles within the courtyard. She could not look on any longer, as Jeron was making his way down the last flight of stairs.

Catching up to him, she relayed her observations.

"Jeron, it looks like the fighting has stopped, and one side is rounding up the other."

"Which side rounds up the other?" he asked with clear apprehension.

"I don't know the Demarian colours, how can I tell?"

"Lorian forces will have white tunics, maybe some purple will be visible on the white. Demarians will be blue, mostly"

Hollyglade's face dropped, and she felt her trepidation rise. She did not want to tell him what she had seen. Sensing her hesitance, he turned to look at her, reading on her face the answer she was afraid to utter.

"Then the capital is in Demarian hands," he fretted, shaking his head. They were now only half a flight of stairs from the tower foyer, and could hear the structure above gradually continuing to crumble. Jeron looked at Hollyglade, brought a finger to his lips to signal her to remain quiet, and waved her close to him.

"There may be guards, or Demarian forces around the corner down there. We will need to get by them, and into a secret set of tunnels, the door to which is hidden behind some woodwork below us."

She nodded and drew the sword she had slung on her back. Jeron reached his hand out and grabbed her forearm to stop her from heading down the stairs.

"No. Take him," he whispered as he indicated to dGerrie "You may be powerful with magic, but I am trained with the sword, and I know my home. Take him, and I'll make sure we have a clear path."

Hollyglade hesitated for a moment, as the sounds of the tower collapsing drew closer, and the floor began to shake.

Jeron set dGerrie down on the stairs, and took the sword from her, drawing one of the daggers from the scabbard as well.

"Can you lift him? If you can bring him down behind me, it will save us time." He did not wait for an answer. "We must be swift" he whispered as he grinned, turned down the stairs, and descended silently on his bare feet.

Hollyglade knelt down, wincing in pain as her knee complained of its still healing wounds. With all the strength she could muster, she pulled at dGerrie's arms to try to get him onto her shoulders. He groaned as she shoved her back under his chest, and she stopped to look at his face. His eyelids remained shut, but she could see his eyes shifting side to side beneath them. Something caught her attention from below, as the sounds of crumbling stone and mortar continued to draw near from above.

The sounds of metal crashing against metal, rang through the stairwell in a short series, followed by the sound of a yelp and a body hitting the floor. Hollyglade, pulled the remaining dagger from the scabbard and held it out, straddling dGerrie defensively. She glanced down at her friend to see his eyes begin to flutter, but quickly turned back to the stairs below her as she heard footsteps. Her heart pounded as the footfalls approached, and she tightened her grip on the dagger. She coiled herself to spring forward as she heard the man coming closer, knowing he would come into view any second.

Hollyglade flinched so intensely that she nearly fell over as she stopped herself mid strike upon seeing the barefooted Jeron round the corner. Then she felt hands on her thighs, and looked down to see dGerrie trying to pull himself up, reaching for a weapon hidden in his jerkin.

"dGerrie!" she cried "Stop, you'll hurt yourself. It's alright, he's a friend," she said as she grabbed his shoulders, steadying him.

"Come on, we have to move!" urged Jeron, in a somewhat hushed, yet forceful tone.

Hollyglade slid the dagger back into its sheath, and put an arm around dGerrie to balance him.

"Can you walk?"

"I think so." he replied, "Who are you?" he asked, looking at Jeron.

"I'm the one who's going to get us out of the city, but only if we move quickly. This way." Jeron signalled for them to follow, and returned back to the foyer.

Hollyglade braced dGerrie as best she could, and they moved down to the bottom of the tower.

"Sprout, what happened back there? Where's that Sorcerer? Who is this man with you?" he asked while flinching and groaning his way down the last few steps.

"He's a friend. I'll introduce you properly later. The Sorcerer's gone, I'm pretty sure. I'll explain as much as I can once we're out of this tower."

The shaking in the floor began to increase drastically, and Jeron shouted from around the corner.

"Hollyglade, help me move this!"

Jeron was trying to pull a large display cabinet away from the wall beneath the stairs. It was wedged in by the partially collapsed stone work, and he was struggling to move it. Letting go of her friend's arm, Hollyglade came to Jeron's side and took hold of the cabinet above where he was pulling on it. Together, they strained against the wedged cabinetry, trying to force it out from under the stairway. It would not come completely away from the wall, as they were only able to create a thin space between the wood and stone.

"Let me in there," interrupted dGerrie, as he came to where Hollyglade and Jeron were fighting with the cabinet. He had found a short spear which had been dropped by a guard, and was now aiming to use it to pry the cabinet away from the wall.

"We'll do it together," offered Jeron, grabbing hold of the spear below where dGerrie had his grip on it. "On three." dGerrie nodded his agreement, and together they applied pressure to the crack.

After several moments of straining against the stubborn woodwork, it finally shifted about half a foot further away from the wall. As it did, the entire foundation of the tower began to shake violently.

"That's going to have to do! Everyone, into the tunnel, now!" shouted Jeron as he squeezed through the crack, pulling on Hollyglade's wrist as he went. She followed him in while turning back to take ahold of dGerrie's hand, not letting him fall behind. As dGerrie slid one leg and arm through the crack, and tried to suck in his chest to follow Hollyglade into the tunnel, his jerkin and tunic became caught, and his hand slipped from her grip.

"dGerrie!" she yelled. "Jeron, wait," she called after him, wrenching her arm free of his grasp.

"It's my tunic," shouted dGerrie, as he tried desperately to force himself through the small opening "it's caught front and back!"

Hollyglade grabbed his jerkin and pulled as hard as she could, but could not free him from whatever it was that hooked him in place. Jeron returned and felt around where dGerrie's front and back sides contacted the wall and the cabinet.

"Can you slide your hips through?" he asked dGerrie.

With a grunt, and some strain, dGerrie managed to slide his hips into the tunnel, and stepped through with his back leg, leaving himself nearly horizontal.

"I still can't get all the way through!" he shouted, his head, and one shoulder still out in the foyer under the stairs. Hollyglade looked through the opening to see debris raining down just beyond the edge of the staircase, and shouted

"Hurry! It's all coming down!"

Hearing the urgency in her voice, Jeron grabbed dGerrie around the waist

"dGerrie, put your arms over your head, and try to slip out of your clothes!"

dGerrie raised his arms up, yelping in pain as his left shoulder injury burned like fire under the strain of simply being lifted. Jeron pulled at his waist, and dGerrie fought his way out of his tunic and jerkin, sliding into the dark tunnel. As he came through into the tunnel, the sounds of the collapsing tower crescendoed with crashes, snapping wood, and falling stone. Dust and small pieces of debris shot through the small crack into the tunnel, covering the group in fragments of the tower walls.

After several moments, the tunnel became quiet.

As the young King stood at the side of the plinth which held his father's now occupied throne, he bit his lip and began to tremble. He did his best to hide the fear and trepidation which had begun to well up inside him. He rubbed his hands together and looked around for someone else he knew, someone he might trust to help him. *Where is that damned sorcerer? He promised that he would stop this. Now what am I supposed to do?* he thought to himself, still reeling from the disbelief in what he was seeing as he looked at King Dermond Riaghlad sitting on the throne he had occupied for such a short time.

As Harford Peaksoul drifted deeper into his own despair, the sound of the crumbling tower increased in volume. The young King and the Master of his Royal forces, turned to look out the window facing the tower. As they did so, to their shock and dismay, the roof of the tower gave way and collapsed in on itself, sending a sound wave that echoed loudly throughout the throne room.

Immediately panic filled the Keep, and those assembled began to take defensive positions around the exits. After a moment, it was clear that the sound did not originate in the throne room, and soldiers were sent to find out where the sound had come from. Quentin Wendal was quick to arrive at Harford's side.

"Your Grace," he said in a hushed tone, "this may be the distraction we need." Wendal took a quick look around the room to see if anyone was paying them direct attention.

"What do you mean?" Harford asked, his voice betraying his trepidation.

"There is still a chance to get you out of the capital."

"How? To what end?"

Quentin Wendal placed and hand on the young King's shoulder and leaned close.

"You are still the rightful King, and we may still be able to regroup over a short time, and retake this kingdom. But we can not do it with you imprisoned."

Harford was numb from his disheartenment, and did not know how to reply. He had been through so much is such a short time. The loss of his father, brother, friends, and now his throne, piled high upon his small shoulders. The weight of all his failures, all that he had been responsible for, everyone he had let down, pressed him into a malaise. He had lost the ability to care about himself, having had everything and everyone else he cared for ripped from him. He sighed, and looked at Quentin Wendal, who was eyeing exits and the distribution of Demarian guards.

"I guess," Harford mumbled. "What difference does it make? Take me wherever you like. One place is as good as another."

With a look of apprehensive concern battling urgent incentive, Wendal nudged Harford toward the back of the plinth where large tapestries hung adorning the rear wall of the throne room.

"Your Grace, we must be quick. When, and if, the opportunity presents itself, we must not hesitate."

Harford shrugged. There was nothing left within him that he could call upon to respond to the urgency his Master of the Royal Forces conveyed. As they stood and watched for someone to return with a report, or some other indication of what had caused the explosive sound wave, the tension in the room was palpable. Several of the Demarian commanders, along with King Dermond himself, gave repeated glances at Harford and Wendal as they took part in some serious looking discussion. Harford turned his attention to the windows at the side of the hall, taking in the starlight of the new moon's night, wishing he were somewhere far away from where he stood, a defeated and deposed unprepared ruler.

As the young King looked up at the tower, to where the Sorcerer's apartment had been, to where he had supposedly worked on his promised solution to the Kingdom's woes, Harford remembered something odd.

"Lord Wendal," he whispered "did you see that light that was coming from the tower? There was never a window there before."

Quentin Wendal stepped around the deposed king, and looked up at the tower, to see if what the King was describing could still be seen. As he did so, the remaining levels of the tower began to crumble with increased momentum, and the entire tower began to cave in upon itself. In a matter of seconds, what remained of the tower collapsed to the ground, sending debris and dust in all directions.

The accompanying sound was deafening, and the rumbling vibrations that rippled through the floor as a result sent everyone in the hall scattering in fear and panic. Without hesitation, Quentin Wendal shoved Harford behind one of the large tapestries depicting his father Jerold, kneeling before the King of Demaria, the very man who now occupied the Lorian throne room, in a gesture of peace and friendship.

Once behind the curtain, Wendal drew something small from within his sleeve, felt along the wall for something hidden within it's texture, and slipped the key into a tiny keyhole. Silently, a hidden door opened inward, and Quentin Wendal turned to the King with a finger to his lips, pulling him to enter the hidden passage. Without a word, both the young King, and the Master of his Royal Forces, slipped out of the throne room, while the sounds of panic, and the echoes of the booming crash of the crumbled tower filled the hall.

Once inside the tunnel, Wendal picked something small off the wall and sparked a torch to light. Lifting the torch from it's sconce, he took Harford by the hand and pulled him along the pathway.

"Where are we? I did not know this was here."

"No one knew this was here. Not even your father. There

is a series of secret tunnels throughout the palace and the city, the knowledge of which is passed from one Master of the Royal forces to another. Though some of the older tunnels beneath the city are known to others, the ones in the palace itself are kept secret for unlikely events such as this. We will take this passage here, and follow it until it joins one leading out of the city. There, we will meet Lords Marnon and Ventrent, and a small contingent of guards, who will join us in escorting you to Stonehome."

"But how will we get past the Demarians who are outside the city?" asked Harford, expressing genuine concern.

"It will be a risk, Your Grace, but we will disguise ourselves as merchants, and travel incognito. We must assume covert dress and names, and we must travel lightly. We must not refer to each other by any titles." He stopped, and looked the young King in the eye. "Until the time is right, I am no longer a Lord, and you are no longer a King."

Harford's jaw dropped slightly as he grappled with the gravity of the sudden change in position. As he fell into his own thoughts, Wendal once again urged him along. Harford was unsure of how he felt. He had never wanted the responsibility of ruling, never been prepared for it emotionally, nor practically. Now that it had been taken from him, he was feeling both a relief and a profound sense of loss. What would his people suffer under the rule of a foreign invader? Would they be enslaved, or worse? Was there any chance at all of mounting a resistance, a rebellion? These questions rolled around in Harford's mind as they wound their way through the narrow passageway, and progressed downward beneath Whiterock.

After several twists and turns, they came to a transition of sorts, where the stone masonry of the castle's interior foundations gave way to rock. They descended several rough-hewn stairways, Wendal occasionally turning back to give Harford a signal to remain quiet. Finally, they came to a wooden door set in the stone, where Wendal signalled for them to stop and remain silent. The lord pressed his ear to the door, and listened for several moments.

After a long pause, he placed his hand on the door, and scratched it lightly, and then waited. A scratching sound came from the other side, and Wendal turned to Harford and nodded. Taking hold of the latch that hung on the inside of the door, Wendal lifted it and pulled the door in toward himself. As the door opened, Harford noted that the outside of the door looked like it had been cut from one piece of stone, with lines of moss running through its crack, giving it the appearance of something old and untouched.

Wendal stepped out through the opening and waved for the young King to follow. Upon stepping out from the tunnel, Harford found himself in the forested area just outside the city walls. They were greeted by Lord Marnon, who shook Wendal's hand in a silent greeting, and passed him a scabbard with a sword and dagger. Lord Marnon bowed to the young King, and indicated which direction he desired him to head.

"Have you secured transportation?" Wendal inquired of Marnon in a low whisper.

"Yes, though it is some little ways away. We dared not risk the sound of wagon wheels in the night."

"How many men have we?"

"I managed to round up only nine. The rest of those who had been assigned to escort us, should we have had need of it, we can assume have either been killed or captured. We will need to rely on some stealth."

"What of Lord Ventrent?"

"I know not," Marnon replied, with a look of dismay.

"Have you some change of clothing? We dare not be seen dressed as we are."

"Yes. Just here," Marnon indicated a sack held by one of the men, who was dressed rather shabbily, and without any visible weapons.

Wendal nodded and took the sack, reaching in to pull out an assortment of brown and grey pants, tunics, shirts and other rough looking clothing. Handing a pile of clothes to Harford, Wendal began to undress. Taking the bundled raggedy costume, Harford wrinkled his nose at the smell and dropped the clothing on the ground, stepping back from it.

"I am not wearing that!" he said in a voice dangerously over a whisper.

Marnon brought a finger to his lips, and a put hand over Harford's mouth.

"We are not secure here, young man. And in truth, if you want to live, you are not wearing that," he said, pointing to Harford's finely tailored suit in the royal colours of white and blue.

"Young man?" retorted Harford, raising his voice further against the hand attempting to quiet him down. "I am your King, and you shall address me as 'My King', or 'Your Grace' as it pl…"

Marnon had heard enough and grabbed Harford around the shoulders, spun his back into his chest, and covered the young King's mouth. Into Harford's ear, he whispered

"You are no King. You have no Kingdom. The land you stand on now belongs to Demaria. If you ever want to get it back, to become King once more, you will shut your mouth, and do as you are told, boy. There is no room here for the etiquette you previously enjoyed. We are all farmers, on our way back to our fields now that the battle is over. Do you hear me, boy?"

He let go of the young King's mouth for a moment to let him answer. Harford was overwhelmed. He had grown up in the finest of riches, clothing tailored freshly every week, food plentiful and cooked to his liking, servants to attend to his every wish. Having done much to remain separated from them his entire life, the prospect of spending a single moment appearing as a low born serf, pushed him over the edge of reason. He began to flail against the lord's grip, kicking, and screaming into the hand that clamped back over his mouth. He felt someone pull off his boots and stockings.

In a fit of rage, Harford bit down on the hand covering his mouth and jerked himself loose from the hold Marnon had on him, turned and looked for somewhere to run. He took one step back toward the castle he longed to go back to, which contained the rooms he yearned to go seal himself within.

Harford felt something hit the back of his head.

Everything went black.

After several moments listening to the sounds of debris settling beyond the tight opening they had squeezed through, Hollyglade felt around herself to find her bearings. She felt for the wall behind her, and pushed herself up to lean her back against it while sitting on the floor. Feeling herself over to search for injury, she found several new sore spots, but none that seemed to be bleeding, nor any bones that seemed broken or bruised.

"dGerrie, Jeron. Are you there?" she whispered, praying there would be responses from both of them.

Jeron responded quickly

"I'm here. Are you alright?"

"I'm fine. A little bruised, but nothing serious. Where's dGerrie?"

"I'm here too. Though, I've felt better," he responded with clearly audible difficulty.

Hollyglade's hearing told her that he was just a few feet away, and she felt her way over to him.

"Do you have anything we can make some light with?" she asked him as she found him pulling himself up to sit against the wall.

"I don't think so. Maybe we can get a spark from some of this stone with a dagger, but what might we put the spark to?"

Jeron responded through a cough, fighting the dust in the air.

"Most of these tunnels have torches along the wall every so often. If we can locate one, we may be able to light it." He stood up, braced himself on the wall, and started to feel his way along it, searching for a sconce.

Hollyglade felt dGerrie over, finding several obvious

wounds.

"We have to patch you up. You're losing blood."

"I'll be fine." he replied as he tried to push himself up off the floor and into a standing position

"Let's just get moving."

It was a tremendous struggle to gain verticality, and as dGerrie fought to get to his feet, the many injuries he had sustained in the last days made themselves known. He cried out in agony as he straightened his damaged leg, felt shooting pain course through his body, and though the tunnel was pitch black he saw stars. As his strength left him, dGerrie faltered and began to sink to the floor. Feeling him swoon, Hollyglade grabbed hold of him under his armpit, and steadied him with her hands, leaning him against the wall.

"Jeron!" she rasped in a low, yet urgent voice "He needs help, and we can't stay here. Either you need to find us a torch, or we need to move in the dark." She heard the sound of cloth tearing, and then metal striking stone. Turning to the sound, she saw sparks jump from one of the blades Jeron was using to try to light something on the floor. In the fraction of moment when the sparks flew, she could see the size of the tunnel, and the rubble blocking the way they had come.

Another spark. Nothing.

Again.

Finally, the piece of cloth Jeron had ripped from his sleeve caught, and began to glow. He picked up the cloth by the far end and lay it over the dagger's blade, turning the dagger in his hand to roll up the cloth. Holding it sideways, he lifted it above his head to cast light about the tunnel.

In the low light, Hollyglade could see as well as if it were a bright summer's day. She turned to dGerrie, and examined him head to toe, taking a closer look at the several wounds oozing blood.

"We need to cover those wounds, Stilt. Otherwise you're in for an untimely slumber, and maybe worse."

"I'm fine," he insisted.

"You're not. And besides, we have a few moments. No

one's going to come digging us out anytime soon, so we might as well patch you up before we try to sneak out of Magnaville." She turned to look for Jeron, finding him visually searching the tunnel.

"Aha!" exclaimed Jeron under his breath, "the genuine article." He pulled a torch from a sconce on the wall, and transferred the flame to it. Dropping the cloth off the end of the dagger, he returned to where Hollyglade and dGerrie leant against the wall.

"You look a little rough, my friend," Jeron confessed as he examined dGerrie, "but we owe you our thanks, and I wish to return some help to you, as I am able"

dGerrie nodded in reply, and looked to Hollyglade as he attempted to seat himself on a chunk of stone which had landed next to him. Looking up to Jeron, he extended his hand.

"dGerrie Theurbeault," he said, introducing himself.

"Jeron Jeroldsen Peaksoul, at your service," replied the Prince, taking dGerrie's hand in his.

"Who? What? The!?" dGerrie stammered.

Jeron smiled and took hold of dGerrie's other arm, to help steady him in his seat, as he knelt down beside him. Hollyglade took off the ground blanket she had been using as a makeshift jerkin, and set it on the floor of the tunnel. Taking the dagger from Jeron, she made a cut at the shoulder of her shirt, and tore off the sleeve.

"Yes, that Jeron," she said, as she cut the sleeve into several lengths.

"I heard you were dead."

"I heard I was dead, too," he replied with a smirk. "I only found that out a day or so ago. I was somewhat surprised, as I had felt rather alive. But for now, that rumour will have to stay the truth."

dGerrie looked up at him as Hollyglade began to bandage his open wounds.

"Why would you let that stand? You are the rightful King, are you not? Couldn't you just go upstairs and show yourself to gain the throne?"

Jeron chuckled at the thought as he switched sides with Hollyglade to allow her to tend to dGerrie's side and arm.

"If I knew what the outcome would be of such a bold play, I may just take your advice. The reality is, as far as we can tell, that Demaria now occupies Loria. I heard the city bells, and the Demarian horn of truce. That could only mean that King Dermond was successful in taking the castle, and therefore the capital. My appeal would need to be to him if I were to take such a risk, and though I know he and my father loved each other, one can never be sure that such love is not secured by mutual military might. No, I must flee, regroup, and wait for some sign that the time is right to reveal myself."

Hollyglade finished tying the last bandage, and placed a hand on dGerrie's cheek, turning his face to hers. She looked deep into his eyes in an effort to determine his lucidity. He seemed diminished, but still present, and so she let out a small breath of relief. Taking his hand, she held his gaze.

"Political aspirations can wait, you two," she said, not taking her eyes off him. "dGerrie, I thought I'd lost you. Again. I can't take anymore worrying. Let's get out of here before the sun comes up. We should still have some hours with which to put some distance between us and this place."

"Can you stand?" Jeron asked

"I will stand, and I'll walk. Just try to stop me," he declared as he pushed himself up. "Now, your royalness. Lead the way," he said with a hint of joviality, trying his best to lighten the mood and take his own mind off the pain he was dealing with.

"Just Jeron," he replied with a smile. "At least, until we get outside the tunnels, and then I'll have to come up with something less conspicuous."

Hollyglade handed dGerrie the blanket to cover his now exposed torso, and held out her hand to steady him. He nodded, slipped the blanket over his head, and began to move away from the wall.

Moving slowly, the group set off down the tunnel. Jeron

taking steps gingerly on his bare feet, dGerrie limping slowly and leaning on both Hollyglade and the walls, and Hollyglade doing her best to support dGerrie while favouring her injured knee and sore feet.

The tunnel wound its way downward for quite some time without encountering a side passage or intersection of any kind. After a while, it changed from laid brick and stone, to a rough-cut passage through the white bedrock upon which the capital sat. After what seemed like just under half an hour, the tunnel came to an intersection, where Jeron paused and waited for the other two to come close.

"Alright, now comes a choice," he said, looking each of them in the eye. "We can either take this tunnel, which leads to the coast, and hope to find a ship we can board to head either North toward, and ideally beyond, Demaria, or South to Sudara, or possibly the far lands beyond it." He paused, letting those options sit with his companions for a moment.

"Or, we can take this passage which will let us out in the Westwood, and travel over land in any direction we choose. Though it would be difficult to secure transport by sea, we could move quite far, quite fast, and could give anyone a wide berth should we find a vessel we can commandeer for ourselves. Land presents more options in terms of direction and destination, but more hazards as well."

Hollyglade looked at both of them, then to the passage that lead to the Westwood.

"Land. I must take the path to land."

dGerrie looked back at her, hearing the resoluteness in her voice.

"You have a plan. I can hear it."

"Yes, I do, but I can't ask you to come with me."

"You can, Sprout. But you don't have to. I'm with you. I finally found you, I'm not letting you out of my sight."

She smiled and nodded, hearing the resolve in his voice. They both looked to Jeron, awaiting his response. He took a breath, and stared at the floor for a few moments, then nodding his head, he found Hollyglade's gaze and met it with his own.

"I owe you my life. Regardless of what plans I have for myself, I must at least see you to some sort of relative safety. I'm with you. My plans can, and must wait."

Hollyglade was taken aback somewhat, as she could never have imagined someone with any status, let alone a prince, wanting to throw their lot in with her. She had no words to offer in response to the commitment each of these men had offered her. She had not even revealed where it was that she hoped to venture to. She stood, holding dGerrie, not knowing what to say, when Jeron broke the silence.

"Well, I'd like to know exactly where we are going, as I'm sure it'll be interesting, but first we must get out of here. Come. There will be more time for talk later, if all goes well. We have a fair way to go before we can pretend to feel safe." He turned and headed down the tunnel leading to the Westwood, a sword in one hand and the torch in the other, waving for his companions to follow. The tunnel wound its way through the bedrock beneath Magnaville, taking the trio further away from Whiterock, and the destruction that had nearly taken their lives.

As they moved through the passages, Hollyglade felt a mix of relief and tension. Having survived the Sorcerer's attempt to steal her very essence, she was grateful to be alive and whole, and that her friends, both old and new, had survived with her. But now, they would face unknown dangers once they left the relative security of the hidden tunnels under the city.

They reached the end of the tunnels in just under an hour, and paused to catch their breath before taking the risk of venturing out into the relative openness of the Westwood. At the door leading out, Jeron signalled for them to wait, and to remain silent as he pressed his ear to the door to listen, and held it there for quite a long time. Once he was certain it would be safe, he pulled away from the door, and sat down with Hollyglade and dGerrie.

"I can not hear anyone outside the door, but I do not trust

that we will have a completely clear exit. There may be some foes to evade or confront once we exit. How fare you both?"

dGerrie looked to Hollyglade, indicating he had the same question for her. She looked to Jeron

"I'm well enough, at least physically, but without more weapons to go around, and with my relative rawness in the use of them, my hope is for stealth. That is one area of skill where I may outclass the both of you." She looked back to her injured friend "It's you I worry about, dGerrie. You have saved us, and me for I can't even recall how many times it is now, but you don't look well."

dGerrie met her gaze with a smile, though it was somewhat forced through the ongoing ordeal of his injuries.

"I'll manage. I must. It's of no advantage for us to remain here." He turned to Jeron with a gravity in his expression "Jeron, how well do you know the area we step into? Do you have a plan for us, in terms of which direction to take? We must find shelter, food, and water. We should all do well with some rest and sustenance."

Jeron nodded pensively as he shifted his gaze away in consideration of their immediate needs.

"I agree, friend. We must recover some strength before attempting to travel too far. There may be a haven for us nearby. I remember a set of small caves where I used to play as a child, somewhere near where this tunnel lets us out. But I must admit that my memory of their exact location is a little lacking."

Hollyglade perked up at the suggestion of the caves.

"Do you refer to a system of caves among an alder grove, where a small stream flows out from the main mouth?" She asked with a hint of eagerness.

"Yes, that sounds like them. Do you know them?"

"I do!" she replied. "I had no idea that there was a secret tunnel that let out in the same wood."

"Nor should you," chuckled Jeron. "They would not be secret if you did."

Hollyglade smiled for the first time in what felt like a

lifetime, and stood up.

"You two stay here. I'll scout quietly and quickly. I'll find the caves and return to lead you there via the safest route."

"Sprout," dGerrie interjected, "I don't want to let you out of my sight again. I can't handle the thought."

"Stilt," she replied reassuringly, "I am well enough to move undetected past whatever eyes or ears may be about, especially in the dark of the new moon. You forget, that as a Giantish girl, I need no light by which to navigate, and as an Elvish girl, I shall be swift and silent. Let me save you now." Her posture and tone displayed an adamance neither man could argue with.

"Alright," Jeron agreed "we shall trust our escape to you. You have saved me once already. I shall not look to find reason to doubt you now." He stood with her and took her hand in his. "I will stay to see what I may do to aid him. Take this."

He offered her the sword.

"It's of no use to me. I am at best clumsy with such a blade."

"Then take this, at least," dGerrie said, holding out the sheathed dagger. "You're not going out there without some sort of blade."

She nodded and took the weapon, sliding it into her belt. She then knelt down, placed a hand on either side of dGerrie's face, and pressed her forehead to his.

"Thank you, brother," she whispered. "I'll be back for you before you know it."

He placed a hand on her shoulder, and smiled.

Standing up and giving a look of acknowledgement to Jeron, Hollyglade moved to the door with him.

"When you return, do not knock on the door. Scratch it like a cat, but gently. I will acknowledge you in the same way." he whispered.

She nodded, and grabbed him around the shoulders, giving him a quick hug, and then turned to the door. Without words, he opened the door slowly, and let her out, closing it carefully behind her.

"Your Grace!" shouted Yerin Greln, "King Harford is missing!"

The War Marshall ran to the King, who was in the process of gathering his Lords and commanders after the collapse of the Tower of Whiterock.

"What?!" the King snapped in surprise and anger, "Where has he gone? How did we lose him?"

The War Marshall stood still, though he wanted to step back from the suddenly bristling conqueror.

"My King, it seems that he has slipped away in the confusion created by the collapse of the tower. I have dispatched the closest cohorts to begin the search, and would like your leave to expand the number of soldiers assigned to find him. He can not have gone very far."

"Do it. Take as many men as you require. Set up checkpoints on all roads out of the city, all gates to the castle and the city walls, and restrict all vessels from leaving the harbour." The King paused, and took a look around the throne room. "And War Marshall, it appears we are searching for Lord Quentin Wendal also. Furthermore, if that Sorcerer we've heard about is spotted, he is to be chained and brought before me. I'll have no such manipulator free to roam about in either of my Kingdoms. Make haste, War Marshall."

"At once, Your Grace." Yerin Greln spun and hurried out of the throne room to oversee the search and set up of checkpoints.

The King returned to his previous meeting

"Lord Birk, you are to organize the surrender of the Lorian troops. They are to be treated with respect and dignity. Weapons are to be surrendered, but those who are willing to swear their fealty to Demarian rule, shall be paid their wage from the Lorian coffers and allowed to retain their position, serving Demarian rule of occupied Loria. Once vetted, any such men shall be returned to active duty. Any non-military civilians, if unarmed, may return to their homes and occupations once cleared through vetting." He paused and looked each Lord and Commander in the eye. "Remember Lords, Commanders, though our cause was just, we were the invaders, and the aggressors. To the innocent civilians of Loria, we may be seen as greedy conquerors. Treat these people with the respect the late King Jerold held for them, and make sure that everyone under your command does the same."

Each of the gathered lords and commanders nodded their acknowledgment.

"Good. Get to it men," he said, dismissing them.

"Lord Orban, Lord Birk, stay please."

The two lords remained and gave a slight bow

"How may I serve, Your Grace?" offered Orban.

"My Lord Orban, I need someone here to administrate. I can not remain here in Loria too long, though I will stay at least a while, and I require someone to discover all details of the young King's rule since the passing of his father. Find the minutes from his Vestry's assemblies, and the written copies of any decrees he that have been made by this boy. It is well known that he had begun to shift this Kingdom into some disarray as of late, and I shall need to know what we must do, and undo, in order to stabilize our rule over it."

"I shall begin right away, Your Grace."

"Good. Assign someone to look into the Lorian finances, and have them report to you. We must know how much strain the crown is under, especially if we are to treat their Royal Forces as they deserve."

"As you wish, Your Grace." Orban bowed and left, calling several of his aides to follow.

Lord Birk straightened his posture, and awaited the King's acknowledgement. King Dermond motioned for him to follow, and walked over to one of the windows facing the fallen tower.

"Birk, we need to know the truth about Prince Jeron. It was surely no Demarian who interfered with him. We must know if he is alive or dead, and who orchestrated his fate.

Does the young Harford deserve blame? Was he manipulated? Was it done without his knowledge? I must know the answers to these questions. Use whatever means you must to find the truth"

"It will be done, Your Grace." replied the lord "What of those who are responsible, should I find them? What shall be their fate?"

"Justice, my Lord. But fair justice. I shall decide their fate, if and when you find them. Get to it. I desire to give these people the truth soon, so that designs on rebellion have fewer incentives."

"Your, Grace." The lord bowed, and left the King alone.

King Dermond Riaghlad stood looking out over the rubble of the collapsed tower for some time. His thoughts were disturbed as he grappled with the rationale for the invasion that brought him there. Oh Jerold, my old friend, what took you from this life so soon? I had hoped you would outlive me. I had hoped to die in the midst of peace. I had hoped our friendship would rub off on our neighbours to the north and south. What a mess we've made, your son and me.

The King returned to the dais. Breathing deeply, savouring his victory and looking out over the city, King Dermond Riaghlad once more settled onto the throne of Loria.

EPILOGUE

The morning air was crisp, and the snow blanketed the ground, settled upon the trees, and painted the landscape in purest white. The sun was rising, and shone through the thin clouds. Though it had only been snowing a few days, the forest was silent of the bird calls normally welcoming the dawn during the summer months. Far back from the mouth of the cave, beside the creek that flowed out from deep within the ground, a small fire burned, well enough back from the opening not to be visible from outside the cavern.

"No, don't shave it! You need to hide your identity still. You are the rightful King, but you still need to stay hidden in the short term. Besides, I like it."

He smiled, and put the blade back in the pocket of the jerkin he had managed to take from a sleeping Demarian soldier.

"I must say, I'm still having a hard time wrapping my head around the fact you eat animals. I mean, you can hear them, talk to them basically, right? Does it not feel like eating a friend?"

"Listen, Jeron," Hollyglade replied with a smirk "they are what they are. It's not their intelligence that allows me to connect with them, it's my gift. One does not need to read the thoughts of a lamb led to the slaughter to know that it would rather not die and be eaten." She took another bite of the rabbit leg and shook her head at him playfully.

"I just can't imagine it. I think I'd have a hard time with it."

"That's because you and I have never had that connection." dGerrie replied for her. "We've grown up not knowing what animals think or feel, so it's easy to be blissfully ignorant. She's grown up knowing what they think all along, so it's just normal for her. We have all arrived at the same place, even though we have traveled different roads to get here."

"You're a wise man, dGerrie." he chuckled. "I'm going to

miss you."

Hollyglade met Jeron's eyes

"Are you sure this is the best plan? Are you sure you won't come with us?"

"It is, and I am. Though I would love to see the mountains again, and meet the Elder Folk you seek there, I must search out the good men whom I can trust would honour me as rightful King. There are sure to be many men who remain loyal to my house, my father, and the Kingdom itself. If I am ever to return Loria to freedom, it must start here, and it must start without delay. Though the word we have all overheard these last few days is that King Dermond has treated the people kindly, he is not their King. They do not deserve a foreign conqueror. They deserve their own, true King."

Hollyglade smiled, uplifted by his steadfast love for his people.

"We're going to miss you too."

"Thank you, Holly. I'm gladdened to finally see that you are both well enough to travel. You have a long road ahead of you."

dGerrie drew up the corner of his mouth, in a coy half smile.

"We aren't taking roads, remember?"

"I worry how long that will take you, and for the fact that tracks stay in snow for longer than people think."

"We have time on our side now. No one knows we live, and no one other than that dead sorcerer, and that coward of a bounty hunter, even knows who we are. You can only follow a track if you find the track. We'll be fine. We'll use roads when it's in our interest, but don't forget, the animals have their roads too."

"Holly, are you sure you can trust the Gnomish? The Elvish? You've never spent any time with them, and though I can't say much about the Gnomish, I can say that the Elvish don't tolerate half-breeds. How do you imagine you'll get them to accept you?"

She nodded in agreement with his assessment of the

challenges that lay before her in the high Elvish alpine. She had struggled to answer the question in her own mind, of where to go and whom to seek out for guidance. She knew that she must learn to use the power within her, to control the gift her father and mother had given their lives to preserve. She knew that the Elvish had great knowledge of innate magical abilities, and that the Gnomish were said to be tolerant of anyone who could manage to survive a winter on the peaks of the Southern Range. Those options both seemed to hold value, and risk. She had also contemplated seeking out the Wizards, perhaps even Artache himself, yet the idea of becoming some sort of specimen to be studied turned her stomach. No, she had a different plan.

"I am going to the Elvish Highlands, but not for the Elvish, nor the Gnomish." She replied.

"The Giantish? But aren't they beyond the mountains altogether? Do you mean to travel through the Elvish lands in stealth to find your mother's people?"

"Not them either. No, I'll travel to the Elvish Highlands, for what I seek is there. But it is not the Elvish, Giantish, nor Gnomish whom I seek. I wish I could tell you, truly, but you must not know. My father told me where to find the one I seek when I was a child, but I remember clearly that he told me I must never share the knowledge of who it is that I travel to find."

"How do you know that this is the right person to look for? The right person to teach you?"

"He was the one that taught my father how to save me, how to preserve me in my mother's belly until I breathed the air and became whole. Though I did not know it then, I know now that such knowledge is ancient, and beyond what the Wizards, or even the Elvish could share with me. Though I don't remember exactly the description of the route which my father related to me, I know I must try. I must seek that path."

Jeron saw the depth of her resolve, the fierceness of her determination, and could not hope to sway her. Such a hope was not within his mind, as he stood and pulled his pack onto his shoulders, and adjusted his scabbard. Stepping around the smoldering fire, he smiled and took her in an embrace.

"You are a true friend, and I admire you. I owe you my life, and whether they know it yet or not, this Kingdom is indebted to you. Farewell Hollyglade. May we meet again soon."

She lowered her head to rest upon the top of his, and hugged him tightly.

"We will meet again, my King. And when we do, we'll laugh about it all, eat some rabbit, and sit by the sea in the open air."

"I'd like that very much."

He pulled away gently, and turned to dGerrie.

"Take care of her. I can't think of a better man for the job, but don't let that go to your head. Don't let her out of your sight." He held out his hand, and dGerrie took it, pulled him close, and hugged him.

Stepping back, dGerrie looked the Prince in the eye.

"You go worry about forming a proper rebellion. None of this weak half-hearted junk that failed in the North so many years ago. I'll take care of Sprout, and she'll probably take care of me too." The three of them chuckled as they picked up their packs and turned for the entrance to the caves.

With one last silent look to each other, Jeron set his mind toward the sea in the east, and Hollyglade and dGerrie intent on the mountains in the west. They smiled to each other one last time, and then parted ways.

"You know we might never see him again, Sprout."

"We will. But we'll be different, and so will he."

She smiled and placed her hand under his arm.

Here ends the first Chronicles of Hollyglade Wayrender.
The story will continue.

ABOUT THE AUTHOR

Steve Barker lives in Canmore, Alberta and drives a school bus for work while living in the Canadian Rocky Mountains with his wife and two children. Writing is a passion fueled by his life of adventurous rock climbing, ice climbing, backcountry camping, and mountaineering. A dynamic storyteller, Steve Barker uses a remarkable combination of wondrous vocabulary, magnificent detail, and engaging description, to personally connect you to his characters in the fantasy genre.

www.ingramcontent.com/pod-product-compliance
Lightning Source LLC
Chambersburg PA
CBHW050324200626
46810CB00023B/2502